Uniform Justice

Donna Leon

Uniform
Justice

Atlantic Monthly Press
New York

First published in the United Kingdom in 2003 by William Heinemann, London, England

Published simultaneously in Canada
Printed in the United States of America

FIRST AMERICAN EDITION

Library of Congress Cataloging-in-Publication Data

Leon, Donna.
    Uniform justice / Donna Leon.
        p. cm.
    ISBN 0-87113-903-0
    1. Brunetti, Guido (Fictitious character)—Fiction. 2. Police—Italy—Venice—Fiction. 3. Military education—Fiction. 4. Military cadets—Fiction. 5. Venice (Italy)—Fiction. I. Title.

PS3562.E534U55 2003
813'.54—dc21   2003044326

Atlantic Monthly Press
841 Broadway
New York, NY 10003

03 04 05 06 07   10 9 8 7 6 5 4 3 2 1

for Hedi and Agustí Janés

In uomini, in soldati
sperare fedeltà?

You expect fidelity
in men, in soldiers?

Così fan tutte

—Mozart

1

Thirst woke him. It was not the healthy thirst that follows three sets of tennis or a day spent skiing, thirst that comes slowly: it was the grinding, relentless thirst that comes of the body's desperate attempt to replenish liquids that have been displaced by alcohol. He lay in his bed, suddenly awake, covered with a thin film of sweat, his underwear damp and clinging.

At first he thought he could outwit it, ignore it and fall back into the sodden sleep from which his thirst had prodded him. He turned on his side, mouth open on the pillow, and pulled the covers up over his shoulder. But much as his body craved more rest, he could not force it to ignore his thirst nor the faint nervousness of his stomach. He lay there, inert and utterly deprived of will, and told himself to go back to sleep.

For some minutes he succeeded, but then a church bell somewhere towards the city poked him back to consciousness. The idea of liquid seeped into his mind: a glass of sparkling mineral water, its sides running with condensation; the drinking fountain in the corridor of his elementary school; a paper cup filled with Coca-Cola. He needed liquid more than anything life had ever presented to him as desirable or good.

Again, he tried to force himself to sleep, but he knew he had lost and now had no choice but to get out of bed. He started to think about which side of bed to get out of and whether the floor of the corridor would be cold, but then he pushed all of these considerations aside as violently as he did his blankets and got to his feet. His head throbbed and his stomach registered resentment of its new position relative to the floor, but his thirst ignored them both.

He opened the door to his room and started down the corridor, its length illuminated by the light that filtered in from outside. As he had feared, the linoleum tiles were harsh on his naked feet, but the thought of the water that lay ahead gave him the will to ignore the cold.

He entered the bathroom and, driven by absolute need, headed to the first of the white sinks that lined the wall. He turned on the cold tap and let it run for a minute: even in his fuddled state he remembered the rusty warm taste of the first water that emerged from those pipes. When the water that ran over his hand was cold, he cupped both hands and bent down towards them. Noisy as a dog, he slurped the water and felt it moving inside him, cooling and saving him as it went. Experience had taught him to stop after the first few mouthfuls, stop and wait to see how his troubled stomach would respond to the surprise of liquid without alcohol. At first, it didn't like it, but youth and good health made up for that, and then his stomach accepted the water quietly, even asked for more.

Happy to comply, he leaned down again and took eight or nine large mouthfuls, each one bringing more relief to his tortured body. The sudden flood of water triggered something in his stomach, and that in turn triggered something in his brain, and he grew dizzy and had to lean forward, hands propped on the front of the sink, until the world grew quiet again.

He put his hands under the still flowing stream and drank again. At a certain point, experience and sense told him any more would be risky, so he stood up straight, eyes closed, and dragged his wet palms across his face and down the front of his T-shirt. He lifted the hem and wiped at his lips; then, refreshed and feeling as if he might again begin to contemplate life, he turned to go back to his room.

And saw the bat, or what his muddled senses first perceived as a bat, just there, off in the distance. It couldn't be a bat, for it was easily two metres long and as wide as a man. But it had the shape of a bat. It appeared to suspend itself against the wall, its head perched above black wings that hung limp at its sides, clawed feet projecting from beneath.

He ran his hands roughly over his face, as if to wipe away the sight, but when he opened his eyes again the dark shape was still there. He backed away from it and, driven by the fear of what might happen to him if he took his eyes from the bat, he moved slowly in the direction of the door of the bathroom, towards where he knew he would find the switch for the long bars of neon lighting. Befuddled by a mixture of terror and incredulity, he kept his hands behind him, one palm flat and sliding ahead of him on the tile wall, certain that contact with the wall was his only contact with reality.

Like a blind man, he followed his seeing hand along the wall until he found the switch and the long double row of neon lights passed illumination along one by one until a daylike brightness filled the room.

Fear drove him to close his eyes while the lights came flickering on, fear of what horrid motion the bat-like shape would be driven to make when disturbed from the safety of the near darkness. When the lights grew silent, the young man opened his eyes and forced himself to look.

Although the stark lighting transformed and revealed the

3

shape, it did not entirely remove its resemblance to a bat, nor did it minimize the menace of those trailing wings. The wings, however, were revealed as the engulfing folds of the dark cloak that served as the central element of their winter uniform, and the head of the bat, now illuminated, was the head of Ernesto Moro, a Venetian and, like the boy now bent over the nearest sink, racked by violent vomiting, a student at San Martino Military Academy.

2

It took a long time for the authorities to respond to the death of Cadet Moro, though little of the delay had to do with the behaviour of his classmate, Pietro Pellegrini. When the waves of sickness abated, the boy returned to his room and, using the *telefonino* which seemed almost a natural appendage, so often did he use and consult it, he called his father, on a business trip in Milano, to explain what had happened, or what he had just seen. His father, a lawyer, at first said he would call the authorities, but then better sense intervened and he told his son to do so himself and to do it instantly.

Not for a moment did it occur to Pellegrini's father that his son was in any way involved in the death of the other boy, but he was a criminal lawyer and familiar with the workings of the official mind. He knew that suspicion was bound to fall upon the person who hesitated in bringing a crime to the attention of the police, and he also knew how eager they were to seize upon the obvious solution. So he told the boy – indeed, he could be said to have commanded him – to call the authorities instantly. The boy, trained in obedience by his father and by two years at San Martino, assumed that the authorities were those in charge of the school and thus went downstairs to report to his commander the presence of a dead boy in the third floor bathroom.

The police officer at the Questura who took the call when it came from the school asked the name of the caller, wrote it down, then asked him how he came to know about this dead person and wrote down that answer, as well. After hanging up, the policeman asked the colleague who was working the switchboard with him if they should perhaps pass the report on to the *Carabinieri*, for the Academy, as a military institution, might be under the jurisdiction of the *Carabinieri* rather than the city police. They debated this for a time, the second one calling down to the officers' room to see if anyone there could solve the procedural problem. The officer who answered their call maintained that the Academy was a private institution with no official ties to the Army – he knew, because his dentist's son was a student there – and so they were the ones who should respond to the call. The men on the switchboard discussed this for some time, finally agreeing with their colleague. The one who had taken the call noticed that it was after eight and dialled the interior number of his superior, Commissario Guido Brunetti, sure that he would already be in his office.

Brunetti agreed that the case was theirs to investigate and then asked, 'When did the call come in?'

'Seven twenty-six, sir,' came Alvise's efficient, crisp reply.

A glance at his watch told Brunetti that it was now more than a half-hour after that, but as Alvise was not the brightest star in the firmament of his daily routine, he chose to make no comment and, instead, said merely, 'Order a boat. I'll be down.'

When Alvise hung up, Brunetti took a look at the week's duty roster and, seeing that Ispettore Lorenzo Vianello's name was not listed for that day nor for the next, he called

Vianello at home and briefly explained what had happened. Before Brunetti could ask him, Vianello said, 'I'll meet you there.'

Alvise had proven capable of informing the pilot of Commissario Brunetti's request, no doubt in part because the pilot sat at the desk opposite him, and so, when Brunetti emerged from the Questura a few minutes later, he found both Alvise and the pilot on deck, the boat's motor idling. Brunetti paused before stepping on to the launch and told Alvise, 'Go back upstairs and send Pucetti down.'

'But don't you want me to come with you, sir?' Alvise asked, sounding as disappointed as a bride left waiting on the steps of the church.

'No, it's not that,' Brunetti said carefully, 'but if this person calls back again, I want you to be there so that there's continuity in the way he's dealt with. We'll learn more that way.'

Though this made no sense at all, Alvise appeared to accept it; Brunetti reflected, not for the first time, that it was perhaps the absence of sense that made it so easy for Alvise to accept. He went docilely back inside the Questura. A few minutes later Pucetti emerged and stepped on to the launch. The pilot pulled them away from the *Riva* and toward the *Bacino*. The night's rain had washed the pollution from the air, and the city was presented with a gloriously limpid morning, though the sharpness of late autumn was in the air.

Brunetti had had no reason to go to the Academy for more than a decade, not since the graduation of the son of a second cousin. After being inducted into the Army as a lieutenant, a courtesy usually extended to graduates of San Martino, most of them the sons of soldiers, the boy had progressed through the ranks, a source of great pride to his father and equal confusion to the rest of the family. There was no military tradition among the Brunettis nor among his mother's family, which is not to say that the family had never had anything to do with the military. To their cost, they had, for it was the generation of Brunetti's parents that had not only fought the last war but had had large parts of it fought around them, on their own soil.

Hence it was that Brunetti, from the time he was a child, had heard the military and all its works and pomps spoken of with the dismissive contempt his parents and their friends usually reserved for the government and the Church. The low esteem with which he regarded the military had been intensified over the years of his marriage to Paola Falier, a woman of leftish, if chaotic, politics. It was Paola's position that the greatest glory of the Italian Army was its history of cowardice and retreat, and its greatest failure the fact that, during both world wars, its leaders, military and political, had flown in the face of this truth and caused the senseless deaths of hundreds of thousands of young men by relentlessly pursuing both their own delusory ideas of glory and the political goals of other nations.

Little that Brunetti had observed during his own undistinguished term of military service or in the decades since then had persuaded him that Paola was wrong. Brunetti realized that not much he had seen could persuade him that the military, either Italian or foreign, was much different from the Mafia: dominated by men and unfriendly to women; incapable of honour or even simple honesty beyond its own ranks; dedicated to the acquisition of power; contemptuous of civil society; violent and cowardly at the same time. No, there was little to distinguish one organization from the other, save that some wore easily recognized uniforms while the other leaned toward Armani and Brioni.

The popular beliefs about the history of the Academy were known to Brunetti. Established on the Giudecca in 1852 by Alessandro Loredan, one of Garibaldi's earliest supporters in the Veneto and, by the time of Independence, one of his generals, the school was originally located in a large building on the island. Dying childless and without male heirs, Loredan had left the building as well as his family *palazzo* and fortune in trust, on the condition that the income be used to support the military Academy to which he had given the name of his father's patron saint.

Though the oligarchs of Venice might not have been wholehearted supporters of the Risorgimento, they had nothing but enthusiasm for an institution which so effectively assured that the Loredan fortune remained in the city. Within hours of his death, the exact value of his legacy was known, and within days the trustees named in the will had selected a retired officer, who happened to be the brother-in-law of one of them, to administer the Academy. And so it had continued to this day: a school run on strictly military lines, where the sons of officers and gentlemen of wealth could acquire the training and bearing which might prepare them to become officers in their turn.

Brunetti's reflections were cut off as the boat pulled into a canal just after the church of Sant' Eufemia and then drew up at a landing spot. Pucetti took the mooring rope, jumped on to the land, and slipped the rope through an iron circle in the pavement. He extended a hand to Brunetti and steadied him as he stepped from the boat.

'It's up here, isn't it?' Brunetti asked, pointing towards the back of the island and the lagoon, just visible in the distance.

'I don't know, sir,' Pucetti confessed. 'I have to admit I come over here only for the Redentore. I don't think I even know where the place is.' Ordinarily, no confession of the provincialism of his fellow Venetians could surprise Brunetti, but Pucetti seemed so very bright and open-minded.

As if sensing his commander's disappointment, Pucetti added, 'It's always seemed like a foreign country to me, sir. Must be my mother: she always talks about it like it's not part of Venice. If they gave her the key to a house on the Giudecca, I'm sure she'd give it back.'

Thinking it wiser not to mention that his own mother had often expressed the same sentiment and that he agreed with it completely, Brunetti said only, 'It's back along this canal, near the end,' and set off in that direction.

Even at this distance, he could see that the large *portone* that led into the courtyard of the Academy stood open: anyone could walk in or out. He turned back to Pucetti. 'Find out when the doors were opened this morning and if there's any record of people entering or leaving the building.' Before Pucetti could speak, Brunetti added, 'Yes, and last night, too, even before we know how long he's been dead. And who has keys to the door and when they're closed at night.' Pucetti didn't have to be told what questions to ask, a welcome relief on a force where the ability of the average officer resembled that of Alvise.

Vianello was already standing just outside the *portone*. He acknowledged his superior's arrival with a slight raising of his chin and nodded to Pucetti. Deciding to use whatever advantage was to be gained by appearing unannounced and in civilian clothes, Brunetti told Pucetti to go back down to the boat and wait ten minutes before joining them.

Inside, it was evident that word of the death had already spread, though Brunetti could not have explained how he knew this. It might have been the sight of small groups of boys and young men standing in the courtyard, talking in lowered voices, or it might have been the fact that one of them wore white socks with his uniform shoes, sure sign that he had dressed so quickly he didn't know what he was doing. Then he realized that not one of them was carrying books. Military or not, this was a school, and students carried books, unless, that is, something of greater urgency had intervened between them and their studies.

One of the boys near the *portone* broke away from the group he was talking to and approached Brunetti and Vianello. 'What can I do for you?' he asked, though, from the tone, he might as well have been demanding what they were doing there. Strong-featured and darkly handsome, he was almost as tall as Vianello, though he couldn't have been out of his teens. The others followed him with their eyes.

Provoked by the boy's tone, Brunetti said, 'I want to speak to the person in charge.'

'And who are you?' the boy demanded.

Brunetti didn't respond but gave the boy a long, steady glance. The young man's eyes didn't waver, nor did he move back when Brunetti took a small step towards him. He was dressed in the regulation uniform – dark blue trousers and jacket, white shirt, tie – and had two gold stripes on the cuffs of his jacket. In the face of Brunetti's silence, the boy shifted his weight then put his hands on his hips. He stared at Brunetti, refusing to repeat his question.

'What's he called, the man in charge here?' Brunetti asked, as if the other had not spoken. He added, 'I don't mean his name, I mean his title.'

'Comandante,' the boy was surprised into saying.

'Ah, how grand,' Brunetti said. He wasn't sure whether the boy's behaviour offended his general belief that youth should display deference to age or whether he felt particular irritation at the boy's preening belligerence. Turning to Vianello, he said, 'Inspector, get this boy's name,' and moved toward the staircase that led to the *palazzo*.

He climbed the five steps and pushed open the door. The foyer had a floor patterned with enormous diamonds made from boards of different woods. Booted feet had worn a path to a door in the far wall. Brunetti crossed the room, which was unexpectedly empty, and opened the door. A hallway led toward the back of the building, its walls covered with what he assumed to be regimental flags. Some of them bore the lion of San Marco; others carried different animals, all equally aggressive: teeth bared, claws unsheathed, hackles raised.

The first door on the right had only a number above it, as

did the second and third. As he walked by the last of them, a young boy, certainly not more than fifteen, came out into the hall. He was surprised to see Brunetti, who nodded calmly and asked, 'Where's the office of the Comandante?'

His tone or his manner sparked a Pavlovian response in the boy, who jumped to attention and snapped out a salute. 'Up one flight, sir. Third door on the left.'

Brunetti resisted the temptation to say, 'At ease.' With a neutral, 'Thank you', he went back toward the staircase.

At the top, he followed the boy's instructions and stopped at the third door on the left. COMANDANTE GIULIO BEMBO, read a sign next to the door.

Brunetti knocked, paused and waited for an answer, and knocked again. He thought he'd take advantage of the absence of the Comandante to have a look at his office, and so he turned the handle and entered. It is difficult to say who was more startled, Brunetti or the man who stood in front of one of the windows, a sheaf of papers in his hand.

'Oh, I beg your pardon,' Brunetti said. 'One of the students told me to come up and wait for you in your office. I had no idea you were here.' He turned towards the door and then back again, as if confused as to whether he should remain or leave.

The man in front of the window was facing Brunetti, and the light that shone in from behind him made it almost impossible for Brunetti to distinguish anything about him. He could see, however, that he wore a uniform different from that of the boys, lighter and with no stripe down the side of the trousers. The rows of medals on his chest were more than a hand span wide.

The man set the papers on his desk, making no attempt to approach Brunetti. 'And you are?' he asked, managing to sound bored with the question.

'Commissario Guido Brunetti, sir,' he said. 'I've been sent to investigate the report of a death here.' This was not strictly true, for Brunetti had sent himself to investigate, but he saw no reason why the Comandante should be told this. He stepped forward and extended his hand quite naturally, as though he were too dull to have registered the coolness emanating from the other man.

After a pause long enough to indicate who was in charge, Bembo stepped forward and extended his hand. His grip was firm and gave every indication that the Comandante was restraining himself from exerting his full force out of consideration for what it would do to Brunetti's hand.

'Ah, yes,' Bembo said, 'a commissario.' He allowed a pause to extend the statement and then went on, 'I'm surprised my friend Vice-Questore Patta didn't think to call me to tell me you were coming.'

Brunetti wondered if the reference to his superior, who was unlikely to appear in his office for at least another hour, was meant to make him tug humbly at his forelock while telling Bembo he would do everything in his power to see that he was not disturbed by the investigation. 'I'm sure he will as soon as I give him my preliminary report, Comandante,' Brunetti said.

'Of course,' Bembo said and moved around his desk to take his chair. He waved what was no doubt a gracious hand to Brunetti, who seated himself. Brunetti wanted to see how eager Bembo was to have the investigation begin. From the way the Comandante moved small objects around on the top of his desk, pulled together a stack of papers and tapped them into line, it seemed that he felt no unseemly haste. Brunetti remained silent.

'It's all very unfortunate, this,' Bembo finally said.

Brunetti thought it best to nod.

'It's the first time we've had a suicide at the Academy,' Bembo went on.

'Yes, it must be shocking. How old was the boy?' Brunetti asked. He pulled a notebook from the pocket of his jacket and bent the covers back when he found an empty page. He patted his pockets then, with an embarrassed smile, leaned forward and reached for a pencil that lay on the Comandante's desk. 'If I may, sir,' he said.

Bembo didn't bother to acknowledge the request. 'Seventeen, I believe,' he said.

'And his name, sir?' Brunetti asked.

'Ernesto Moro,' Bembo replied.

Brunetti's start of surprise at the mention of one of the city's most famous names was entirely involuntary.

'Yes,' Bembo said, 'Fernando's son.'

Before his retirement from political life, Dottor Fernando Moro had for some years served as a Member of Parliament, one of the few men universally acknowledged to have filled that position honestly and honourably. The wags of Venice insisted that Moro had been moved from various committees because his honesty proved inconvenient to his colleagues: the instant it became evident that he was immune to the temptations of money and power, his incredulous fellow parliamentarians found reason to reassign him. His career was often cited as evidence of the survival of hope in the face of experience, for each chairman who found Moro appointed to his committee was certain that, this time, he could be induced to back those policies most certain to line the pockets of the few at the expense of the many.

But none of them, in three years, had apparently succeeded in corrupting Moro. Then, only two years ago, he had suddenly, and without explanation, renounced his parliamentary seat and returned full time to private medical practice.

'Has he been informed?' Brunetti asked.

'Who?' Bembo asked, clearly puzzled by Brunetti's question.

'His father.'

Bembo shook his head. 'I don't know. Isn't that the job of the police?'

Brunetti, exercising great restraint, glanced at his watch

and asked, 'How long ago was the body discovered?' Though he strove for neutrality, he failed to keep reproach out of his voice.

Bembo bristled. 'This morning some time.'

'What time?'

'I don't know. Shortly before the police were called.'

'How shortly before?'

'I have no idea. I was called at home.'

'At what time?' Brunetti asked, pencil poised over the page.

Bembo's lips tightened in badly disguised irritation. 'I'm not sure. About seven, I'd say.'

'Were you already awake?'

'Of course.'

'And was it you who called the police?'

'No, that had already been done by someone here.'

Brunetti uncrossed his legs and leaned forward. 'Comandante, the call is registered as having come at seven twenty-six. That's about half an hour after you were called and told the boy was dead.' He paused to allow the man time to explain, but when Bembo made no attempt to do so, Brunetti continued. 'Could you suggest an explanation for that?'

'For what?'

'For the delay of a half an hour in informing the authorities of a suspicious death at the institution you direct.'

'Suspicious?' Bembo demanded.

'Until the medical examiner has determined the cause of death, any death is suspicious.'

'The boy committed suicide. Anyone can see that.'

'Have you seen him?'

The Comandante did not answer immediately. He sat back in his chair and considered the man in front of him. Finally he answered, 'Yes. I have. I came here when they called me and went to see him. He'd hanged himself.'

'And the delay?' Brunetti asked.

Bembo waved the question away. 'I have no idea. They must have thought I would call the police, and I was sure they had.'

Letting this pass, Brunetti asked, 'Do you have any idea who called?'

'I just told you I don't know,' Bembo said. 'Surely they must have given their name.'

'Surely,' Brunetti repeated and returned to the subject. 'But no one has contacted Dottor Moro?'

Bembo shook his head.

Brunetti got to his feet. 'I'll go and see that someone does.'

Bembo didn't bother to stand. Brunetti paused for a moment, curious to see if the Comandante would enforce his sense of the loftiness of his position by glancing down at something on his desk while he waited for Brunetti to leave. Not so. Bembo sat, empty hands resting on the top of his desk, eyes on Brunetti, waiting.

Brunetti slipped his notebook into the pocket of his jacket, placed the pencil carefully on the desk in front of Bembo, and left the Comandante's office.

3

Outside Bembo's office, Brunetti moved a few metres away from the door and pulled out his *telefonino*. He punched in 12 and was asking for Moro's number when his attention was caught by loud male voices coming up the stairway.

'Where's my son?' a loud voice demanded. A softer voice replied, but the other voice insisted, 'Where is he?' Saying nothing, Brunetti broke the connection and slipped the phone back into his pocket.

As he approached the stairs, the voices grew even louder. 'I want to know where he is,' the original voice shouted, refusing to be placated by whatever it was that was said to him.

When Brunetti started down the flight of stairs, he saw at the bottom a man of about his own age and size and recognized him instantly, having both seen his photo in the papers and been presented to him at official functions. Moro's face was blade-thin, his cheekbones high and tilted at a Slavic angle. His eyes and complexion were dark and in sharp contrast to his hair, which was white and thick. He stood face to face with a younger man dressed in the same dark blue uniform worn by the boys in the courtyard.

'Dottor Moro,' Brunetti said, continuing down the steps in their direction.

The doctor turned and looked up at Brunetti but gave no sign of recognition. His mouth was open and he appeared to breathe only with difficulty. Brunetti recognized the effect of shock and mounting anger at the opposition the young man was giving him.

'I'm Brunetti, sir. Police,' he said. When Moro made no response, Brunetti turned to the other man and said, 'Where's the boy?'

At this reinforcement of the demand, the young man gave in. 'In the bathroom. Upstairs,' he said, but grudgingly, as if neither man had the right to ask anything of him.

'Where?' Brunetti asked.

Vianello called from the staircase above them, waving back towards where he had come from, 'He's up here, sir.'

Brunetti glanced at Moro, whose attention was now directed at Vianello. He stood rooted to the spot, his mouth still roundly open and his breathing still audible to Brunetti.

He stepped forward and took the doctor's arm in his. Saying nothing, Brunetti led him up the stairs after the retreating back of the slowly moving Vianello. At the third floor, Vianello paused to check that they were following, then moved down a corridor lined with many doors. At the end he turned right and continued down an identical one. Vianello opened a door with a round glass porthole. He caught Brunetti's glance and gave a small nod, at the sight of which Moro's arm tightened under Brunetti's hand, though his steps did not falter.

The doctor passed in front of Vianello as though the Inspector were invisible. From the doorway, Brunetti saw only his back as he walked toward the far end of the bathroom, where something lay on the floor.

'I cut him down, sir,' Vianello said, putting a hand on his superior's arm. 'I know we're not supposed to touch anything, but I couldn't stand the idea that anyone who came to identify him would see him like that.'

Brunetti clasped Vianello's arm and had time to say only 'Good', when a low animal noise came from the back of the room. Moro half lay, half knelt beside the body, cradling it in his arms. The noise came from him, beyond speech and beyond meaning. As they watched, Moro pulled the dead boy closer to him, gently moving the lolling head until it rested in the hollow between his own neck and shoulder. The noise turned to words, but neither Vianello nor Brunetti could understand what the man said.

They approached him together. Brunetti saw a man not far from himself in age and appearance, cradling in his arms the body of his only son, a boy about the same age as Brunetti's own. Terror closed his eyes, and when he opened them he saw Vianello, kneeling behind the doctor, his arm across his shoulders, close to but not touching the dead boy. 'Let him be, Dottore,' Vianello said softly, increasing his pressure on the doctor's back. 'Let him be,' he repeated and moved slowly to support the boy's weight from the other side. Moro seemed not to understand, but then the combination of command and sympathy in Vianello's voice penetrated his numbness, and, aided by Vianello, he lowered the upper half of his son's body to the floor and knelt beside him, staring down at his distended face.

Vianello leaned over the body, lifted the edge of the military cape, and pulled it over the face. It wasn't until then that Brunetti bent down and put a supporting hand under Moro's arm and helped him rise unsteadily to his feet.

Vianello moved to the other side of the man, and together they left the bathroom and headed down the long corridor and then down the stairs and out into the courtyard. When they emerged, groups of uniformed boys still stood about. All of them glanced in the direction of the three men who emerged from the building and then as quickly glanced away.

Moro dragged his feet like a man in chains, capable of only the shortest steps. Once he stopped, shook his head as if in answer to a question neither of the others could hear, and then allowed himself to be led forward again.

Seeing Pucetti emerge from a corridor on the other side of the courtyard, Brunetti raised his free hand and signalled him over. When the uniformed officer reached them, Brunetti stepped aside and Pucetti slipped his arm under Moro's, who seemed not to register the change. 'Take him back to the launch,' Brunetti said to both of them, and then to Vianello, 'Go home with him.'

Pucetti gave Brunetti an inquiring glance.

'Help Vianello take the doctor to the boat and then come back here,' Brunetti said, deciding that Pucetti's intelligence and native curiosity, to make no mention of his nearness in age to the cadets, would help in questioning them. The two officers set off, Moro moving jerkily, as though unaware of their presence.

Brunetti watched them leave the courtyard. The boys shot occasional glances in his direction, but they had only to catch his eye to look away instantly or to adjust their gaze as though they were busy studying the far wall and really didn't notice him standing there.

When Pucetti came back a few minutes later, Brunetti told him to find out if anything unusual had happened the night before and to get a sense of what sort of boy young Moro had been as well as of how he was regarded by his classmates. Brunetti knew that these questions had to be asked now, before their memories of the previous night's events began to influence one another and before the boy's death had time to register and thus transform everything the cadets had to say about him into the sort of saccharine nonsense that accompanies the retelling of the stories of the saints and martyrs.

Hearing the two-tone wail of an approaching siren, Brunetti went out on to the *Riva* to wait for the scene of crime team. The white police launch drew up to the side of the canal; four uniformed officers stepped off then reached back on board for the boxes and bags filled with their equipment.

Two more men then stepped off. Brunetti waved to them, and they picked up their equipment and started in his direction. When they reached him, Brunetti asked Santini, the chief technician, 'Who's coming?'

All of the men or the scene of crime team shared Brunetti's preference for Dottor Rizzardi, so it was with a special tone of voice that Santini answered, 'Venturi', consciously omitting the man's title.

'Ah,' answered Brunetti before he turned and led the men into the courtyard of the Academy. Just inside, he told them the body was upstairs, then led them to the third floor and along the corridor to the open door of the bathroom.

Brunetti chose not to go back inside with them, though not out of a professional concern with the purity of the scene of the death. Leaving them to it, he returned to the courtyard.

There was no sign of Pucetti, and all of the cadets had disappeared. Either they had been summoned to classes or had retreated to their rooms: in either case, they had removed themselves from the vicinity of the police.

He went back up to Bembo's office and knocked at the door. Hearing no response, he knocked again, then tried the handle. The door was locked. He knocked again but no one answered.

Brunetti walked back to the central staircase, stopping to open each of the doors in the corridor. Behind them stood classrooms: one with charts and maps on the walls, another with algebraic formulae covering two blackboards, and a third with an enormous blackboard covered by a complicated diagram filled with arrows and bars, the sort of design usually found in history books to illustrate troop movements during battles.

In ordinary circumstances, Brunetti would have paused to study this, as, over the decades, he had read accounts of scores, perhaps hundreds, of battles, but today the diagram and its meaning held no interest for him, and he closed the door. He climbed to the third floor where, decades ago, the servants would have lived, and there he found what he wanted: the dormitories. At least that was what he thought they had to be: doors set not too close to one another, a printed card bearing two family names slipped into a neat plastic holder to the left of each.

He knocked at the first. No response. The same with the second. At the third, he thought he heard a faint noise from inside and so, without bothering to read the names on the card, he pushed the door open. A young man sat at a desk in front of the single window, his back to Brunetti, moving about in his chair as though trying to escape from it or perhaps in the grip of some sort of seizure. Brunetti stepped into the room, reluctant to approach and startle the boy into some worse reaction but alarmed by his violent motions.

Suddenly, the boy bent his head towards the desk, thrust out his arm, and slapped his palm on the surface three times, singing out, 'Yaah, yaah, yaah,' drawing out the final noise until, as Brunetti could hear even across the room, the drummer played a final extended riff, which the boy accompanied, beating out the rhythm with his fingers on the edge of his desk.

Into the pause between tracks, Brunetti barked, his voice intentionally loud, 'Cadet.'

The word cut through the low hiss of the headphones and the boy jumped to his feet. He turned towards the voice, his right hand leaping toward his forehead in salute, but he caught it in the wire of the headphones and the Discman crashed to the floor, dragging the headphones after it.

The impact seemed not to have dislodged the disc, for Brunetti could still hear the bass, loud even halfway across the room. 'Hasn't anyone ever told you how much that will damage your hearing?' Brunetti asked conversationally. Usually, when he put this same question to his own children, he pitched his voice barely above a whisper, the first few times successfully tricking them into asking him to repeat himself. Wise to him now, they ignored him.

The boy slowly lowered his hand from his forehead, looking very confused. 'What did you say?' he asked, then added, by force of habit, 'sir.' He was tall and very thin, with a narrow jaw, one side of which looked as if it had been shaved with a dull razor, the other covered with signs of persistent acne. His eyes were almond shaped, as beautiful as a girl's.

Brunetti took the two steps that brought him to the other side of the room, and noticed that the boy's body tightened in response. But all Brunetti did was bend down to pick up the Discman and headphones. He set them carefully on the boy's desk, marvelling as he did at the spartan simplicity of the room: it looked like the room of a robot, not a young man, indeed, of two young men, if he was to believe the evidence provided by bunk beds.

'I said loud music can damage your hearing. It's what I tell my children, but they don't listen to me.'

This confused the boy even more, as if it had been a long time since an adult had said anything to him that was both normal and understandable. 'Yes, my aunt tells me that, too.'

'But you don't listen?' Brunetti asked. 'Or is it that you don't believe her?' He was honestly curious.

'Oh, I believe her all right,' the boy said, loosening up sufficiently to reach down and press the OFF button.

'But?' Brunetti insisted.

'It doesn't matter,' the boy said with a shrug.

'No, tell me,' Brunetti said. 'I'd really like to know.'

'It doesn't matter what happens to my hearing,' the boy explained.

'Doesn't matter?' Brunetti asked, utterly at a loss to grasp his meaning. 'That you go deaf?'

'No, not that,' he answered, paying real attention to Brunetti and apparently now interested in making him understand. 'It takes a lot of years for something like that to happen. That's why it doesn't matter. Like all that Global Warming stuff. Nothing matters if it takes a long time.'

It was obvious to Brunetti that the boy was in earnest. He said, 'But you're in school, studying for a future career – I presume in the military. That's not going to happen for a number of years, either; doesn't that matter?'

The boy answered after a few moments' reflection. 'That's different.'

'Different how?' asked a relentless Brunetti.

The boy had relaxed now with the ease of their conversation and the seriousness with which Brunetti treated his answers. He leaned back against the top of his desk, picked up a packet of cigarettes and held it out to Brunetti. At his refusal the boy took one and patted around on the top of his desk until he found a plastic lighter hidden under a notebook.

He lit the cigarette and tossed the lighter back on to the desk. He took a long drag at the cigarette. Brunetti was struck by how very hard he tried to appear older and more sophisticated than he was; then the boy looked at Brunetti and said, 'Because I can choose about the music but I can't about the school.'

Sure that this made some sort of profound difference to the boy but unwilling to spend more time pursuing it, Brunetti asked, 'What's your name?' using the familiar *tu*, as he would with one of his children's friends.

'Giuliano Ruffo,' the boy answered.

Brunetti introduced himself, using his name and not his title, and stepped forward to offer his hand. Ruffo slid from the desk and took Brunetti's hand.

'Did you know him, the boy who died?'

Ruffo's face froze, all ease fled his body, and he shook his head in automatic denial. As Brunetti was wondering how it was that he didn't know a fellow student in a school this small, the boy said, 'That is, I didn't know him well. We just had one class together.' Ease had disappeared from his voice, as well: he spoke quickly, as if eager to move away from the meaning of his words.

'What one?'

'Physics.'

'What other subjects do you take?' Brunetti asked. 'What is it for you, the second year?'

'Yes, sir. So we have to take Latin and Greek and Mathematics, English, History, and then we get to choose two optional subjects.'

'So Physics is one of yours?'

'Yes, sir.'

'And the other?'

The answer was a long time in coming. Brunetti thought the boy must be trying to work out what this man's hidden motive was in asking all of these questions. If Brunetti had a motive, it was hidden even from himself: all he could do at this point was try to get a sense of things at the school, to catch the mood of the place; all of the information he gained had more or less the same amorphous value and its meaning would not become clear until later, when each piece could be seen as part of some larger pattern.

The boy stabbed out his cigarette, eyed the packet, but did not light another. Brunetti repeated, 'What is it, the second one?'

Reluctantly, as if confessing to something he perhaps construed as weakness, the boy finally answered, 'Music.'

'Good for you,' came Brunetti's instant response.

'Why do you say that, sir?' the boy asked, his eagerness patent. Or perhaps it was merely relief at this removal to a neutral subject.

Brunetti's response had been visceral, so he had to consider what to say. 'I read a lot of history,' he began, 'and a lot of history is military history.' The boy nodded, prodding him along with his curiosity. 'And historians often say that soldiers know only one thing.' The boy nodded again. 'And no matter how well they might know that one thing, war, it's not enough. They've got to know about other things.' He smiled at the boy, who smiled in return. 'It's the great weakness, knowing only that one thing.'

'I wish you'd tell my grandfather that, sir,' he said.

'He doesn't believe it?'

'Oh, no, he doesn't even want to hear the word "music", at least not from me.'

'What would he rather hear – that you'd been in a duel?' Brunetti asked, not at all uncomfortable at undermining the concept of grandparental authority.

'Oh, he'd love that, especially if it were with sabres.'

'And you went home with a scar across your cheek?' Brunetti suggested.

They laughed at the absurdity, and it was like this, easy and comfortably united in gentle mockery of military tradition, that Comandante Bembo found them.

4

'Ruffo!' a voice barked from behind Brunetti.

The boy's smile vanished and he straightened up to stand as stiff as one of the pilings in the *laguna*, his heels clacking together at the same instant as his stiff fingers snapped to his forehead in salute.

'What are you doing here?' Bembo demanded.

'I don't have a class this hour, Comandante,' Ruffo answered, staring straight ahead.

'And what were you doing?'

'I was talking to this gentleman, sir,' he said, eyes still on the far wall.

'Who gave you permission to talk to him?'

Ruffo's face was a mask. He made no attempt to answer the question.

'Well?' demanded Bembo in an even tighter voice.

Brunetti turned to face the Comandante and acknowledged his arrival with a gentle nod. Keeping his voice mild, he asked, 'Does he need permission to speak to the police, sir?'

'He's a minor,' Bembo said.

'I'm not sure I follow you, sir,' Brunetti said, careful to smile to show his confusion. He could have understood if Bembo had said something about military rank or the need to respond only to orders from a direct superior, but to cite the boy's youth as a reason why he should not talk to the police displayed what seemed to Brunetti an inordinate attention to legal detail. 'I'm not sure I see how Cadet Ruffo's age is important.'

'It means his parents should be with him when you talk to him.'

'Why is that, sir?' Brunetti asked, curious to hear Bembo's reason.

It took a moment for Bembo to find it. Finally he said, 'To see that he understands the questions you ask.'

His doubts as to the boy's ability to understand simple questions hardly spoke well of the quality of instruction on offer at the school. Brunetti turned back to the cadet, who stood rigid, arms rod-like at his side, his chin a stranger to his collar. 'You understood what I asked you, didn't you, Cadet?'

'I don't know, sir,' the boy answered, keeping his eyes on the wall.

'We were talking about his classes, sir,' Brunetti said, 'and Cadet Ruffo was telling me how much he enjoyed Physics.'

'Is this true, Ruffo?' the Comandante demanded, not the least concerned that he was openly doubting Brunetti's veracity.

'Yes, sir,' the boy answered. 'I was telling the gentleman that I had two elective subjects and how much I liked them.'

'Don't you like the required subjects?' Bembo demanded. Then, to Brunetti: 'Was he complaining about them?'

'No,' Brunetti answered calmly. 'We didn't discuss them.' He wondered, as he spoke, why Bembo should be so concerned at the mere possibility that a student had said something negative about his classes. What else would a student be expected to say about his classes?

Abruptly Bembo said, 'You can go, Ruffo.' The boy saluted and, ignoring Brunetti's presence, walked out of the room, leaving the door open after him.

'I'll thank you to let me know before you question any of my cadets again,' Bembo said in an unfriendly voice.

Brunetti hardly thought it worth contesting the point, so agreed that he would. The Comandante turned towards the door, hesitated for a moment as though he wanted to turn back and say something to Brunetti, but then thought better of it and left.

Brunetti found himself alone in Ruffo's room, feeling in some way invited there as a guest and thus bound by the rules of hospitality, one of which was never to betray the host's trust by invading the privacy of his home. The first thing Brunetti did was to open the front drawer of the desk and remove the papers he found there. Most of them were notes, what appeared to be rough drafts for essays the boy was writing; some were letters.

'*Dear Giuliano,*' Brunetti read, entirely without shame or scruple. '*Your aunt came to see me last week and told me you were doing well in school.*' The calligraphy had the neat roundness of the generation previous to his own, though the lines wandered up and down, following an invisible path known only to the writer. It was signed 'Nonna'. Brunetti glanced through the other papers, found nothing of interest, and put them all back into the drawer.

He opened the doors of the closet next to Ruffo's desk and checked the pockets of the jackets hanging there; he found nothing but small change and cancelled vaporetto tickets. There was a laptop computer on the desk, but he didn't even waste his time turning it on, knowing he would have no idea what to do with it. Under the bed, pushed back against the wall, he saw what looked like a violin case. The books were what he would have expected: textbooks, a driver's manual, a history of AC Milan and other books about soccer. The bottom shelf held musical scores: Mozart's violin sonatas and the first violin part of one of the Beethoven string quartets. Brunetti shook his head in bemusement at the contrast between the music in the Discman and the music on the shelf. He opened the door to the closet that must belong to Ruffo's roommate and cast his eye across the surface of the second desk, but he saw nothing of interest.

Struck again by the neatness of the room, the almost surgical precision with which the bed was made, Brunetti toyed for a moment with the idea of drugging his son Raffi and having him brought down here to be enrolled. But then he remembered what it was that had brought him to this room, and levity slipped away on silent feet.

The other rooms were empty or, at least, no one responded to his knocking, so he went back towards the bathroom where the boy had been found. The scene of crime team was at work, and the body still lay there, now entirely covered with the dark woollen cloak.

'Who cut him down?' Santini asked when he saw Brunetti. 'Vianello.'

'He shouldn't have done that,' another of the technicians called from across the room.

'That's exactly what he told me,' Brunetti answered.

Santini shrugged. 'I would have done it, too.' There were affirmative grunts from two of the men.

Brunetti was about to ask what the crew thought had happened, when he heard footsteps. He glanced aside and saw Dottor Venturi, one of Rizzardi's assistants. Both men nodded, as much acknowledgement of the other's presence as either was willing to give.

Insensitive to most human feelings that were not directed towards him, Venturi stepped up close to the body and set his medical bag by the head. He went down on one knee and drew the edge of the cloak from the boy's face.

Brunetti looked away, back into the showers, where Pedone, Santini's assistant, was holding a plastic spray bottle up towards the top of the right-hand wall. As Brunetti watched, he squirted cloud after tiny cloud of dark grey powder on to the walls, moving carefully from left to right and then back to his starting point to repeat the process about twenty centimetres below.

By the time all the walls were coated, Venturi was back on his feet. Brunetti saw that he had left the boy's face uncovered.

'Who cut him down?' was the first thing the doctor asked.

'One of my men. I told him to,' Brunetti answered and bent down to draw the edge of the cape back across the boy's face. He rose up again and looked at Venturi, saying nothing.

'Why did you do that?'

Appalled at the question, Brunetti ignored it, irritated that he had to speak to a man capable of asking it He asked, 'Does it look like suicide?'

Venturi's long pause made it obvious that he wanted to exchange discourtesies with Brunetti, but when Santini turned to him and said, 'Well?' the doctor answered, 'I won't have any idea until I can take a look at his insides.' Then, directly to Santini, 'Was there a chair, something he could stand on?'

One of the other technicians called over, 'A chair. It was in the shower.'

'You didn't move it, did you?' Venturi demanded of him.

'I photographed it,' the man answered. speaking with glacial clearness. 'Eight times, I think. And then Pedone dusted it for prints. And then I moved it so it wouldn't get in his way when he dusted the shower stall.' Pointing with his chin to a wooden chair that stood in front of one of the sinks, he added, 'That's it, over there.'

The doctor ignored the chair. 'I'll have my report sent to

you when I'm finished,' he said to Brunetti, then picked up his bag and left.

When Venturi's footsteps had died away, Brunetti asked Santini, 'What does it look like to you?'

'He *could* have done it himself,' the technician answered. He pointed to some marks that stood out from the darker grey of the coating on the walls of the shower. 'There are two long swipes across the wall here, at about shoulder height. He could have done that.'

'Would that have happened?'

'Probably. It's instinct: no matter how much they want to die, the body doesn't. '

Pedone, who had been openly listening to this, added, 'It's clean, sir. No one had a fight in there, if that's what you're wondering about.'

When it seemed that his partner wasn't going to add anything, Santini continued: 'It's what they do, sir, when they hang themselves. Believe me. If there's a wall near them, they try to grab it; can't help themselves.'

'It's the way boys do it, isn't it, hanging?' Brunetti asked, not looking down at Moro.

'More than girls, yes,' Santini agreed. His voice took on an edge of anger and he asked, 'What was he – seventeen? eighteen? How could he do something like that?'

'God knows,' Brunetti said.

'God didn't have anything to do with this,' Santini said angrily, though it was unclear whether his remark called into question the deity's charity or his very existence. Santini went out into the hall, where two white-coated attendants from the hospital waited, a rolled-up stretcher leaning against the wall between them. 'You can take him now,' he said. He remained outside while they went in, put the boy on the stretcher, and carried him from the room. When they were abreast of Santini, he put up a monitory hand. They stopped, and he leaned down to pick up the end of the dark blue military cloak that was dragging on the ground behind the stretcher. He tucked it under the boy's leg and told the attendants to take him out to the boat.

5

Recognizing it as the temptation of moral cowardice, Brunetti pushed aside the desire to join the others on the police boat to the hospital and from there to the Questura. Perhaps it was the flash of terror when he first saw the boy's body, or perhaps it was Brunetti's admiration for the elder Moro's inconvenient honesty, but something there was that urged Brunetti to get a more complete picture of the boy's death. The suicides of young boys were ever more frequent: Brunetti had read somewhere that, with almost mathematical regularity, they increased in times of economic well-being and decreased when times were bad. During wars, they virtually disappeared. He assumed his own son was as subject to the vagaries of adolescence as any other boy: carried up and down on the waves of his hormones, his popularity, or his success at school. The idea of Raffi's ever being driven to suicide was inconceivable, but that must be what every parent thought.

Until evidence suggested that the boy's death had not been suicide, Brunetti had no mandate to question anyone about any other possibility: not his classmates, still less his parents. To do so would be the worst sort of ghoulish curiosity as well as a flagrant misuse of his power. Admitting all of this, he went out into the courtyard of the Academy and, using the *telefonino* he had remembered to bring with him, called Signorina Elettra's direct line at the Questura.

When she answered, he told her where he was and asked that she check the phone book for Moro's address, which he thought must be in Dorsoduro, though he couldn't remember why he associated the man with that *sestiere*.

She asked no questions, told him to wait a moment, then said the number was unlisted. There elapsed another minute or two, then she gave him the Dorsoduro address. She told him to wait, then told him the house was on the canal running alongside the church of Madonna della Salute. 'It's got to be the one next to the low brick one that has the terrace with all the flowers,' she said.

He thanked her, then made his way back up the stairs to the dormitory rooms on the top floor and went along the still-silent corridor, checking the names outside of the doors. He found it at the end: MORO/CAVANI. Not bothering to knock, Brunetti entered the room. Like that of Ruffo, the room was clean, almost surgical: bunk beds and two small desks opposite them, nothing left in sight to clutter up their surfaces. He took a pen from the inside pocket of his jacket and used it to open the drawer of the desk nearest him. With the pen he flipped open the notebook that lay inside. Ernesto's name was on the inside of the cover and the book was filled with mathematical formulae, written out in a neat, square hand. He shoved the notebook to the back of the drawer and opened the one beneath it, with much the same result, though this one contained exercises in English.

He shoved the drawer closed and turned his attention to the closet between the two desks. One door had Moro's name on it. Brunetti pulled it open from the bottom with his foot.

Inside, there were two uniforms in dry cleaning bags, a denim jacket, and a brown tweed coat. The only things he found in the pockets were some small change and a dirty handkerchief.

A bookcase contained nothing more than textbooks. He lacked the will to take down and examine each of them. He took one final look around the room and left, careful to hook his pen in the handle to pull the door shut.

He met Santini on the steps and told him to check Moro's room then left the school and went down to the edge of the Canale della Giudecca. Turning right, he started to walk along the *Riva*, intending to catch a *vaporetto*. As he walked, he kept his attention on the buildings on the other side of the canal: Nico's Bar and, above it, an apartment he had spent a lot of time in before he met Paola; the church of the Gesuati, where once a decent man had been pastor; the former Swiss Consulate, the flag gone now. Have even the Swiss abandoned us? he wondered. Ahead was the Bucintoro, the long narrow boats long gone, evicted by the scent of Guggenheim money, Venetian oarsmen gone to make space for even more tourist shops. He saw a boat coming from Redentore and hurried on to the *imbarcadero* at Palanca to cross back to the Zattere. When he got off, he looked at his watch and realized that it really did take less than five minutes to make the trip from the Giudecca. Even so, the other island still seemed, as it had ever seemed, as far distant as the Galapagos.

It took less than five minutes to weave his way back to the broad *campo* that surrounded La Madonna della Salute, and there he found the house. Again resisting the impulse to delay, he rang the bell and gave his title and name.

'What do you want?' a woman's voice asked.

'I'd like to speak to Dottor Moro,' he said, announcing at least the most immediate of his desires.

'He can't see anyone,' she said shortly.

'I saw him before,' Brunetti said, then added, in the hope that it would give force to his request, 'at the school.' He waited to see if this would have any effect on the woman, but then went on, 'It's necessary that I speak to him.'

She made a noise, but it was cut off by the electrical buzz of the door release, leaving Brunetti to guess at its nature. He pushed open the door, passed quickly through a hallway, and stopped at the bottom of a staircase. At the top, a door opened and a tall woman came out on to the landing. 'Up here,' she said.

When he reached the top of the stairs, she turned and led him into the apartment, closed the door behind him, then turned back to face him. He was struck at first by the fact that, though surely not as old as he, she had white hair, cut short just above her shoulders. It contrasted sharply with her skin, dark as an Arab's, and with her eyes, as close to black as he had ever seen eyes be.

She put out her hand. 'I'm Luisa, Fernando's cousin.'

Brunetti took her hand and gave his name and position. 'I realize this is a terrible time,' he began, planning how best to speak to her. Her posture was rigid, her back as straight as if she had been told to stand against a wall. She kept her eyes on his as they spoke.

When Brunetti added nothing to this self-evident truth, she asked, 'What do you want to know?'

'I'd like to ask him about his son's state of mind.'

'Why?' she demanded. Brunetti thought the answer to that should have been obvious, and was taken aback by the vehemence with which she asked the question.

'In a case such as this,' he began evasively, 'it's necessary to know as much as possible about how the person was feeling and behaving, whether there were perhaps any signs . . .'

'Of what?' She cut him off, making no attempt to disguise her anger or her contempt. 'That he was going to kill himself?' Before Brunetti could answer, she went on, 'If that's what you mean, for God's sake, then say so.' Again she didn't wait for an answer. 'The idea's ridiculous. It's disgusting. Ernesto would no sooner kill himself than I would. He was a healthy boy. It's insulting to suggest that he would.' She closed her eyes and pressed her lips together, fighting to regain control of herself.

Before Brunetti could say that he had made no insinuation of any kind, Dottor Moro appeared in a doorway. 'That's enough, Luisa,' he said in a soft voice. 'You shouldn't say any more.'

Though the man had spoken, it was the face of the woman Brunetti studied. The stiffness of her posture lessened, and her body inclined in her cousin's direction. She raised one hand towards him but made no move to touch him. Instead, she nodded once, ignored Brunetti completely, and turned away. Brunetti watched as she walked down the corridor and through a door at the end.

When she was gone, Brunetti turned his attention to the doctor. Though he knew this was impossible, Moro had aged a decade during the brief time that had elapsed since Brunetti had last seen him. His skin was pasty, his eyes dull and reddened with tears, but it was in his posture that Brunetti perceived most change, for it had taken on the forward-leaning curvature of an old man.

'I'm sorry to intrude on your grief, Dottore,' Brunetti began, 'but I hope that by speaking to you now, I won't have to trouble you again.' Even to Brunetti, schooled as he was in the ways of professional mendacity, this sounded so forced and artificial as to distance him from the other man and his sorrow.

Moro waved his right hand in the air, a gesture that might just as easily have been dismissal as acknowledgement. He wrapped his arms around his stomach and bowed his head.

'Dottore,' he went on, 'in the last few days or weeks, had

your son done anything that would lead you to suspect that he might have been considering anything like this?' Moro's head was still bowed so Brunetti could not see his eyes, nor had he any idea if the doctor was paying attention.

He continued, 'Dottore, I know how difficult this must be for you, but it's important that I have this information.'

Without looking up, Moro said, 'I don't think you do.'

'I beg your pardon,' Brunetti said.

'I don't think you have any idea of how difficult this is.'

The truth of this made Brunetti blush. When his face had grown cool again, Moro had still not bothered to look at him. After what seemed to Brunetti a long time, the doctor raised his head. No tears stood in his eyes, and his voice was as calm as it had been when he spoke to his cousin. 'I'd be very grateful if you'd leave now, Commissario.' Brunetti began to protest, but the doctor cut him off by raising his voice, but only in volume: his tone remained calm and impersonal. 'Please don't argue with me. There is nothing at all that I have to say to you. Not now, and not in the future.' He took his arms from their protective position around his middle and let them fall to his sides. 'I have nothing further to say.'

Brunetti was certain that it was futile to pursue the matter now, equally certain that he would return and ask the same question again after the doctor had had time to overcome his immediate agony. Since he had learned of the boy's death, Brunetti had been assailed by the desire to know if the man had other children, but couldn't bring himself to ask. He had some sort of theoretical belief that their existence would serve as consolation, however limited. He tried to put himself in Moro's place and understand what solace he would find in the survival of one of his own children, but his imagination shied away from that horror. At the very thought, some force stronger than taboo seized him, numbing his mind. Not daring to offer his hand or to say anything further, Brunetti left the apartment.

From the Salute stop, he took the Number One to San Zaccaria and started back toward the Questura. As he approached it, a group of teenagers, three boys and two girls, cascaded down the Ponte dei Greci and came towards him, arms linked, laughter radiating out from them. Brunetti stopped walking and stood in the middle of the pavement, waiting for this exuberant wave of youth to wash over him. Like the Red Sea, they parted and swept around him: Brunetti was sure they hadn't even noticed him in any real sense; he was merely a stationary obstacle to be got round.

Both of the girls had cigarettes in their hands, something that usually filled Brunetti with the desire to tell them, if they valued their health and well-being, to stop. Instead, he turned and looked after them, filled with a sense of almost religious awe at the sight of their youth and joy.

By the time he reached his office, the feeling had passed. On his desk he found the first of the many forms that were generated by any case of suicide; he didn't bother to fill it out. It was only after he heard from Venturi that he would know how to proceed.

He called down to the officers' room, but neither Vianello nor Pucetti was there. He dialled Signorina Elettra's extension and asked her to begin a complete search through all the sources available to her, official and unofficial, for information on Fernando Moro's careers as both a doctor and a Member of Parliament. Saying that she had already begun, she promised to have something for him later in the day.

The thought of lunch displeased him: food seemed an irrelevant extravagance. He felt a gnawing desire to see his family, though he knew his current mood would render him so solicitous as to make them uncomfortable. He called Paola and told her he couldn't make it home for lunch, saying that something had come up at the Questura that would keep him there and, yes, yes, he'd eat something and be home at the regular time.

'I hope it's not too bad,' Paola said, letting him know that she had registered his tone, however neutral he had tried to make his words.

'I'll see you later,' he said, still unwilling to tell her what had happened. 'Hug the kids for me,' he said before he hung up.

He sat at his desk for a few minutes, then drew some papers towards him and looked at them, reading through the words, understanding each one but not certain he understood what they intended to say. He set them aside, then pulled them back and read them again; this time the sentences made sense to him, though he could see no reason why anyone should find their messages important.

He went to the window and studied the crane that stood constant guard over the church and the restoration that had yet to begin. He had read or been told once how much the equally motionless cranes that loomed over the empty shell of the opera house cost the city to maintain each day. Where did all the money go? he wondered. Who was it that reaped such enormous profits from so much inactivity? Idly, keeping his mind occupied with matters other than the death of young men, he began rough calculations. If the cranes cost five thousand Euros a day, it would cost the city almost two million Euros to keep them there a year, whether they worked or not. He stood for a long time, numbers moving around in his head in far greater activity than had been shown by any of those cranes for some time.

Abruptly he turned away and went back to his desk. There was no one to call, so he left his office, went downstairs and out of the Questura. He walked to the bar at the foot of the bridge, where he had a *panino* and a glass of red wine and let the words of the day's newspaper pass under his eyes.

6

Though he prevaricated as much as he could, Brunetti still had no choice but eventually to return to the Questura. He stopped in the officers' room to look for Vianello and found him there with Pucetti. The younger officer started to get to his feet, but Brunetti waved him back. There was only one other policeman in the room, sitting at a desk off to one side, talking on the phone.

'Anything?' he asked the two seated policemen.

Pucetti glanced at Vianello, acknowledging his right to speak first.

'I took him back,' the Inspector began, 'but he wouldn't let me go in with him.' He shrugged this away and asked, 'You, sir?'

'I spoke to Moro and to his cousin, who was there with him. She said the boy couldn't have killed himself, seemed pretty insistent on it.' Something kept Brunetti from telling the others how easy it had been for Moro to dismiss him.

'His cousin, you said?' Vianello interrupted, echoing his neutrality.

'That's what she told me.' The habit of doubt, Brunetti reflected, the habit of seeking the lowest possible common moral denominator, had been bred into all of them. He wondered if there were some sort of psychological equation which correlated years of service with the police and an inability to believe in human goodness. And whether it was possible, or for how long it would be possible, to go back and forth between his professional world and his private world without introducing the contamination of the first to the second.

His attention was recalled by Vianello, who had just finished saying something.

'Excuse me?' Brunetti said.

'I asked if his wife was there,' Vianello repeated.

Brunetti shook his head. 'I don't know. No one else came in while I was there, but there's no reason she would want to talk to me.'

'Is there a wife?' Pucetti asked, emphasizing the first word.

Rather than admit that he didn't know, Brunetti said, 'I asked Signorina Elettra to see what she can find out about the family.'

'There was something in the papers about them, I think,' Vianello said. 'Years ago.' Brunetti and Pucetti waited for him to continue, but all the Inspector finally said was, 'I don't remember, but I think it was something about the wife.'

'Whatever it is, she'll find it,' Pucetti declared.

Years ago, Brunetti would have responded with condescension to Pucetti's childlike faith in Signorina Elettra's powers, as one would to the excesses of the peasant believers in the liquefaction of the blood of San Gennaro. Himself presently numbered among that unwashed throng, he made no demurral.

'Why don't you tell the Commissario what you've told me?' Vianello asked Pucetti, drawing him back from his devotions and Brunetti back from his reflections.

'The *portiere* told me that the gate is kept locked after ten at night,' the young officer began, 'but most faculty members have keys, and students who stay out later than that have to ring him to let them in.'

'And?' Brunetti asked, sensing Pucetti's reservations.

'I'm not sure,' Pucetti answered, then explained. 'Two of the boys I spoke to, separately, that is, seemed to make fun of the idea. I asked why, and one of them smiled and went like this,' Pucetti concluded, raising the thumb of his right hand towards his mouth.

Brunetti registered this but left it to Pucetti to continue. 'I'd say the boys are right and he's a drunk, the *portiere*. It was what – eleven in the morning when I spoke to him, and he was already halfway there.'

'Did any of the other boys mention this?'

'I didn't want to push them on it, sir. I didn't want any of them to know just what I had learned from the others. It's always better if they think I already know everything there is to know: that way, they think I'll know when they lie. But I got the feeling that they can get in and out when they please.'

Brunetti nodded for him to continue.

'I'm not sure I learned much more than that, sir. Most of them were so shocked that all they could do was ask more questions,' Pucetti answered.

'What exactly did you ask them?' Brunetti inquired.

'What you told me to, sir: how well they knew Moro and if they had spoken to him in the last few days. None of them could think of anything special the boy had said or done, nor that he had been behaving strangely, and none of them said that Moro had been a particular friend.'

'And the faculty?' Brunetti asked.

'Same thing. None of the ones I spoke to could remember anything strange about Moro's behaviour in the last few days, and all of them said he was a fine, fine boy but were quick to insist that they really didn't know him very well.'

All three of them recognized the phenomenon: most people refused to know anything. It was rare for any person who was subject to questioning or interrogation to admit to familiarity with the subject of police inquiries. One of the texts Paola had dealt with in her doctoral thesis was a medieval one entitled *The Cloud of Unknowing*. For an instant Brunetti pictured it as a warm, dry place to which all witnesses and potential witnesses fled in lemming-like terror and where they huddled until no single question remained to be asked.

Pucetti went on. 'I wanted to speak to his roommate, but he wasn't there last night, nor the night before.' Seeing interest in their faces, he explained, 'Twenty-three boys, including Moro's roommate, were on a weekend trip to the Naval Academy in Livorno. Soccer. The game was Sunday afternoon, and then they spent yesterday and this morning going to classes there. They don't get home until this evening.'

Vianello shook his head in tired resignation. 'I'm afraid this is all we're going to get from any of them.' Pucetti shrugged in silent agreement.

Brunetti stopped himself from remarking that it was what they could expect from a public which viewed authority and all who attempted to impose it as adversaries. He had read enough to know that there were countries whose citizens did not perceive their government as an inimical force, where they believed, instead, that the government existed to serve their needs and respond to their wishes. How would he react if someone he knew were to maintain this to be true here, in this city, in this country? Religious mania would be less convincing proof of mental imbalance.

Vianello and Pucetti were to go back that afternoon and question the rest of the boys and the remaining faculty. Leaving it at that, Brunetti told them he would be up in his office, and left.

Curiosity and the desire to see Signorina Elettra and learn what she had managed to discover led him off the stairs at her floor and into her small office. Here he had the sensation that he had stepped into a jungle or a forest: four tall trees with enormous leaves, broad, dark green and shiny, stood in terracotta pots against the back wall. With their darkness as a backdrop, Signorina Elettra, today dressed in colours usually seen only on Buddhist monks, sat at her desk. The total effect was of an enormous piece of exotic fruit exposed in front of the tree from which it had fallen.

'Lemons?' he asked.

'Yes.'

'Where did you get them?'

'A friend of mine just directed *Lulu* at the opera. He had them sent over after the last performance.'

'*Lulu*?'

She smiled. 'The very same.'

'I don't remember lemons in *Lulu*,' he said, puzzled, but willing, as ever, to be graced with illumination.

'He set the opera in Sicily,' she explained.

'Ah,' Brunetti whispered, trying to remember the plot. The music, mercifully, was gone. At a loss for what else to say, he asked, 'Did you go and see it?'

She took so long to answer that, at first, he thought he had somehow offended her with the question. Finally, she said, 'No, sir. My standards are very low, of course, but I do draw the line at going to the opera in a tent. In a parking lot.'

Brunetti, whose aesthetic principles were entrenched well behind that same line, nodded and asked, 'Have you been able to find out anything about Moro?'

Her smile was fainter, but it was still recognizably a smile. 'Some things have come in. I'm waiting for a friend in Siena to tell me more about the wife Federica.'

'What about her?' Brunetti asked.

'She was involved in an accident there.'

'What kind of accident?'

'Hunting.'

'Hunting? A woman in a hunting accident?' he asked, his disbelief audible.

She raised her eyebrows as if to suggest that anything at all was possible in a world where *Lulu* was set in Sicily, but instead said, 'I shall pass over the glaring sexism in that remark, Commissario.' She paused a didactic moment, then continued, 'It happened a couple of years ago. She was staying with friends in the countryside near Siena. One afternoon, while she was out for a walk, she was shot in the leg. Luckily, she was found before she bled to death and taken to the hospital.'

'Was the hunter ever found?'

'No, but it was hunting season so they assumed that a hunter had heard her and thought she was an animal and shot at the noise without seeing what it was.'

'And didn't bother to come and see what he had shot?' an indignant Brunetti asked. He added another question. 'Or when he saw what he had shot, he didn't help her or call for help?'

'It's what they do,' she said, her voice matching his own in indignation. 'You read the papers, don't you, every year when the season opens, about the way three or four of them get shot on the first day? It goes on all during hunting season. It's not only the ones who stumble over their own guns and blow their brains out.' Brunetti thought her tone was devoid of anything approaching sympathy as she said this. 'They shoot one another, too,' she went on, 'and get left to bleed to death because no one wants to run the risk of being arrested for having shot someone.'

He started to speak, but she cut him off and added, 'As far as I'm concerned, it can't happen often enough.'

Brunetti waited for her to calm down and retract her words but then decided to leave the issue of her feelings toward hunters unexamined and asked, 'Were the police called? When she was shot?'

'I don't know. That's what I'm waiting for – the police report.'

'Where is she now?' Brunetti asked.

'That's something else I'm trying to find out.'

'She's not with her husband?'

'I don't know. I had a look at the files at the Comune, but she's not listed as resident at his address, even though they own the apartment jointly.' So habituated had Brunetti become to her useful criminality that it did not for an instant trouble him that a person with greater sympathy for legal precision would translate her phrase, 'had a look at' as 'broke into'.

There could certainly be many explanations for why Moro's wife was not registered as resident at his Dorsoduro address, though the most obvious interpretation was that she did not live with her husband. 'Let me know when you get hold of the report on the shooting,' he said, wondering if this would launch her into further denunciation. Like most Venetians, Brunetti had no interest in hunting, judging it an endeavour that was expensive, inconvenient, and excessively loud. Further, experience as a policeman as well as his habit of reflecting upon human behaviour had too often suggested a frightening correlation between a man's interest in firearms and feelings of sexual inadequacy.

'It could have been a warning,' she said without preamble.

'I know,' he answered, having thought this the instant she told him about the shooting. 'But of what?'

7

The scepticism that had seeped into Brunetti's bones over the years forced him to suspect that Signora Moro's accident might have been something other than that. She must have cried out when she was shot, and the sound of a woman's scream would surely have brought any hunter running. Low as his opinion of hunters was, Brunetti could not believe that one of them would leave a woman lying on the ground, bleeding. That conviction led him to the consideration of what sort of person would be capable of doing so, which in its turn led him to consider what other sorts of violence such a person might be capable of.

He added to these speculations the fact that Moro had served in Parliament for some time but had resigned about two years ago. Coincidence could link events either in kind or subject or time: the same sort of thing happened to different people or different things happened to the same person, or things happened at the same time. Moro had resigned from Parliament around the time his wife was injured. Ordinarily, this would hardly arouse suspicion, even in someone as instinctively mistrustful as Brunetti, were it not that the death of their son provided a point from which to begin a process of speculative triangulation around the ways in which the third event might be related to the other two.

Brunetti thought of Parliament in the way most Italians thought of their mothers-in-law. Not due the loyalties created by ties of blood, a mother-in-law still demanded obedience and reverence while never behaving in a manner that would merit either. This alien presence, imposed upon a person's life by sheerest chance, made ever-increasing demands in return for the vain promise of domestic harmony. Resistance was futile, for opposition inevitably led to repercussions too devious to be foreseen.

He lifted the phone and dialled his home number. When the machine answered after four rings, he hung up without speaking, bent down to his bottom drawer, and took out the phone book. He flipped it open to the Ps and kept turning pages until he found Perulli, Augusto. He tossed the book back into the drawer and dialled the number.

After the third ring a man's voice answered. 'Perulli.'

'This is Brunetti. I need to speak to you.'

After a long pause, the man said, 'I wondered when you'd call.'

'Yes,' was Brunetti's only response.

'I can see you in half an hour. For an hour. Then not until tomorrow.'

'I'll come now,' Brunetti said.

He kicked the drawer shut and left his office, then the Questura. Because he had half an hour, he chose to walk to Campo San Maurizio, and because he was early, he chose to stop and say hello to a friend in her workshop. But his mind was on things other than jewellery, so he did little more than exchange a kiss and promise to bring Paola to dinner some time soon; then he crossed the *campo* and headed up towards the Grand Canal.

He had last been to the apartment six years ago, near the end of a long investigation of a trail of drug money that led from the noses of adolescents in New York to a discreet account in Geneva, a trail that paused long enough in Venice to invest in a couple of paintings meant to join the money in the vault of that eminently discreet bank. The money had made its way safely through the empyrean realms of cyberspace, but the paintings, made of less celestial matter, had been stopped at Geneva airport. One by Palma il Vecchio and the other by Marieschi and thus both part of the artistic heritage of the country, neither could be exported, at least not legally, from Italy.

A mere four hours after the discovery of the paintings, Augusto Perulli had called the *Carabinieri* to report their theft. No proof could be found that Perulli had been informed of their discovery – a possibility that would raise the unthinkable idea of police corruption – and so it was decided that Brunetti, who had gone to school with Perulli and had remained on friendly terms with him for decades, should be sent to talk to him. That decision had not been taken until the day after the paintings were found, by which time the man who was transporting them had somehow been released from police custody, though the precise nature of the bureaucratic oversight permitting that error had never been explained to the satisfaction of the Italian police.

When Brunetti finally did talk to his old schoolfriend, Perulli said that he had become aware of the paintings' disappearance only the day before but had no idea how it could have happened. When Brunetti asked how it could be that only two paintings had been taken, Perulli prevented all further questioning by giving Brunetti his word of honour that he knew nothing about it, and Brunetti believed him.

Two years later, the man who had been detained with the paintings was again arrested by the Swiss, this time for trafficking in illegal aliens, and this time in Zurich. In the hope of making a deal with the police, he admitted that he had indeed been given those paintings by Perulli, and asked to take them across the border to their new owner, but by then Perulli had been elected to Parliament and was thus exempt from arrest or prosecution.

'*Ciao*, Guido,' Perulli said when he opened the door to Brunetti, extending his hand.

Brunetti was conscious of how theatrical was his own hesitation before he took Perulli's hand: Perulli was equally conscious of it. Neither pretended to be anything but wary of the other, and both were open in studying the other for signs of the years that had passed since their last meeting.

'It's been a long time, hasn't it?' Perulli said, turning away and leading Brunetti into the apartment. Tall and slender, Perulli still moved with the grace and fluidity of the youth he had shared with Brunetti and their classmates. His hair was still thick, though longer than he had worn it in the past, his skin smooth and taut, rich with the afterglow of a summer spent in the sun. When was it that he had begun searching the faces of the acquaintances of his youth for the telltale signs of age? Brunetti wondered.

The apartment was much as Brunetti remembered it: high-ceilinged and well-proportioned, sofas and chairs inviting people to sit at their ease and speak openly, perhaps indiscreetly. Portraits of men and women from former eras hung on the walls: Perulli, he knew, spoke of them casually, suggesting that they were ancestors, when in reality his family had for generations lived in Castello and dealt in sausage and preserved meat.

New were the ranks of silver-framed photos that stood on a not particularly distinguished copy of a sixteenth-century Florentine credenza. Brunetti paused to examine them and saw reflected in them the trajectory of Perulli's career: the young man with his friends; the university graduate posed with one of the leaders of the political party to which Perulli had then given allegiance; while the adult man stood arm in arm with a former mayor of the city, the Minister of the Interior, and the Patriarch of Venice. Behind them, in an even more elaborate frame, Perulli's face smiled from the cover of a news magazine that had since abandoned publication. This photo, and Perulli's need that people see it, filled Brunetti, against his will, with an enormous sadness.

'Can I offer you something?' Perulli asked from the other side of the living room, standing in front of a leather sofa and clearly wanting to settle this before he sat down.

'No, nothing,' Brunetti said. 'Thanks.'

Perulli sat, pulling fussily at both legs of his trousers to keep them from stretching at the knees, a gesture Brunetti had observed before, but only in the old. Did he sweep the bottom part of his overcoat aside before he sat down on the vaporetto?

'I don't suppose you want to pretend we're still friends?' Perulli asked.

'I don't want to pretend anything, Augusto,' Brunetti said. 'I just want to ask you a few questions, and I'd like you to give me honest answers.'

'Not like the last time?' Perulli asked with a grin he tried to make boyish but succeeded only in making sly. It caused Brunetti a moment's uncertainty: there was something different about Perulli's mouth, about the way he held it.

'No, not like the last time,' Brunetti said, surprised at how calm he sounded, calm but tired.

'And if I can't answer them?'

'Then tell me so, and I'll go.'

Perulli nodded, and then said, 'I didn't have any choice, you know, Guido.'

Brunetti acted as though the other hadn't spoken and asked, 'Do you know Fernando Moro?'

He watched Perulli react to the name with something stronger than mere recognition.

'Yes.'

'How well do you know him?'

'He's a couple of years older than we are, and my father was a friend of his, so I knew him well enough to say hello to on the street or maybe go and have a drink with, at least when we were younger. But certainly not well enough to call him a friend.' Some sense warned Brunetti what was going to come next, so he was prepared to hear Perulli say, 'Not like I know you,' and so did not respond.

'Did you see him in Rome?'

'Socially or professionally?'

'Either.'

'Socially, no, but I might have run into him a few times at Montecitorio. But we represented different parties, so we didn't work together.'

'Committees?'

'No, we worked on different ones.'

'What about his reputation?'

'What about it?'

Brunetti restrained the sigh that seeped up from his chest and answered neutrally, 'As a politician. What did people think of him?'

Perulli uncrossed his long legs and immediately recrossed them the opposite way. He lowered his head and raised his hand to his right eyebrow and rubbed at it a few times, something he had always done when he considered an idea or had to think about his response. Seeing Perulli's face from this new angle, Brunetti noticed that something was different about the angle of his cheekbones, which seemed sharper and more clearly defined than they had been when he was a student. His voice, when he finally spoke, was mild. 'I'd say people generally thought he was honest.' He lowered his hand and tried a small smile, 'Perhaps too honest.' He enlarged the smile, that same engaging smile that girls, then women, had proven unable to resist.

54

'What does that mean?' Brunetti asked, striving to fight against the anger he felt growing in response to the sniggling tone of Perulli's answers.

Perulli didn't answer immediately, and as he thought about what to say or how to say it, he pursed his lips into a tight little circle a few times, a gesture Brunetti had never noticed in him before. Finally he said, 'I suppose it means that he was sometimes difficult to work with.'

That told Brunetti nothing, so he asked again, 'What does that mean?'

Perulli couldn't restrain a quick gleam of anger as he looked across at Brunetti, but when he spoke his voice was calm, almost too calm. 'To the people who disagreed with him, it meant that it was impossible to persuade him to look at things from a different point of view.'

'Meaning their point of view?' Brunetti asked neutrally.

Perulli did not rise to the bait and, instead, said only, 'From any point of view different from the one he had decided on.'

'Did you ever have this experience with him?'

Perulli shook the idea away with a negative motion of his head. 'I told you, we never worked on the same committees.'

'What committees did he work on?' Brunetti asked.

Perulli put his head back against the top of his chair and closed his eyes, and Brunetti could not stop himself from thinking that the gesture was consciously posed to show the energy Perulli was willing to expend in order to answer the question.

After what seemed an inordinately long time, Perulli said, 'As far as I can remember, he was on the committee that examined the Post Office, and one that had something to do with farming, and a third one . . .' He broke off and glanced at Brunetti with a very small, private smile, then he continued, 'I don't really remember what that one was. Maybe the mission in Albania, all that humanitarian aid stuff, or maybe the one about farmers' pensions. I can't be sure.'

'And what did these committees do?'

'What all of them do,' Perulli said, his voice honestly surprised that a citizen should need to ask. 'They study the problem.'

'And then?'

'Make recommendations.'

'To whom?'

'To the government, of course.'

'And then what happens to their recommendations?'

'They're examined and studied, and a decision is made. And if it's necessary, a law is passed or the existing law is changed.'

'As simple as that, eh?' Brunetti said.

Perulli's smile didn't have time to blossom fully before the frost of Brunetti's tone blighted that smile.

'You can joke if you want, Guido, but it's not easy, running a country like this.'

'You really think you run it?'

'Not I, personally,' Perulli said in a tone that suggested some regret at this fact. 'Of course not.'

'All of you together, then? The people in Parliament?'

'If not we, then who?' Perulli demanded, voice rising to something that resembled indignation but was closer to anger.

'Indeed,' Brunetti said simply. After a long pause, he went on, his voice perfectly normal, 'Do you know anything else about these committees, perhaps who else served on them?'

Deprived of an immediate target for his displeasure by Brunetti's sudden change of subject, Perulli hesitated before he answered. 'I'm not sure there's much to be said about any one of them. They aren't important, and usually new members or those who aren't well connected get appointed to them.'

'I see,' Brunetti said neutrally. 'Do you know any of the other people who served on these committees?'

He was afraid he had pushed Perulli too far and that the man might dismiss his question or refuse to give him any more time, but after a moment the parliamentarian answered, 'I know one or two of them, but not at all well.'

'Could you talk to them?'

'About what?' Perulli asked, immediately suspicious.

'Moro.'

'No.' His answer was immediate.

'Why not?' Brunetti asked, though he was sure he knew the answer.

'Because, when you called, you said you wanted to ask me some questions. You didn't say you wanted me to start doing your job for you.' As he spoke, Perulli's voice grew more heated. He looked at Brunetti, who said nothing, and that silence seemed to be enough to unleash even more of Perulli's anger. 'I don't know why you want to know about Moro, but it's a good thing someone's going to take a closer look at him.' Red spots the size of golf balls flashed into being on his cheeks.

'Why?' Brunetti asked.

Again, Perulli uncrossed his legs, but this time he leaned forward, towards Brunetti, the forefinger of his right hand jabbing the space between them. 'Because he's a sanctimonious bastard, always talking about fraud and dishonesty and . . .' Here Perulli's voice changed, deepening and dragging out the final syllables of words in a way Brunetti realized was very much like Moro's. 'Our responsibility to the citizen,' he went on, the imitation suddenly becoming sarcastic exaggeration. 'We can't continue to treat our offices, this Parliament, as though it were a trough and we a herd of pigs,' Perulli intoned. It was clear to Brunetti that he was again quoting Moro.

Brunetti thought the other man would go on: Augusto had never known when a joke had gone on long enough. But Perulli surprised him by lapsing into silence, though he couldn't resist the temptation to goad Brunetti by saying, 'If he's done something, it's no surprise to me: he's no different from any one of us.'

'With your front trotters in the trough?' Brunetti asked mildly.

He might just as well have slapped the other man across the face. Perulli lurched forward, his right hand aiming for Brunetti's throat, but he had forgotten the low table between them. It caught Perulli just below the knees and sent him sprawling across and then beyond it.

Brunetti had risen to his feet while Perulli was clattering across the table. Seeing him on the floor, stunned, he started to reach down to help him to his feet but then stopped himself. Curious, he stepped to one side and bent over to look closer. Perulli's hair had fallen forward, and Brunetti could see the little round, puckered scar just behind the left ear. Gratified to have detected the cause of Perulli's youthful appearance, he stood and waited, and when he saw Perulli pull his knees up under him and place his hands flat on the floor on either side of him, Brunetti turned and left the apartment.

8

When he got outside and looked at his watch, Brunetti was surprised to see that it was almost five. He found himself very hungry and geographically halfway between work and home. He didn': know what he'd find to eat at home, and by the time he got there and had something, it would be too late to bother to go back to the Questura. He sent the feet of memory up towards San Marco, recallirg every bar or trattoria he knew on the way, then, at the thought of what he would encounter in that direction, he replotted the trip via Campo Sant' Angelo and back through Campo San Fantin. Knowing it was absurd and aware that he had himself chosen to forgo lunch, he was assaulted by a wave of self-pity: he was doing his job as best he knew how, and he found himself hungry at a time when it would be impossible to get a meal.

He remembered then one of the few stories his father ever told about the war, though he recalled it in a garbled fashion, for it had never been told the same way twice. At some point, marching across Lower Saxony in the days just after the end of the war, his father and two companions had been befriended by a stray dog that emerged from under a bombed house to follow them. The next day, they ate the dog. Over the course of decades, this story had taken on talismanic powers for Brunetti, and he found himself unable to keep his mind from it whenever anyone talked about food in a way he thought too precious, as though it were a fashion accessory rather than a basic need. All he had to do was hear one of Paola's friends go on about her delicate digestion and how she couldn't even bear to buy vegetables that had been displayed next to garlic, and the story came to mind. He remembered, years ago, sitting across the table from a man who told the other guests how impossible it was for him to eat any meat that had not come from his own butcher, that he could taste the difference in quality instantly. When the man finished the story, and after he had received the required accolade for his delicacy of palate, Brunetti had told the story of the dog.

He cut through to Campo San Fantin and stopped in a bar for two *tramezzini* and a glass of white wine. While he was there, an attractive dark-haired woman came in for a coffee wearing a tight leopard-patterned coat and an outrageous black hat that looked like a black pizza balanced on a skullcap. He studied her for a moment as she sipped at her coffee; indeed, he joined every man in the bar in studying her. All of them, he concluded, joined with him in giving thanks that she had come in to lift their hearts and brighten their day.

Cheered by having seen her, he left the bar and walked back to the Questura. As he entered his office, he saw a folder lying on his desk, and when he opened it he was astonished to discover the autopsy report on Ernesto Moro. His immediate reaction was to wonder what Venturi was up to, what manoeuvre or power play he might be involved in and against whom. His speed in having performed the autopsy could be explained only as an attempt to win Brunetti's favour, and that favour could be of use to the pathologist only if he were planning to move against some rival or perceived rival either in the police or the medical system.

Brunetti refused to speculate further about Venturi's motives and directed his attention to the report. Ernesto Moro had been in excellent health at the time of his death, entirely free of any sign of disease, not a single cavity in his teeth, though there was evidence of previous orthodontic work. His left leg had been broken in the past, perhaps as long as ten years ago, but had healed completely; tonsils and appendix were still present.

The cause of death was strangulation. There was no way to judge how far his body had fallen before the noose had tightened around his throat, but it had not been sufficient to break his neck, so the boy had strangled to death. It had not been, Venturi stated, a quick process: the rope had caused extensive bruising of the front and right side of his neck. This suggested that his last moments had been spent in instinctive convulsions against the tightening cord. There followed the exact dimensions of the shower stall in which his body had been found and the possible extension of arms as long as his. Brunetti thought of those sweeping marks on the wall of the shower.

From the evidence of the food in the boy's stomach, it was likely that he had died some time between midnight and three in the morning. There was no evidence of drug use, and it seemed that he had consumed only a moderate amount of wine with his last meal, probably no more than one glass and certainly not enough to cloud his judgement in any way.

Brunetti put the papers back in the folder and left it lying open on his desk. The report said everything just as it said nothing. He tried to subtract the knowledge that Signora Moro had been shot and view her son's death as a separate event. The obvious possible motives were thus some disappointment the boy had suffered or the desire to pay someone back for a perceived injury. Once the mother was put back into the equation, the possible motives expanded exponentially. Instead of being viewed as the prime mover in the action, the boy became a means and some other person the mover.

Following this filament of vague speculation, Brunetti saw that the mother's survival suggested she was not the prime target, which left Moro himself. But even that, he realized, led nowhere: until he had an idea of what Moro might be a target of, or for whom, all speculation was as flimsy as the jumbled bits and pieces of information upon which he chose to base it.

The arrival of Signorina Elettra put an end to his fragmentary musings. 'You saw that?' she asked as she came in, nodding towards the autopsy report.

'Yes. What do you make of it?'

'I can't understand it, why a boy like that would kill himself. It doesn't make any sense at all.'

'It's not so unusual, I'm afraid, kids killing themselves.'

His remark seemed to cause her pain. She stopped in front of his desk, another folder in one hand. 'But why?'

'I spoke to one of the cadets over there. He said there was no way to be sure about the future, or that there even would be one for them.'

'That's nonsense,' she snapped angrily. 'Of course there's always a future.'

'I'm just repeating what he told me.'

'A cadet?' she asked.

'Yes.'

She was silent for a long time, then finally said, 'I went out with one of them for a while.'

Immediately curious, Brunetti asked, 'When you were a student?'

Her mouth moved in a sly smile: 'Not last week, certainly.' Then she went on, 'Yes, when I was eighteen.' She looked down at the floor in a moment's reflection and then said, 'No, as a matter of fact, I was only sixteen. That explains it.'

He knew a set-up line when he heard it. 'Explains what?'
'How I could have put up with him.'

Brunetti half rose in his chair and gestured towards the
other. 'Have a seat, please.' She swept one hand behind her as
she sat, straightening her skirt, then placed the folder flat on
her lap.

'What did you have to put up with?' he asked, puzzled by
the idea of Signorina Elettra as a person capable of enduring
anything she didn't wish to.

'I was going to say that he was a Fascist and that they all
were, and probably still are today, but it might not be true of
all of them. So I'll say only that *he* was a Fascist, and a bully,
and a snob and that most of his friends were, too.' From long
experience of her, Brunetti could sense when Signorina
Elettra was doing no more than practising verbal *solfeggi* and
when she was preparing to launch into an aria; he detected
signs of the second.

'But you see that only now?' he asked, offering her the
briefest of *recitativi* as a means of prompting the aria.

'We used to see them, my friends and I, swanning around
the city in their capes, and we thought they were the most
exciting, wonderful boys in the world. Whenever one of them
spoke to one of us, it was as though the heavens had opened
to allow a god to descend. And then one of them . . .' she
began. Then, seeking the proper words, she changed her
mind and went on, 'I began going out with one of them.'

'Going out?' he inquired.

'For a coffee, for a walk, just to go down to the Giardini to
sit on a bench and talk.' With a rueful smile, she corrected
herself. 'To listen, that is.' She smiled across at him. 'I believe
one could employ a new noun here, sir: a listen, instead of a
conversation. That's what I had whenever we met: a listen.'

'Perhaps it was a quicker way for you to get to know him,'
Brunetti suggested drily.

'Yes,' she said brusquely. 'I got to know him.'

He didn't know quite what question to ask. 'And what was it that makes you say those things about him?'

'That he was a snob and a Fascist and a bully?'

'Yes.'

'You know Barbara, don't you?' she asked, mentioning her older sister.

'Yes.'

'She was in medical school at the time, living in Padova, so I didn't see much of her except on the weekends. I'd been going out with Renzo for about three weeks when she came home one weekend, and I asked her to meet him. I thought he was so wonderful, so clever, so thoughtful.' She snorted at the memory of her own youth and went on. 'Imagine that, thoughtful. At eighteen.' She took a deep breath and smiled at him, so he knew that this story was going to have a happy ending.

'Whenever we were together, he talked about politics, history, all those things I'd heard Barbara and my parents talk about for so long. Nothing he said sounded much like what they said. But he had dark blue eyes, and he had a car at home, in Milano, a convertible.' Again, she smiled at the memory of the girl she had been, and sighed.

When she seemed reluctant to continue, he asked, 'And did Barbara meet him?'

'Oh yes, and they hated one another after three words. I'm sure he thought she was some sort of Communist cannibal, and she must have thought he was a Fascist pig.' She smiled again at him.

'And?'

'One of them was right.'

He laughed outright and asked, 'How long did it take you to realize it?'

'Oh, I suppose I knew it all along, but he did have those eyes. And there was that convertible.' She laughed. 'He carried a photo of it in his wallet.'

At first, it was difficult for Brunetti to picture a Signorina Elettra capable of this folly, but after a moment's reflection, he realized that it didn't surprise him all that much.

'What happened?'

'Oh, once Barbara started on him, when we got home, it was as if – how do they describe it in the Bible? – as if "the scales fell from my eyes"? Well, it was something like that. All I had to do was stop looking at him and start listening to what he said and thinking about it, and I could see what a vicious creep he was.'

'What sort of things?'

'The same things people like him are always saying: the glory of the nation, the need to have strong values in the family, the heroism of men in war.' She stopped here and shook her head again, like a person emerging from rubble. 'It's extraordinary, the sort of things a person can listen to without realizing what nonsense it is.'

'Nonsense?'

'Well, when the people who say it are still children, I suppose it's nonsense. It's when adults say it that it's dangerous.'

'What became of him?'

'Oh, I don't know. I imagine he graduated and went into the Army and ended up torturing prisoners in Somalia. He was that kind of person.'

'Violent?'

'No, not really, but very easily led. He had all of the core beliefs. You know the sort of things they say: honour and discipline and the need for order. I suppose he got it from his family. His father had been a general or something, so it's all he'd ever been exposed to.'

'Like you, only different?' Brunetti asked, smiling. He knew her sister, and so he knew what the politics of the Zorzis were.

'Exactly, only no one in my family has ever had a good

word to say about discipline or the need for order.' The pride with which she said this was unmistakable.

He started to ask another question, but she got to her feet, as though suddenly conscious of how much she had revealed, and leaned forward to place the file on his desk. 'That's what's come in, sir,' she said with a briskness that was strangely dissonant with the easy familiarity of their conversation up to that point.

'Thank you,' he said.

'It should all be clear, but if you need any explanation, call.'

He noticed that she didn't tell him to come down to her office or to ask her to come up to explain. The geographical limits of their formality had been re-established.

'Certainly,' he said, and then repeated, as she turned toward the door, 'Thank you.'

9

The folder contained photocopies of newspaper articles about Fernando Moro's careers as doctor and politician. The first seemed to have led to the second: he had first caught the public eye about six years ago, when, as one of the inspectors commissioned to examine the quality of hospital care in the Veneto, he had submitted a report calling into question the statistics issued by the provincial government, statistics which boasted one of the lowest patient to doctor ratios on the continent. It was the Moro Report which indicated that the low figure resulted from the inclusion in the statistics of three new hospitals, facilities which were planned to provide medical care at the highest level. Money had been allocated for their construction, and that money had been spent, and thus the statistics included these hospitals and factored in all of the services they were planned to provide. The resulting figures were a three-day marvel, for the Veneto was thus shown to have the best health care in Europe.

It was Fernando Moro's report that pointed out the

inconvenient fact that those three hospitals, however grandiose their plans, however extensive their staffs, and however varied the services they were meant to provide, had never actually been built. Once their services were subtracted from the tabulations, the health care provided to the citizens of the Veneto fell to where its patients were accustomed to judging it to be: somewhat below that of Cuba, though certainly above that of Chad.

In the aftermath of the report, Moro had been lauded as a hero by the press and had become one in the popular mind, but he found that the administration of the hospital where he worked had decided that his many talents would be better utilized if he were to take over the administration of the old people's home attached to the hospital. His protest that, as an oncologist, he would be better employed in the hospital's oncology ward was brushed aside as false humility, and his lateral transfer was confirmed.

This in its turn led to his decision to attempt to achieve public office before his name dropped from public memory; perhaps a tactical decision, but a no less successful one for that.

Moro had once remarked that his long familiarity with terminal illness was perhaps the best preparation he could have had for a career in Parliament. Late at night and only when among old and trusted friends, he was rumoured to expand upon that metaphor, a fact which was not long in filtering back to his fellow parliamentarians. This might well have affected the nature of the committees to which he was appointed.

As he read the newspaper articles, all purporting to be neutral presentation of fact but all tinted by the political affiliation of the particular paper or journalist, Brunetti realized that he was colouring the articles with the hues of his own memory. He had known, or at least heard, about Moro for years, and as he tended to share the man's political leanings, he knew he was prejudiced in the man's favour and that he presupposed his honesty. He knew just how dangerous this sort of thinking was, especially for a policeman, yet Moro was hardly a suspect: the totality of his grief excluded him from any suspicion of involvement in his son's death. 'Or else I've never had a son; or else I've never had a soul,' Brunetti caught himself whispering out loud.

He looked up at the door, embarrassed to have been so distracted by his thoughts, but no one was there. He continued reading: the other articles merely repeated the essential information contained in the first few. Regardless of how insinuating the tone of some of the journalists, no matter how carefully they constructed their specious explanations of Moro's behaviour, not even the dullest reader could doubt the man's integrity.

The tone of innuendo became even stronger in some of the articles dealing with Moro's sudden withdrawal from Parliament, a decision he refused to attribute to anything other than 'personal reasons'. The first article, written by one of the best-known apologists of the Right, raised the rhetorical question of the sort of connection that might exist between Moro's resignation and the arrest, two weeks before, of one of the last members of the Baader-Meinhof Gang. 'None, probably,' Brunetti found himself whispering again, as had become his annoying habit when reading this particular adornment of the free press.

The shooting of Moro's wife was mentioned in two small articles, neither of which did more than report the barest facts of the case. The second article, however, provided the name of the people with whom she was staying at the time of the shooting.

He picked up the phone and dialled 12, then asked for the number of Giovanni Ferro in Siena or in the province of Siena. There were two, and he took down both numbers.

He dialled the first number and a woman answered.

'Signora Ferro?'

'Who's calling, please?'

'This is Commissario Guido Brunetti, in Venice,' he said.

He heard a startled gasp and then she asked, voice tight and fast and apparently beyond her control, 'Is it Federica?'

'Federica Moro?' he asked.

The woman was evidently too shaken to do more than answer, 'Yes.'

'Signora, nothing's happened to her, please believe me. I'm calling to ask about the incident two years ago.' She said nothing, but Brunetti could hear her rapid breathing on the other end of the line. 'Signora, can you hear me? Are you all right?'

There was another long silence, and he was afraid she was going to hang up or already had, but then her voice came back, 'Who did you say you were?'

'Commissario Guido Brunetti. I'm with the police in Venice, Signora.' Again, silence. 'Signora, can you hear me?'

'Yes,' she said, 'I can hear you.' There was another long pause, and then the woman said, 'I'll call you back', and was gone, leaving Brunetti with the memory of her terror and the strong aspirants of her Tuscan speech.

And indeed, thought Brunetti, as he replaced the receiver, why should she believe that he was who he said he was? There was no way to prove it, and the call was being made about a woman who had been shot and whose assailant, presumably, had never been found by the police Brunetti claimed to represent.

The phone rang after a few minutes. He picked it up on the first ring and gave his name.

'Good,' she said. 'I wanted to be certain.'

'That's very wise of you, Signora,' he said. 'I hope you're reassured that I am who I said I was.'

'Yes,' she agreed, then went on, 'What do you want to know about Federica?'

'I'm calling about the shooting because there's a case it might be related to. The newspapers said that she was staying with you and your husband when it happened.'

'Yes.'

'Could you tell me something more about it, Signora?'

Yet again there was a long pause, and then the woman asked, 'Have you spoken to her?'

'Signora Moro?'

'Yes.'

'No, I haven't, not yet.' He waited for her to speak.

'I think you should talk to her,' Signora Ferro said.

There was something in the way she said the last word that warned Brunetti not to dispute this. 'I'd very much like to,' he agreed amiably. 'Could you tell me where I might find her?'

'Isn't she there?' the woman asked, the nervousness flooding back into her voice.

He adopted his most soothing tone. 'You're the first person I've called, Signora. I haven't had time to try to locate Signora Moro.' He felt like an explorer on a glacier who suddenly sees an enormous crevasse yawn open in front of him: so far he had said nothing about the death of Signora Moro's son and to do so at this point would be impossible. 'Is she here with her husband?'

Her voice became bland and noncommittal. 'They're separated,' she said.

'Ah, I didn't know that. But is she still here in Venice?'

He could all but follow her thoughts as she considered this. A policeman would find her friend; sooner or later, he'd find her. 'Yes,' she finally answered.

'Could you give me the address?'

Slowly she answered: 'Yes, wait while I get it, please.' There was a soft tap as she set the phone down, then a long silence, and then the woman was back. 'It's San Marco 2823,' she said, then gave him the phone number, as well.

Brunetti thanked her and was considering what else he could ask her when the woman said, 'What you need to do is let the phone ring once and then call back. She doesn't want to be disturbed.'

'I can understand that, Signora,' he said, the memory of Ernesto Moro's limp body suddenly appearing to him like the ghost of one of Ugolino's sons.

The woman said goodbye and hung up, leaving Brunetti, he realized, in possession of little more information than he had had before he made the call.

He was aware of how dark his office had become. The late afternoon sun had faded away, and he doubted that he could any longer see the numbers on the phone clearly enough to dial them. He walked over to the switch by the door and turned on the light and was surprised by the unaccustomed order he had established on his desk while talking to Signora Ferro: a stack of folders sat at the centre, a piece of paper to one side, a pencil placed across it in a neat horizontal. He thought of the obsessive neatness of his mother's house in the years before she lapsed into the senility in whose embrace she still lay, and then the explosion of disorder in the house during the last months before she was taken from it.

Seated at his desk again, he was suddenly overcome by exhaustion and had to fight the impulse to lay his head on the desk and close his eyes. It had been more than ten hours since they had been called to the school, hours during which death and misery had soaked into him like liquid into blotting paper. Not for the first time in his career he found himself wondering how much longer he could continue to do this work. In the past, he had comforted himself with the belief that a vacation would help, and often his physical removal from the city and the crimes he saw there did in fact serve to lift his mood, at least for the time he was away. But he could think of no removal in time or space that wculd lift from him the sense of futility that he now felt assailing him from every side.

He knew he should try to call Signora Moro, willed himself to reach for the phone, but he could not do it. Who was it whose gaze could turn people to stone? The Basilisk? Medusa? With serpents for hair and an open, glaring mouth. He conjured up an image of the tangled, swirling locks, but could not remember who had painted or sculpted them.

His departure from the Questura had the feel of flight about it, at least to Brunetti. His chair remained pushed back from his desk, his door open, the papers set neatly at the centre of his desk, while he fled the place and went home in a state not far from panic.

His nose brought him back to his senses. As he opened the door to the apartment he was greeted by aromas from the kitchen: something roasting, perhaps pork; and garlic, so pervasive it suggested that an entire field of garlic had been seized and tossed into the oven along with the pork.

He hung up his jacket, remembered that he had left his briefcase in his office and shrugged off the thought. He paused at the door to the kitchen, hoping to find his family already seated at the table, but the room was empty, except for the garlic, the odour of which seemed to be coming from a tall pot boiling over a low flame.

Devoting his entire attention to the smell, he attempted to remember where he had smelled it before. He knew it was familiar, as a melody is familiar even when a person cannot remember the piece from which it comes. He tried to separate the scents: garlic, tomato, a touch of rosemary, something fishy like clams or shrimp – probably shrimp – and, perhaps, carrots. And the garlic, a universe of garlic. He summoned up the sensation he had experienced in the office, of his spirit being steeped in misery. He breathed deeply, hoping that the garlic would drive the misery out. If it could drive away vampires, then surely it could work its herbal magic against something as banal as misery. He stood propped against the jamb, his eyes closed, inhaling the scents, until a voice behind him said, 'That is not the proud stance of a defender of justice and the rights of the oppressed.'

Paola appeared beside him, kissed his cheek without really looking at him, and slipped past him into the kitchen.

'Is that Guglielmo's soup?'

'The very same,' Paola said, lifting the lid from the pot and taking a long wooden spoon from the counter to stir at the contents. 'Twelve heads of garlic,' she whispered, her voice filled with something that approached awe.

'And we've survived it every time,' Brunetti added.

'Proof of divine intervention, I think,' Paola suggested.

'And, if Guglielmo is to be believed, a sure cure for worms and high blood pressure.'

'And an even surer way to get yourself a seat on the vaporetto tomorrow.'

Brunetti laughed, feeling his tension begin to evaporate. He remembered their friend Guglielmo, who had served as military attaché in Cairo for four years, during which time he had studied Arabic, converted to Coptic Christianity, and made a fortune smuggling archaeological artefacts out of the country on military aeroplanes. Devoted to food, he had taken with him, when he left, a broad variety of recipes, most of which called for inordinate quantities of garlic.

'Is it true that they've found dried-up garlic in mummy coffins?' Brunetti asked, pushing himself away from the door.

'You'd probably find it in the pockets of Guglielmo's dress uniform, too,' Paola observed, replacing the lid and taking her first good look at her husband. Her voice changed. 'What's the matter with you?'

He tried to smile but failed. 'Bad day.'

'What?'

'A suicide that might not be.'

'Who?'

'A boy.'

'How old?'

'Seventeen.'

The death, the gender and the age stopped Paola in her tracks. She took a deep breath, shook her head as if to dismiss superstitious possibility, and put her hand on his arm. 'Tell me about it.'

For a reason he didn't understand, perhaps the same superstition, Brunetti didn't want to have to look at Paola as he told her about Ernesto Moro, so he busied himself with taking down two glasses and getting a chilled bottle of Tocai out of the refrigerator. As he went through the business of opening the bottle, he spoke, deliberately slowing his actions so that they would last as long as the explanation he had to give. 'He was a student at the San Martino. We had a call this morning, and when we got there, we found him hanging in the shower. Vianello did, that is.'

He poured two glasses of wine and handed one to Paola, who ignored it and asked, 'Who was he?'

'Fernando Moro's son.'

'Dottor Moro?'

'Yes,' Brunetti said and pressed the glass into her hand until she accepted it.

'Does he know?'

Brunetti turned away from her, set his glass down, and opened the refrigerator, searching for something he could eat by way of distraction. His back to her, he went on, 'Yes.'

She said nothing while he rooted around and found a plastic container of olives, which he opened and placed on the counter. As soon as he saw them, dark and plump in their yellow oil, he lost the taste for them and picked up his glass again. Conscious of Paola's attention, he glanced at her.

'Did you have to tell him?'

'He came while I was there with the boy's body, then I went and talked to him at his home.'

'Today?' she asked, unable to disguise what was either astonishment or horror.

'I wasn't there long,' he said and regretted the words the instant they were out of his mouth.

Paola shot him a look, but what she saw on his face made her let his remark pass without comment. 'The mother?' she asked.

'I don't know where she is. Someone said she was here, in the city, but I couldn't call her.' Perhaps it was the way he said 'couldn't' that caused Paola not to question him about this, either.

Instead, she asked, 'What makes you think it might not be?'

'Habit,' he ventured.

'The habit of doubt?' she asked.

'I suppose you could call it that,' Brunetti answered and finally allowed himself a sip of wine. Cool, tight on his tongue, it gave him little comfort, though it reminded him that comfort did exist in the world.

'Do you want to talk about it?' Paola asked, sipping for the first time at her own wine.

'Later, perhaps. After dinner.'

She nodded, took another sip, and set the glass down. 'If you want to go and read for a while, I'll set the table. The kids should be home soon,' she began, and both of them were conscious of the word 'kids' and the casual assertion it made that things had at least remained the same for them, their family safe. Like a horse suddenly breaking stride to avoid a hole below its front foot, her voice jogged over into artificial jollity and she added, 'And then we'll eat.'

Brunetti went into the living room. He placed his glass on the table, sat on the sofa, and picked up his book, Anna Comnena's life of her father, the Emperor Alexius. Half an hour later, when Chiara came in to tell her father that dinner was ready, she found him on the sofa, his book lying open and forgotten in his lap, as he stared out at the rooftops of the city.

10

Much as Brunetti hoped that talking to Paola about the boy's death would serve to lessen the horror with which it filled him, it did not. In bed, Paola curled beside him, he told her the events of his day, struck by the grotesqueness of their bedtime talk. When he finished, not hiding from her the anguish that had caused him to flee from his office without trying to contact Signora Moro, she propped herself up on one elbow and looked down at his face.

'How much longer can you do this, Guido?' she asked.

In the dim moonlight, he glanced at her, then returned his attention to the opposite wall, where the mirror glowed dimly in the light reflected from the tiles of the terrace.

She allowed a certain time to pass in silence, and then asked, 'Well?'

'I don't know,' he answered. 'I can't think about that until this is finished.'

'If it's decided he committed suicide, then isn't it already finished?' she asked.

'I don't mean finished that way,' he said dismissively. 'I mean really finished.'

'Finished for you, you mean?' she asked. At other times, the words would have been a demand, perhaps even a sarcastic observation, but tonight they were only a request for information.

'I suppose so,' he admitted.

'When will that be?'

The accumulated exhaustion of the day enveloped him, almost as if it had decided to wrap its arms around him and lull him to sleep. He felt his eyes close and he rested on those other arms for a moment. The room began to move away from him as he felt himself drawn towards sleep. Suddenly able to see the events affecting the Moro family only as a triangle created by coincidence, he whispered, 'When the lines aren't there,' and gave himself to sleep.

The next morning, he woke to ignorance. The rays of the sun, reflected off the same mirror and on to his face, pulled him from sleep, and in the first moments of waking, he had no memory of the events of the previous day. He moved a bit to the right and his body sensed Paola's absence; he turned his head to the left and saw the bell tower of San Polo, the sunlight so clear upon it that he could make out the grey blobs of cement that held the bricks together. A pigeon glided toward the eaves under the tower roof, spread its wings to reduce speed, and then set itself down in a soft-footed landing. It turned around twice, bobbed about a bit, and then tucked its head under one wing.

Nothing the bird did was reminiscent of the events of the previous day, but as its head disappeared under its wing, Brunetti had a sharp vision of Ernesto Moro's face at the moment that Vianello pulled the hem of his cape across it.

Brunetti got out of bed and, careful to avoid himself in the mirror, went down to the bathroom to take a shower As he stood there, shaving, he had no choice but to confront his own eyes, and the face he saw looking back at him had the weary dullness of every grief-stricken parent he had ever had to speak to. How to explain that a child was dead, and even if it could be explained, what explanation could hope to stem the torrent of grief that must flow from those words?

Paola and the children were long gone, so he left the house, glad of the chance to drink his coffee in the company of a familiar *pasticceria*, with conversation no more demanding than the idle comments someone might make to him. He bought both *Il Tempo* and *Il Gazzettino* at the *edicola* in Campo Santa Marina and went into Didovich for a coffee and a brioche.

CADET AT EXCLUSIVE VENETIAN SCHOOL HANGS HIMSELF, the first paper declared on one of the inner pages, while the front page of the second carried the headline, SON OF EX-PARLIAMENTARIAN FOUND DEAD AT SAN MARTINO. The lower-case headlines informed the people of Venice that the father of the victim had resigned from Parliament after his hotly contested health report had been condemned by the then Minister of Health, that the police were investigating the boy's death, and that his parents were separated. Reading the lead paragraphs, Brunetti was sure that anyone who read them, regardless of the information contained in the article that followed, would already suspect that the parents or the way they lived was somehow related to, if not directly responsible for, the boy's death.

'Terrible, isn't it? This boy?' one of the women at the counter asked the owner, waving her hand towards Brunetti's newspaper. She bit into her brioche and shook her head.

'What's the matter with kids today? They have so much. Why can't they be content with it?' another one answered.

As if on cue, a third woman the same age as the other two, her hair the standard post-menopausal red, set her coffee cup resoundingly back into its saucer and said, 'It's because the parents don't pay attention to them. I stayed home to take care of my children, and so nothing like this ever happened.' A stranger to this culture might well assume that no option was open to the children of working mothers but suicide. The three women nodded in united disapproval at this latest proof of the perfidy and ingratitude of youth and the irresponsibility of all parents other than themselves.

Brunetti folded his paper, paid, and left the *pasticceria*. The same headlines blared forth from the yellow posters taped to the back wall of the *edicola*. In their real grief, attacks like this could do no more than glance off the souls of the Moros: this belief was the only comfort Brunetti could find in the face of this latest evidence of the mendacity of the press.

Inside the Questura, he went directly to his office, where he saw new files lying on his desk. He dialled Signorina Elettra, who answered the phone by saying, 'He wants to see you immediately.'

It no longer surprised him when Signorina Elettra knew that it was he who was calling: she had spent considerable police funds in having Telecom install a new phone line in her office, though the moneys currently available could not provide for anyone except her to have a terminal on which the number of the caller appeared. Nor was he surprised by her use of the pronoun: she granted this distinction only to her immediate superior, Vice-Questore Giuseppe Patta.

'Immediately now?' he asked.

'Immediately yesterday afternoon, I'd say,' she answered.

Brunetti went downstairs and into her office without taking time to examine the folders. He had expected to find Signorina Elettra at her desk, but her office was empty. He stuck his head back outside the door to check to see if she were in the hallway, but there was no sign of her.

Reluctant to present himself to Patta without first having some indication of his superior's mood or what it was Patta wanted to see him about, Brunetti toyed with the idea of going back to his office to read the folders or to the officers' room to see if Vianello or Pucetti were there. As he stood undecided, the door to Vice-Questore Patta's office opened, and Signora Elettra emerged, today wearing what looked very much like a bomber jacket, buttoned tight at the waist, puffy and full over the bust and shoulders; well, a bomber jacket, were bombardiers given to the wearing of uniforms made of apricot-coloured raw silk.

Patta had a clear view from his office into hers. 'I'd like to see you, Brunetti,' he called. Brunetti glanced at Signorina Elettra as he turned toward Patta's door, but the only thing she had time to do was push her lips tightly together in either disapproval or disgust. Like ships in the night, they passed, barely acknowledging the presence of the other.

'Close the door,' Patta said, glancing up and then back at the papers on his desk. Brunetti turned to do so, certain that Patta's use of the word 'please' would provide the clue to what sort of meeting this would be. The fact that Brunetti had time to formulate this thought destroyed any possibility that it was going to be a pleasant interchange of ideas between colleagues. A short delay would be the habitual flick of the whip from a carriage driver: aimed to snap the air and catch the beast's attention without doing it any harm, it was an unconscious assertion of command, not meant to inflict damage. A longer delay would demonstrate Patta's irritation without revealing its cause. The complete absence of the word, as on this occasion, was indicative of either fear or rage: experience had taught Brunetti that the first of these was the more dangerous, for fear drove Patta to the reckless endangerment of other people's careers in his attempt to protect his own. This evaluation was complete long before Brunetti turned to approach his superior, and so the sight of a glowering Patta did not intimidate him.

'Yes, sir?' he asked with a serious face, having learned that neutrality of expression and tone was expected of him in these moments. He waited for Patta to wave him to a chair, consciously imitating the behaviour of a non-Alpha male dog.

'What are you waiting for?' Patta demanded, still without looking at him. 'Sit down.'

Brunetti did so silently and placed his arms in neat horizontals on the arms of the chair. He waited, wondering what scene Patta was going to play and how he was going to play it. A minute passed silently. Patta continued to read through the file that lay open before him, occasionally turning a page.

Like most Italians, Brunetti respected and approved of beauty. When he could, he chose to surround himself with beauty: his wife, the clothes he wore, the paintings in his home, even the beauty of thought in the books he read: all of these things gave him great pleasure. How, he wondered, as he did whenever he encountered Patta after a gap of a week or so, how could a man so very handsome be so utterly devoid of the qualities usually attributed to beauty? The erect posture was solely physical, for the ethical Patta was an eel; the firm jaw bespoke a strength of character that was manifested only in stubbornness; and the clear dark eyes saw only what they chose to see.

Caught in this reflection, Brunetti didn't notice when Patta finally turned his attention to him, nor did he hear the Vice-Questore's first words, tuning in only toward the end '. . . your mistreatment of his students'.

Like a scholar piecing together a coherent meaning from a fragment of text, Brunetti realized that the students must be those at the San Martino Academy, and the only person capable of using the possessive pronoun when speaking of them the Comandante.

'I chanced into the room of one of them, and we discussed his class work. I don't think this can be construed in any way as mistreatment, sir.'

'Not only you,' Patta said, overriding Brunetti and giving no indication that he had bothered to listen to his explanation. 'One of your officers. I was at a dinner last night, and the father of one of the boys said your officer was very rough when he questioned his son.' Patta allowed the full horror of this to sink in before adding, 'The father was at school with General D'Ambrosio.'

'I'm sorry, sir,' Brunetti said, wondering if the boy would go on to complain to his father should he experience rough treatment from the enemy in battle, 'I'm sure if he had known that, he would have shown him more courtesy.'

'Don't try being smart with me, Brunetti,' Patta shot back, displaying a quicker sensitivity to Brunetti's tone than usual. 'I don't want your men in there, strong-arming these boys and causing trouble. These are the sons of some of the best people in the country and I won't have them treated like this.'

Brunetti had always been fascinated by the way the police shuttlecocked back and forth between Patta and all the others who might be seen as responsible for them: when they solved a case or behaved bravely, they were Patta's police, but all cases of misbehaviour, incompetence or negligence were clearly attributable to their behaving like the police of someone else, in this case, Brunetti.

'I'm not sure there's any question of their being mistreated, sir,' Brunetti said mildly. 'I asked an officer to speak to the other students and try to find out if the Moro boy had been behaving strangely or if he had said anything that would indicate he had been thinking about suicide.' Before Patta could interrupt, he went on, 'I thought this would help make it even clearer that the boy had committed suicide.'

'Clearer than what?' Patta asked.

'Than the physical evidence, sir,' Brunetti answered.

For a moment, he thought that Patta was about to say, 'Good.' Surely his face grew less tense and he, too, let out a deep breath. But all he said was, 'Very well. Then let's file it as suicide and let the school begin to get back to normal.'

'Good idea, sir,' said Brunetti, then, as if the idea had just occurred to him, 'But what do we do if the boy's parents aren't satisfied?'

'What do you mean, "aren't satisfied?"'

'Well, the father has a history of causing trouble,' Brunetti began, shaking his head as if thinking of the shocking scepticism towards public institutions demonstrated in the Moro Report. 'And so I wouldn't want to be responsible for a report about his son's death that left anything open to question.'

'Do you think there's a chance of that?'

'Probably not, sir,' Brunetti answered. 'But I wouldn't want to leave something undone that a person as difficult as Moro could point to and ask questions about. He'd be sure to make it look bad for us. And he's certainly a person who gets his fair share of public attention.' Brunetti stopped himself from saying more.

Patta gave all of this some thought and finally asked, 'What do you suggest?'

Brunetti feigned surprise that he should be asked such a thing. He started to speak, stopped, and then went on, giving every evidence that he'd never considered this possibility. 'I suppose I'd try to find out whether he took drugs or showed signs of depression.'

Patta appeared to consider all of this and then said, 'It would be easier for them to bear it if they were certain, I suppose.'

'Who, sir?'

'His parents.'

Brunetti risked a question. 'Do you know them?'

'The father, yes,' Patta said.

Because this was still not followed by an attack on the man, Brunetti dared to ask, 'Then do you think we should go ahead like this, sir?'

Patta sat up straighter and moved a heavy Byzantine coin he used as a paperweight from one side of his desk to the other. 'If it doesn't take too much time, all right.' How typically Patta was this answer: having commissioned the investigation, he had simultaneously assured that any delay would be laid at the feet of someone else.

'Yes, sir,' Brunetti said and got to his feet. Patta turned his attention to a thin file on his desk and Brunetti let himself out.

In the small outer office, he found Signorina Elettra at her desk, head bent over what appeared to be a catalogue. He looked closer and saw a double-page spread of computer screens.

She glanced up and smiled.

'Didn't you just buy one of those?' he asked, pointing to the screen to her right.

'Yes, but they've just come out with new ones, perfectly flat screens, as thin as a pizza. Look,' she said, pointing a scarlet fingernail at one of the photos in the catalogue. Though he found her simile surreal, he had to agree it seemed accurate enough.

He read the first two lines of print and, seeing too many numbers and initials, to make no mention of a word he thought was 'gigabytes' he sped to the bottom where the price was given. 'That's a month's salary,' he said, in astonishment, aware that there was more than a little disapproval in his tone.

'Closer to two,' she added, 'if you get the larger LCD screen.'

'Are you really going to order it?' he asked.

'I've no choice, I'm afraid.'

'Why?'

'I've already promised this one,' she began, indicating her all-but-new computer screen as though it were a bag of old clothing she was asking the cleaning lady to dispose of, 'to Vianello.'

Brunetti decided to let it go. 'There seems to be some connection between the Vice-Questore and Dottor Moro,' he began. 'Do you think you could find out more about that?'

She had returned her attention to the catalogue. 'Nothing easier, sir,' she said, and turned a page.

11

Venice, like every other city in the country, was feeling the consequences of the government's refusal to adopt an immigration policy that was related in any sane way to the realities of immigration. Among the consequences which did not affect Brunetti directly were the thousands of illegal immigrants who profited from the easygoing Italian policy and who then, in possession of Italian documents legitimizing their presence on the continent, passed to northern countries where they would be able to work with some protection under the law. There was also the resulting irritation on the part of other governments at the ease with which the Italians washed their hands of the problem by passing it on to them.

Venice, and Brunetti, had begun to feel the consequences in their own way: the number of pickpocketings had skyrocketed; shoplifting was a problem for even the smallest merchants; and no householder any longer felt that his home was safe from robbery. Since most of these cases passed through the Questura, Brunetti registered the increase, but he felt it lightly, as a person with a mild cold might discover that his temperature has increased a degree or two without feeling any real symptoms. If this increase in petty crime produced any symptoms for Brunetti himself, it was in the amount of paperwork he was obliged to initial and, presumably, read.

It was a period in which there was very little violent crime in the houses or on the streets of Venice, and so Patta, no doubt feeling withdrawal symptoms after his name had not appeared in the *Gazzettino* for more than a week, ordered Brunetti, and requested Signorina Elettra, to prepare a report providing statistics which would show the high clear-up rate of the Venetian police. The report, he stipulated, was to show that the perpetrators of most crimes were found and arrested and that, during the last year, there had been a consequent decrease in crime within the city.

'But that's nonsense,' Brunetti said, when Signorina Elettra informed him of their task.

'No more nonsensical than any other statistic we're provided with,' she said.

His patience short because of the time he knew he'd waste in preparing this report, he asked curtly, 'Like what?'

'Like the statistics about road fatalities,' she said, smiling, patient in the face of his annoyance.

'What about them?' he asked, not really interested, yet doubtful that anything so well documented could be altered.

'If you die a week or more after you're injured in an accident, you didn't die because of the accident,' she said, almost with pride. 'At least, not statistically.'

'Does that mean the hospitals kill you?' he asked, aiming towards irony.

'That's certainly often enough the case, sir,' she said with every appearance of patience. 'I'm not sure just how they list these deaths, but they aren't counted as traffic fatalities.'

Not for an instant did it occur to Brunetti to doubt her. Her idea, however, sent his mind tumbling back to the report they had to prepare. 'Do you think we could use this technique ourselves?'

'You mean, if someone who is murdered takes a week to die, they weren't murdered?' she asked. 'Or if a theft is reported after more than a week, then nothing was stolen?' He nodded, and Signorina Elettra devoted herself to considering the possibility. Finally she answered, 'I'm sure the Vice-Questore would be delighted, though I'm afraid there would be certain difficulties if we were questioned about it.'

He drew his imagination away from these angel flights of mathematics and back to the grim truth of the report they had to write. 'Do you think we can do it and get the results he wants?'

Her voice grew serious. 'I think what he wants won't be hard to give him. All we have to do is exercise caution about the number of crimes reported.'

'What does that mean?'

'That we count only those where people came down here or went to the *Carabinieri* to fill out a formal *denuncia*.'

'What will that achieve?'

'I've told you before, Commissario. People don't bother to report crimes, least of all pick-pocketing or burglary. So when they phone to report it but then don't bother to come down here to fill out the papers, the crime hasn't been reported.' She paused for a moment, allowing Brunetti, who knew just how Jesuitical her reasoning could be, to prepare himself for the consequences towards which this must lead her. 'And if there is no official *denuncia* – which, in a certain sense, means the act never occurred – then I see no reason why we should have to include them in our calculations.'

'What percentage would you estimate people don't bother to report?' he asked.

'I have no way of knowing, sir,' she said. 'After all, it's philosophically impossible to prove a negative.' There followed another pause, and then she said, 'I'd guess a bit more than half.'

'Are or aren't reported?' a surprised Brunetti asked.

'Aren't.'

This time it was Brunetti who paused for a long time before he said, 'That's very lucky for us, isn't it?'

'Indeed,' was her response, then she asked, 'Would you like me to take care of it, sir? He wants it for the newspapers, and they want to be able to say that Venice is a happy island, virtually free from crime, so no one is likely to question my numbers or my accounting.'

'It is, though, isn't it?' he asked.

'What, a happy island?'

'Yes.'

'In comparison with the rest of the country, yes, I think so.'

'How long do you think it will stay like that?'

Signorina Elettra shrugged. As Brunetti was turning to leave her office, she opened her desk drawer and took a few sheets of paper from it. 'I didn't forget about Dottor Moro, sir,' she said as she handed it to him.

He thanked her and left her office. As he walked up the stairs, he saw that it explained the reason for Patta's familiarity with Dr Fernando Moro. There was nothing unusual: Signora Patta's mother had been a patient of Moro's since he had returned to the practice of medicine. Signorina Elettra had not managed to provide copies of her medical records, but she had supplied the dates of her visits to Dottor Moro, twenty-seven in all during the last two years. At the bottom, Signorina Elettra had added, in her own hand: 'Breast cancer.' He checked the date of the last appointment: little more than two months ago.

As with any superior, Vice-Questore Giuseppe Patta was often the subject of speculation among those under his command. His motives for action or inertia were usually transparent: power, its maintenance and aggrandizement. In the past, however, he had proven capable of great weakness, had even been deflected from his headlong pursuit of power, but only when he acted in defence of his family. Brunetti, though often suspicious of Patta and usually deeply contemptuous of his motives, felt nothing but respect for this weakness.

Brunetti had told himself that decency demanded he wait at least two days before attempting to speak again to either of the boy's parents. That time had passed, and he arrived at the Questura that morning with the intention of interviewing one or both of them. Dottor Moro's home phone was answered by a machine. The phone at his practice said that, until further notice, the doctor's patients would be seen by Doctor D. Biasi, whose office hours and phone number were given. Brunetti redialled the first number and left his name and his direct number at the Questura, requesting that the doctor call him.

That left the mother. Signorina Elettra had provided a brief biography. Venetian, like her husband, she had met Moro in *liceo*, then both had gone on to the University of Padova, where Moro opted for medicine, Federica for child psychology. They married when her studies were completed but didn't return to Venice until Moro was offered a place at the Ospedale Civile, when she had opened a private practice in the city.

Their legal separation, which took place with unseemly haste after her accident, had been a surprise to their friends. They had not divorced, and neither appeared to be involved with another person. There was no evidence that they had contact with one another, and any communication they had seemed to take place through their lawyers.

Signorina Elettra had clipped the article about Ernesto's death that had appeared in *La Nuova* to the outside of the folder. He chose not to read it, though he did read the caption under the photo of the family, 'in happier times'.

Federica Moro's smile was the centre of the photo: she stood with her right arm wrapped around the back of her husband, her head leaning on his chest, her other hand ruffling her son's hair. The photo showed them on a beach, in shorts and T-shirts, tanned and bursting with happiness and health; behind them the head of a swimmer bobbed just to her husband's right. The picture must have been taken years ago, for Ernesto was still a boy, not a young man. Federica looked away from the camera, and the other two looked at her, Ernesto's glance open and proud, as who would not be proud to have such an attractive woman as a mother? Fernando's look was calmer, yet no less proud.

One of them, Brunetti thought, must just have said something funny, or perhaps they'd seen something on the beach that made them laugh. Or was it the photographer, perhaps, who had been the clown of the moment? Brunetti was struck by the fact that, of the three of them, Federica had the shortest hair: boyish, only a few centimetres long. It stood in sharp contrast to the fullness of her body and the natural ease with which she embraced her husband.

Who would dare to publish such a photo, and who could have given it to the paper, surely knowing how it would be used? He slipped the clipping free and stuck it inside the folder. The same number Signora Ferro had given him was written on the outside; he dialled, forgetting what she had told him about letting it ring once and hanging up.

On the fourth ring, a woman's voice answered, saying only '*Sì?*'

'Signora Moro?' Brunetti asked.

'*Sì.*'

'Signora, this is Commissario Guido Brunetti. Of the police. I'd be very grateful if you would find the time to speak to me.' He waited for her to reply, then added, 'About your son.'

'Aah,' she said. Then nothing for a long time.

'Why have you waited?' she finally asked, and he sensed that having to ask the question made her angry.

'I didn't want to intrude on your grief, Signora.' When she was silent, he added, 'I'm sorry.'

'Do you have children?' she surprised him by asking.

'Yes, I do.'

'How old?'

'I have a daughter,' he began, then said the rest quickly, 'My son is the same age as yours.'

'You didn't say that at the beginning,' she said, sounding surprised that he should have failed to use such an emotive tool.

Unable to think of anything suitable to say, Brunetti asked 'May I come and speak to you, Signora?'

'Any time you want,' she said, and he had a vision of days, months, years, an entire lifetime stretching away from her.

'May I come now?' he asked.

'It's all the same, isn't it?' she asked; it was a real request for information, not a sarcastic or self-pitying pose.

'It should take me about twenty minutes to get there,' he said.

'I'll be here,' she replied.

He had located her address on the map and so knew which way to walk. He could have taken the boat up towards San Marco, but he chose to walk up the *Riva*, cutting through the Piazza and in front of the Museo Correr. He entered Frezzerie and turned left at the first *calle* on his left. It was the second door on the right, the top bell. He rang it, and with no question asked through the intercom, the door snapped open and he went in.

The entrance hall was damp and dark, though no canal was nearby. He climbed to the third floor and found, directly opposite him, an open door. He paused, called, 'Signora Moro?' and heard a voice say something from inside, so he went in and closed the door behind him. He went down a narrow corridor with a cheap machine-made carpet on the floor, towards what seemed to be a source of light.

A door stood open on his right and he stepped inside. A woman was sitting in a chair on the other side of the room, and light filtered in from two curtained windows that stood behind her. The room smelled of cigarette smoke and, he thought, mothballs.

'Commissario?' she asked, raising her face to look in his direction.

'Yes,' he answered. 'Thank you for letting me come.'

She waved his words away with her right hand, then returned the cigarette it held to her mouth and inhaled deeply. 'There's a chair over there,' she said, exhaling and pointing to a cane-seated chair that stood against the wall.

He brought it over and set it facing her, but not very close and a short distance to one side. He sat and waited for her to say something. He didn't want to seem to stare at her and so he directed his attention to the windows, beyond which he saw, just on the other side of the narrow *calle*, the windows of another house. Little light could get in that way. He turned his attention back to her and, even in this strange penumbra, recognized the woman in the photo. She looked as though she'd been on a crash diet that had drawn the flesh tight on her face and honed the bones of her jaw until they were so sharp that they would soon come slicing through the skin. The same process seemed to have pared her body down to the bare essentials of shoulders, arms, and legs contained in a heavy sweater and dark slacks that accentuated her body's frailty.

It became evident that she was not going to speak, was simply going to sit with him and smoke her cigarette. 'I'd like to ask you some questions, Signora,' he began, and exploded in a sudden fit of nervous coughing.

'Is it the cigarette?' she asked, turning to the table on her right and making to put it out.

He raised a reassuring hand. 'No, not at all,' he gasped but was gripped by another coughing fit.

She stabbed out the cigarette and got to her feet. He started to get to his, doubled over by his coughing, but she waved him back and left the room. Brunetti lowered himself into the chair and continued to cough, tears streaming from his eyes. In a moment, she was back, handing him a glass of water. 'Drink it slowly,' she said. 'Take small sips.'

Still shaking with the attempt to control himself, he took the glass with a nod of thanks and put it to his lips. He waited for the spasms to subside and took a small sip, and then another and another until all of the water was gone and he could breathe freely again. Occasionally, puffs of air rushed from his lungs, but worst was over. He leaned down and set the glass on the floor. 'Thank you,' he said.

'It's nothing,' she answered, taking her place in the chair opposite him. He saw her reach instinctively to the right, towards the pack of cigarettes that lay on the table, and then lower her hand to her lap.

She looked over at him and asked, 'Nerves?'

He smiled. 'I think so, though I don't think I'm supposed to say so.'

'Why not?' she asked, sounding interested.

'Because I'm the policeman, and we're not supposed to be weak or nervous.'

'That's ridiculous, isn't it?'

He nodded, and in that instant recalled that she was a psychologist.

He cleared his throat and asked, 'Could we begin again, Signora?'

Her smile was minimal, a ghost of the one on her face in the photo that still lay on his desk. 'I suppose we have to. What is it you'd like to know?'

'I'd like to ask you about your accident, Signora.'

Her confusion was visible, and he could understand its

cause. Her son was recently dead in circumstances that had
yet to be officially determined, and he was asking her about
something that had happened more than two years ago. 'Do
you mean in Siena?' she finally asked.

'Yes.'

'Why do you want to know about that?'

'Because no one seemed curious about it at the time.'

She tilted her head to one side as she considered his
answer. 'I see,' she finally said, then added, 'Should they have
been?'

'That's what I'm hoping to learn, Signora.'

Silence settled in between them and Brunetti, having no
option, sat and waited to see if she would tell him what had
happened. In the minutes that passed, she glanced aside at
the cigarettes twice, and the second time he almost told her to
go ahead and smoke, that it wouldn't bother him, but he said
nothing. As the silence lengthened, he studied the few objects
he could see in the room: her chair, the table, the curtains at
the window. All spoke of a taste far different from the casual
wealth he had observed in Moro's home. There was no
attempt to suit style to style or do anything more than
provide furniture that would meet the most basic needs.

'I'd gone down to our friends on the Friday morning,' she
said, surprising him when she finally began to speak.
'Fernando was supposed to get there on the last train, at
about ten that night. It was a beautiful day, late autumn but
still very warm, so I decided to go for a walk in the afternoon.
I was about a half a kilometre from the house when I heard a
loud noise – it could have been a bomb for all I knew – and
then I felt a pain in my leg, and I fell down. It wasn't as if
anyone had pushed me or anything: I just fell down.'

She glanced across at him, as if to establish whether he
could possibly find any of this interesting. He nodded and
she went on. 'I lay there, too stunned to do anything. It didn't
even hurt all that much then. I heard noises from the woods

that I had been walking towards. Well, not really woods, perhaps an acre or two of trees. I heard something moving around in there and I wanted to shout for help, but then I didn't. I don't know why, but I didn't. I just lay there.

'A minute or two must have passed, and then, over from where I'd come from, two dogs came running toward me, barking their heads off, came right up to me and started jumping around, barking all the time. I shouted at them to shut up. My leg had started to hurt then, and when I looked at it, I realized I'd been shot, so I knew I had to do something. And then there were these hunting dogs, barking and dancing around me like crazy things.'

She stopped talking for so long that Brunetti was forced to ask, 'What happened then?'

'The hunters came. The men whose dogs they were, that is. They saw the dogs and they saw me on the ground and they thought the dogs had attacked me, so they came running and when they got to us they started kicking the dogs away and hitting at them with the ends of their guns, but the dogs weren't doing anything. They probably saved my life, those dogs.'

She stopped and looked directly at him, as if to ask if he had any questions, and when he said nothing, she went on, 'One of them used his handkerchief and made a tourniquet, and then they carried me to their Jeep, which was just at the edge of the woods. And they took me to the hospital. The doctors there are used to this kind of thing: hunters are always shooting themselves or other hunters down there, it seems.' She paused and then said softly, 'Poor things,' in a voice so filled with real sympathy that he was struck by how vulgar and cheap his conversation with Signorina Elettra sounded in comparison.

'Did they ask you at the hospital how it happened, Signora?'

'The men who found me told them what had happened, so

all I did, when I came out from surgery, was confirm what they'd said.'

'That it was an accident?' he asked.

'Yes.' She said the word with no special tone.

'Do you think it was?' he asked.

Again, there was a long delay before she spoke. 'At the time, I didn't think it could have been anything else. But since then I've started to wonder why whoever it was that shot me didn't come to see what they'd done. If they thought I was some sort of an animal, they would have come to check that they'd killed me, wouldn't they?'

That was what had troubled Brunetti ever since he'd first heard the story.

'And when they heard the dogs and then the other hunters, they would have come to see what all that was about, if they thought someone else was going to take the animal they'd killed.' She let some time pass and then said, 'As I said, I didn't think about any of this at the time.'

'And what do you think now?'

She started to speak, stopped herself, and then said, 'I don't mean to be melodramatic, but I have other things to think about now.'

So did Brunetti. He was wondering if a police report had been filed of the incident, if the two hunters who found her had noticed anyone in the area.

Brunetti could no longer keep her from her cigarettes, so he said, 'I have only one more question, Signora.'

She didn't wait for him to ask it. 'No, Ernesto didn't kill himself. I'm his mother, and I know that to be true. That's another reason why I think it wasn't an accident.' She prised herself from her chair, said, 'If that was your last question . . .' and started towards the door of the room. Her limp was slight, the merest favouring of her right leg when she walked, and as she wore slacks, he had no idea of the damage that had been done to her leg.

He let her lead him to the door of the apartment. He thanked her but didn't offer his hand. Outside, it had grown marginally warmer, and as it was already after noon, Brunetti decided to go directly home for lunch with his family.

12

Brunetti arrived before the children did, so he opted to keep Paola company while she finished preparing the meal. As she set the table, he lifted pot lids and opened the oven, comforted to find nothing but familiar dishes: lentil soup, chicken smothered in red cabbage, and what looked like *radicchio di Treviso.*

'Are you bringing all of your detective skills to bear in examining that chicken?' Paola asked as she set glasses on the table.

'No, not really,' he said, closing the oven and standing upright. 'My investigation has to do with the radicchio, Signora, and whether there are perhaps traces in it of the same pancetta I detected in the lentil soup.'

'A nose as good as that,' she said, coming over and placing the tip of her finger on it, 'could effectively put an end to crime in this city.' She lifted the lid from the soup and stirred it round a bit, then said, 'You're back early.'

'I was over near San Marco and so it didn't make any sense to go back,' he said, taking a sip of mineral water. 'I went to see Signora Moro,' he began, pausing to see if Paola would react. She did not, so he went on, 'I wanted to talk to her about the hunting accident.'

'And?' Paola prodded.

'Someone shot at her from the woods near her friends' house, but then some other hunters came along and took her to the hospital.'

'Are you sure they were other hunters?' Paola asked, giving evidence that her native scepticism had been enhanced by more than two decades of marriage to a policeman.

'It would seem so,' he said, leaving it at that.

Knowing how reluctant he would be to mention him, Paola asked, 'And the boy?'

'She said that he didn't kill himself, and that's all she said.'

'She's his mother,' Paola said. 'Believe her.'

'It's as simple as that?' Brunetti asked, unable to disguise his own scepticism.

'Yes, it's as simple as that. If anyone knew what he was capable of, it's she.'

Unwilling to argue the point, he poured himself another glass of water and wandered over to stand at the window that looked off to the north. From behind him, Paola asked, 'What's she like?'

He thought about the woman, remembered her voice, the eyes that took little interest in seeing him, the paper-thin skin of her neck. 'Reduced,' he finally said. 'She's not a whole person any more.' He thought Paola would ask about this, but she didn't. 'All I saw was a photo of her, taken some years ago, with the boy. And her husband. She still looks like the same person; I mean, you could recognize her from the photo, but there's less of her.'

'That makes sense,' Paola said, 'there *is* less of her.'

He had no idea why he thought Paola would have an answer, but he asked her anyway, 'Will that ever go away, the diminishing?'

It was only then that Brunetti realized that his question would force Paola to think about the death of her own children because the only way to answer the question was to put herself in the other woman's place. He regretted asking the question as soon as he had spoken. He had never had the courage to ask her if she thought about that possibility and, if so, how often. Though he had always found it absurd that parents should worry excessively about the safety of their children, that is, worry in the absence of any real danger, a day did not pass but he worried about his own. The fact that he knew it to be ridiculous, especially in a city without cars, in no way reduced his concern or prevented him from counting out the ways the safety of his children could be imperilled.

Paola's voice broke into his reverie. 'No, I don't think the death of a child is something a person ever recovers from, not fully.'

'Do you think it's worse because she's a mother?' he asked.

She dismissed this with a shake of her head. 'No. That's nonsense.' He was grateful that she chose not to give an example to prove that a father's grief could be as deep.

He turned back from looking at the mountains, and their eyes met. 'What do you think happened?' she asked.

He shook his head, utterly at a loss to make any sense of what had happened to the Moro family. 'All I have is four events: he writes his report, though nothing much comes of it except that he's punished; he gets elected to Parliament and then leaves before his term in office is over; his wife is shot just before he resigns; two years later, his son is found hanged in the bathroom of his school.'

'Does the school mean anything?' Paola asked.

'Mean anything in what way? That it's a military academy?'

'That's the only thing that's unusual about it, isn't it?' she asked. 'That and the fact that they spend the winter walking around the city looking like penguins. And the rest of the year looking like they have a bad smell under their noses.' This was Paola's usual description of snobs and their behaviour. As she had been born to a conte and contessa and had spent her youth surrounded by wealth and titles and the hangers-on who are drawn to both, he figured she'd seen her fair share of snobs.

'I always heard it had a good academic record,' he said.

'Bah,' she exploded, erasing that possibility from the air with a puff of breath.

'I'm not sure that serves as a conclusive counter-argument,' he said. 'Articulate and well-reasoned as it is.'

Paola turned to face him and put her hands on her hips, looking like an actress trying out for the role of Angry Woman. 'My counter-argument might not be conclusive,' she said, 'but I shall do my best to make it articulate.'

'Oh, I love it when you're angry like that, Signora Paola,' he said in a voice he forced up to its highest register. Her hands fell to her sides and she laughed. 'Tell me,' he said, reaching for the bottle of Pinot Noir that stood on the counter.

'Susanna Arici,' she said, 'used to teach there, right after she came back from Rome and was waiting for a job at a state school. She thought that by taking the job she was offered at the Academy, even though it was only part time, she'd at least have entered the state system.' At Brunetti's questioning glance, she explained, 'She thought it was run by the Army, which would make it a state school. But it's entirely private, not attached to the Army in any official way, though it seems it somehow manages to receive quite a bit of state funding. So all she had was a badly paid part-time job. And then when the permanent position came up, they didn't give her the job, anyway.'

'What did she teach, English?' Brunetti had met Susanna a number of times. The youngest sister of a classmate of Paola's, she had gone to Urbino to study, then come back to

Venice to teach, where she still was, happily divorced and living with the father of her second daughter.

'Yes, but for only one year.'

This had been almost ten years ago, so Brunetti asked, 'Couldn't things have changed since then?'

'I don't see why anything should have. Certainly, the public schools have done nothing but get worse, though I imagine the students have remained pretty much the same: I don't see why things in private schools should be any different.'

Brunetti pulled out his chair and sat. 'All right. What did she say?'

'That most of their parents were terrible snobs and that they passed this feeling of superiority on to their sons. To their daughters as well, for all I know, but as the Academy takes only boys ...' Paola's voice trailed off, and for a moment Brunetti wondered if she were going to use this opportunity to launch into a denunciation of single-sex schools that received funds from the state.

She came and stood near him, took his glass of wine and sipped at it, then handed it back to him. 'Don't worry. Only one sermon at a time, my dear.' Brunetti, unwilling to encourage her, stifled a smile.

'What else did she say?' he asked.

'That they felt entitled to everything they had or their parents had and that they believed themselves to be members of a special group.'

'Doesn't everyone?' Brunetti asked.

'In this case,' Paola went on, 'it was more a case that they felt themselves bound only to the group, to its rules and decisions.'

'Isn't that what I just said?' Brunetti asked. 'Certainly we police feel that way. Well, some do.'

'Yes, I suppose so. But you still feel bound by the laws that govern the rest of us, don't you?'

'Yes,' Brunetti agreed, but then his conscience, and indeed his intelligence, forced him to add, 'Some of us.'

'Well, what Susanna said was that these boys didn't. That is, they thought that the only rules that governed them were the rules of the military. So long as they obeyed them and remained loyal to that group, they believed they could pretty much do anything else they wanted.'

Paola studied him as she spoke, and when she saw the attention he gave to what she said, she went on, 'What's more, she said that the teachers, most of whom had a military background, did everything they could to encourage the students to think like this. They told them to think of themselves as soldiers first and foremost.' And then she smiled, though grimly. 'Just think of the pathos of it: they aren't soldiers, aren't associated with the military in any real way, yet they're being taught to think of themselves as warriors, loyal only to the cult of violence. It's disgusting.'

Something that had been nibbling at the edge of his memory finally broke through. 'Was she there when that girl was raped?' he asked.

'No, I think that was a year or two after she left. Why?'

'I'm trying to remember the story. The girl was the sister of one of them, wasn't she?'

'Yes, or a cousin,' Paola said, then shook her head as if that would better summon the memory. 'All I remember is that the police were called to the school and at first it looked as if the girl had been raped. But then it dropped out of the papers like a stone.'

'It's strange, but I don't have a clear memory of it, just that it happened, but none of the details are clear.'

'I think it happened when you were in London on that course,' Paola suggested. 'I remember thinking, at the time, that I had no way of knowing what really happened because you weren't here to tell me, and the only source of information I had was the newspapers.'

'Yes, that must be it,' he agreed. 'I'm sure there's something in the files; there's got to be, at least the original report.'

'Could you find it?'

'I'm sure Signorina Elettra could.'

'But why bother?' Paola suddenly countered. 'There's no surprise here: rich boys, rich parents, so everything goes suddenly quiet and, next thing you know, it's disappeared from the press and, for all I know, from the public record.'

'I can still ask her to have a look,' Brunetti said. Then he asked, 'What else did Susanna say?'

'That she never felt comfortable there. She said there was always an undercurrent of resentment at the fact that she was a woman.'

'No way she could change that, is there?' Brunetti asked.

'They did the next best thing when they hired her replacement,' Paola said.

'Let me guess. A man?'

'Very much so.'

Speaking carefully, always conscious of when he was about to stumble over one of Paola's hobby-horses, he asked, 'It couldn't be a bit of reverse sexism I'm detecting here, could it?'

Paola's look was fierce, but then it disappeared, replaced by a tolerant smile. 'According to Susanna, he spoke English about as well as the average Parisian taxi driver, but he'd been to the Naval Academy in Livorno, so it didn't matter how well he spoke it. For that fact, it probably didn't matter if he spoke it at all. You know the place is just a finishing school for those boys before they step into their fathers' shoes in the Army or into whatever businesses they run, and it's not as if the Army's an institution that makes serious intellectual demands on anyone.' Before Brunetti could question this, Paola said, 'But, yes, it might be that she exaggerated. Susanna does tend to see sexism where it doesn't exist.'

When he got his breath back, Brunetti asked, 'You remember her saying all of this at the time?'

'Of course. I was one of the people who recommended her for the job, so when they let her go, she told me. Why do you ask?'

'I wondered if you've talked to her since this happened.'

'You mean the boy?'

'Yes.'

'No, we haven't spoken in, oh, at least six months. But I remember it, probably because it confirms everything I've ever thought about the military. They have the morals of pit vipers. They'll do anything to cover up for one another: lie, cheat, commit perjury. Just look what happened when those Americans flew into the cable car. You think any of them told the truth? I haven't noticed any of them going to jail. How many people did they kill? Twenty? Thirty?' She made a noise of disgust, poured herself a small glass of wine, but left it untouched on the counter as she went on. 'They'll do anything they want to anyone who isn't a member of the group, and the instant the public begins to ask questions, they all clam up and talk about honour and loyalty and all that other noble shit. It's enough to make a pig vomit.' She stopped talking and closed her eyes, then opened them enough to see her glass of wine and pick it up. She took a small sip, and then a larger one. Suddenly she smiled. 'End of sermon.'

Brunetti had, in his youth, done eighteen months of undistinguished military service, most of it spent hiking in the mountains with his fellow Alpini. His memories, and he admitted that they had acquired the golden patina of age, were chiefly of a sense of unity and belonging entirely different from those his family had given him. As he cast his mind back, the image that came through with greatest clarity was of a dinner of cheese, bread and salami, eaten in company with four other boys in a freezing mountain hut in

Alto Adige, after which they had drunk twc bottles of grappa and sung marching songs. He had never told Paola about this evening, not because he was ashamed of how drunk they had all got, but because the memory could still fill him with such simple joy. He had no idea where the other boys – men now – had gone or what they had done after finishing their military service, but he knew that some sort of bond had been forged in the cold of that mountain hut and that he would never experience anything like it again.

He pulled his mind back to the present and to his wife. 'You've always hated the military, haven't you?'

Her response was instant. 'Give me one reason not to.'

Certain that she would dismiss his memory as the worst sort of male bonding ritual, Brunetti found himself with precious little to say. 'Discipline?' he asked.

'Have you ever ridden on a train with a bunch of them?' Paola asked, then repeated his answer with a little puff of contempt. 'Discipline?'

'It gets them away from their mothers.'

She laughed. 'That's perhaps the only certain good thing it does. Unfortunately, after they have their eighteen months, they all come back home to roost.'

'Is that what you think Raffi will do?' he asked.

'If I have any say,' she began, causing Brunetti to wonder when she had not, 'he won't do military service. It would be better for him to go to Australia and spend eighteen months hitchhiking around the country and working as a dishwasher. He'd certainly learn more by doing that, or by opting to do his service as a volunteer in a hospital, instead.'

'You'd actually let him go off to Australia by himself? For eighteen months? To wash dishes?'

Paola looked at him and, at the expression of real astonishment she read on his face, she smiled. 'What do you think I am, Guido, the mother of the Gracchi, that I must forever hold my children to my bosom as though they were my only jewels? It wouldn't be easy to see him go, no, not at all, but I think it would do him a world of good to go off and be independent.' When Brunetti remained silent, she said, 'At least it would teach him how to make his own bed.'

'He does that already,' a literal-minded Brunetti answered.

'I mean in the larger sense,' Paola explained. 'It would give him some idea that life is not only this tiny city with its tiny prejudices, and it might give him some idea that work is what you do if you want something.'

'As opposed to asking your parents?'

'Exactly. Or your grandparents.'

It was rare for Brunetti to hear Paola make a criticism, however veiled, of her parents, and so he was curious to follow this up. 'Was it too easy for you? Growing up, I mean.'

'No more than it was too hard for you, my dear.'

Not at all sure what she meant by that, Brunetti was about to ask, when the door to the apartment flew open and Chiara and Raffi catapulted into the corridor. He and Paola exchanged a glance, and then a smile, and then it was time to eat.

13

As often happened, Brunetti was immeasurably cheered by having lunch at home in the company of his family. He was never certain if his response was different from that of an animal returned to its den: safe, warmed by the heat of the bodies of its young, slavering over the fresh kill it had dragged home. Whatever the cause, the experience gave him fresh heart and sent him back to work feeling restored and eager to resume the hunt.

The imagery of violence dropped away from him when he entered Signorina Elettra's office and found her at her desk, head bowed over some papers on her desk, chin propped in one hand, utterly relaxed and comfortable. 'I'm not interrupting you, am I?' he asked, seeing the seal of the Ministry of the Interior on the documents and below it the red stripe indicating that the material it contained was classified.

'No, not at all, Commissario,' she said casually slipping the papers inside a file and thus arousing Brunetti's interest.

'Could you do something for me?' he asked, his eyes on

hers; he was careful to avoid lowering them to the label on the front of the file.

'Of course, sir,' she said, slipping the file into her top drawer and pulling a notepad over in front of her. 'What is it?' she asked, pen in hand, smile bright.

'In the files for the Academy, is there anything about a girl who had been raped?'

Her pen clattered to the desk, and the smile disappeared from her lips. Her entire body pulled back from him in surprise, but she said nothing.

'Are you all right, Signorina?' he asked, with concern.

She looked down at the pen, picked it up, made quite a business of replacing the cap and removing it again, then looked up at him and smiled. 'Of course, sir.' She looked at the pad, pulled it closer to her, and poised her pen over it. 'What was her name, sir? And when did it happen?'

'I don't know,' Brunetti began. 'That is, I'm not even sure it happened. It must have been about eight years ago; I think it was when I was at a police seminar in London. It happened at the San Martino. The original report was that the girl had been raped, I think by more than one of them. But then no charges were pressed, and the story disappeared.'

'Then what is it you'd like me to look for, sir?'

'I'm not sure,' Brunetti answered. 'Any sign of something that might have happened, who the girl was, why the story disappeared. Anything at all you can find out about it.'

She seemed to be a long time writing all of this down, but he waited until she was finished. Pen still in her hand, she asked, 'If charges weren't pressed, then it's not likely we'll have anything here, is it?'

'No, it isn't. But I'm hoping that there might be some report of the original complaint.'

'And if there isn't?'

Brunetti was puzzled to find her so hesitant about

following up an investigation. 'Then perhaps the newspapers. Once you have the date, that is,' he said.

'I'll have a look at your personnel file, sir, and find the dates when you were in London,' she said, then looked up from her notebook, face serene.

'Yes, yes,' he said, then, lamely, 'I'll be in my office.'

As he went upstairs, he reconsidered what Paola had said about the military, trying to figure out why he couldn't bring himself to condemn them as universally or as strongly as she did. Part of it, he knew, was because of his own experience under arms, however brief it had been, and the lingering fondness he felt for that period of unexamined comradeship. Perhaps it was nothing more elevated than the instinct of the pack, gathered round the kill, retelling stories of that day's hunt while great gobbets of fat dripped into the fire. But if memory was to be trusted, his loyalty had been to his immediate group of friends and not to some abstract ideal of corps or regiment.

His reading in history had given him many examples of soldiers who died in proud defence of the regimental flag or while performing remarkable acts of heroism to save the perceived honour of the group, but these actions had always seemed wasteful and faintly stupid to Brunetti. Certainly, reading accounts of the actual events or even the words of the decorations bestowed, too often posthumously, upon these brave young men, Brunetti had felt his heart stir in response to the nobility of their behaviour, but the antiphon of pragmatic good sense had always rung out in the background, reminding him that, in the end, these were boys who threw their lives away in order to protect what was nothing more than a piece of cloth. Bold, certainly, and brave, but also foolish to the point of idiocy.

He found his desk covered with reports of one sort or another, the detritus of several days' lack of attention. He wrapped himself in the cloak of duty and, for the next two hours, engaged himself in behaviour as futile as any he thought to criticize on the part of those valiant young men. As he read through accounts of arrests for burglary, pick-pocketing, and the various types of fraud currently practised on the streets of the city, he was struck by how often the names of the people arrested were foreign and by how often their age exempted them from punishment. These facts left him untroubled: it was the thought that each of these arrests guaranteed another vote for the Right that disturbed him. Years ago, he had read a short story, he thought by some American, which ended with the revelation of an endless chain of sinners marching towards heaven along a broad arc in the sky. He sometimes thought the same chain of sinners marched slowly through the skies of Italian politics, though hardly toward paradise.

Stupefied by the boredom of the task, he heard his name called from the door and looked up to see Pucetti.

'Yes, Pucetti?' he said, beckoning the young officer into his office. 'Have a seat.' Glad of the excuse to set the papers aside, he turned his attention to the young policeman. 'What is it?' he asked, struck by how young he looked in his crisp uniform, far too young to have any right to carry the gun at his side, far too innocent to have any idea of how to use it.

'It's about the Moro boy, sir,' Pucetti said. 'I came to see you yesterday, sir, but you weren't here.'

It was close to a reproach, something Brunetti was not used to hearing from Pucetti. Resentment flared in Brunetti that the young officer should dare to take this tone with him. He fought down the impulse to explain to Pucetti that he had decided there was no need for haste. If it was generally believed the police were treating Moro's death as suicide, people might be more willing to speak about the boy openly; besides, he had no need to justify his decisions to this boy. He waited longer than he usually would, then asked simply, 'What about him?'

'You remember the time we were there, talking to the cadets?' Pucetti asked, and Brunetti was tempted to ask if the younger man thought he had arrived at an age where his memory needed to be prodded in order to function.

'Yes,' Brunetti limited himself to saying.

'It's very strange, sir. When we went back to talk to them again, it was as if some of them didn't even know he had been in the same school with them. Most of the ones I talked to told me they didn't know him very well. I spoke to the boy who found him, Pellegrini, but he didn't know anything. He was drunk the night before, said he went to bed about midnight.' Even before Brunetti could ask, Pucetti supplied the information: 'Yes, he'd been at a party at a friend's house, in Dorsoduro. I asked him how he'd got in, and he said he had a key to the *portone*. He said he paid the *portiere* twenty Euros for it, and the way he said it, it sounded like anyone who wants one can buy one.' He waited to see if Brunetti had any questions about this, but then continued, 'I asked his roommate, and he said it was true, that Pellegrini woke him up when he came in. Pellegrini said he got up about six to get some water and that's when he saw Moro.'

'He wasn't the one who called, though, was he?'

'Called us, you mean, sir?'

'Yes.'

'No. It was one of the janitors. He said he'd just got there for work and heard a commotion in the bathroom, and when he saw what had happened, he called.'

'More than an hour after Pellegrini found the body,' Brunetti said aloud.

When Pucetti made no response, Brunetti said, 'What else? Go on. What did they say about Moro?'

'It's in here, sir,' he said, placing a file on Brunetti's desk. He paused, weighing what to say next. 'I know this sounds strange, sir, but it seemed like most of them really didn't care about it. Not the way we would, or a person would, if something like this happened to someone you knew, or you worked with.' He gave this some more thought and added, 'It was creepy, sort of, the way they talked as if they didn't know him. But they all live there together, and take classes together. How could they not know him?' Hearing his voice rise, Pucetti forced himself to calm down. 'Anyway, one of them told me that he'd had a class with Moro a couple of days before, and they'd studied together that night and the following day. Getting ready for an exam.'

'When was the exam?'

'The day after.'

'The day after what? That he died?'

'Yes, sir.'

Brunetti's conclusion was instant, but he asked Pucetti, 'How does that seem to you?'

It was obvious that the young officer had prepared himself for the question, for his answer was immediate. 'People kill themselves, well, at least it seems to me, that they'd do it after an exam, at least they'd wait to see how badly they'd done in it, and then maybe they'd do it. At least that's what I'd do,' he said, then added, 'not that I'd kill myself over a stupid exam.'

'What would you kill yourself over?' Brunetti asked.

Owl-like, Pucetti stared across at his commander. 'Oh, I don't think over anything, sir. Would you?'

Brunetti shook the idea away. 'No, I don't think so. But I suppose you never know.' He had friends who were killing themselves with stress or cigarettes or alcohol, and some of his friends had children who were killing themselves with drugs, but he could think of no one he knew, at least not in this instant, whom he thought capable of suicide. But perhaps that's why suicide fell like lightning: it was always the most unexpected people who did it.

His attention swung back to Pucetti only at the end of what he was saying. '. . . about going skiing this winter.'

'The Moro boy?' Brunetti asked to disguise the fact that his attention had drifted away.

'Yes, sir. And this kid said Moro was looking forward to it, really loved to ski.' He paused to see if his superior would comment, but when he did not, Pucetti went on, 'He seemed upset, sir.'

'Who? This boy?'

'Yes.'

'Why?'

Pucetti gave him a startled glance, puzzled that Brunetti hadn't figured this out yet. 'Because if he didn't kill himself, then someone else did.'

At the look of pleased satisfaction on Brunetti's face as he heard him explain this, Pucetti began to suspect, not without a twinge of embarrassment, that perhaps his superior had figured it out.

14

In the days that followed, Brunetti's thoughts were distracted from the Moro family and its griefs and directed towards the *Casinò*. The police, this time, were not asked to investigate the frequent and refined forms of peculation practised by guests and croupiers, but the accusations brought against the casino's administration for having enriched itself at public expense. Brunetti was one of the few Venetians who bothered to remember that the *Casinò* belonged to the city; hence he realized that any theft or embezzlement of *Casinò* earnings came directly from the funds earmarked for the aid of orphans and widows. That people who spent their lives among gamblers and card-sharks should steal was no surprise to Brunetti: it was only their boldness that occasionally astonished him, for it seemed that all of the ancillary services offered by the *Casinò* – banquets, private parties, even the bars – had quietly been turned over to a company that turned out to be run by the brother of the director.

Since detectives had to be brought in from other cities so as not to be detected as they presented themselves at the *Casinò* in the role of gamblers, and employees had to be found who would be willing to testify against their employers and colleagues, the investigation had so far been a slow and complicated one. Brunetti found himself involved in it at the expense of other cases, including that of Ernesto Moro, where the evidence continued to pile up in support of a judgment of suicide: the crime lab's report on the shower stall and the boy's room contained nothing that could be used to justify suspicions about his death, and none of the statements of students or teachers suggested anything at variance with the view that it was suicide. Brunetti, though unpersuaded by the absence of credible evidence in support of his own view, recalled occasions in the past when his impatience had proven harmful to investigations. Patience, then, patience and calm would be his watchwords.

The magistrate appointed to the investigation of the *Casinò* was on the point of issuing warrants for the arrest of the entire directorate when the mayor's office put out a statement announcing the transfer of the director of the *Casinò* to another position in the city administration, as well as the promotion of his chief assistants to places high in other city services. Further, the two leading witnesses found themselves promoted to positions of importance within the reorganized *Casinò*, whereupon both began to realize that their previous interpretation of events must have been mistaken. Their case in rubble, the police backed away from the gorgeous *palazzo* on the Canal Grande, and the visiting detectives were sent home.

These events resulted in a late-morning summons from Patta, who chastised Brunetti for what he considered an over-aggressive attitude toward the *Casinò* administration. Because Brunetti had at no time felt more than mild disapproval of the behaviour of the suspects – always taking a broad-minded view of crimes against property – Patta's heated words fell upon him with no more effect than spring rainfall upon sodden earth.

It was when his superior turned his attention to the Moro family that he found himself attending to what Patta was saying. 'Lieutenant Scarpa has told me that the boy was considered unstable, and so there's no further need to drag our heels on this. I think it's time we closed the case.'

'By whom, sir?' Brunetti inquired politely.

'What?'

'By whom? Who was it that thought he was unstable?' It was evident from Patta's response that he had not thought it necessary to ask this question: Scarpa's assertion would more than suffice by way of proof.

'His teachers, I imagine. People at the school. His friends. Whoever the lieutenant talked to,' Patta shot off in a quick list. 'Why do you ask?'

'Curiosity, sir. I didn't know the lieutenant was interested in the case.'

'I didn't say he was interested,' Patta said, making no attempt to disguise his disapproval at this latest evidence of Brunetti's inability – though Patta suspected it was his refusal – to do what every good policeman should do: realize when a suggestion was really an order. He took a long breath. 'Whoever it was he talked to, they said that the boy was clearly unstable, and so it's even more likely that it was suicide.'

'That's certainly what the autopsy indicated,' Brunetti affirmed mildly.

'Yes, I know.' Before Brunetti could ask, Patta went on, 'I haven't had time to read it carefully, but the overview is certainly consistent with suicide.'

There was no doubt in Brunetti's mind as to the author of this overview; what was in doubt was why Lieutenant Scarpa should take an interest in a case in which he was not involved.

'Has he had anything else to say about this?' Brunetti asked, trying his best to sound only mildly interested.

'No. Why?'

'Oh, merely that if the lieutenant is so convinced, then we can inform the boy's parents that the investigation is closed.'

'You've already spoken to them, haven't you?'

'Some days ago, yes. But if you remember, sir, you asked me to be sure that no doubt could be cast on our conclusions so the father would have no reason to complain about our work, given that he's already created a great deal of trouble for other agencies of the state.'

'You mean his report?' Patta asked.

'Yes, sir. I was of the understanding that you wanted to be certain he would have no grounds to launch a similar investigation of our handling of his son's death.' Brunetti paused a moment to assess the effect of this, and when he saw the first signs of Patta's uneasiness, he drove in another nail. 'He seems to be someone who has earned the trust of the public, so any complaint he might make would probably be picked up by the press.' He allowed himself a small, dismissive shrug. 'But if Lieutenant Scarpa is satisfied that there's enough evidence to prove to the parents that it was suicide, then there's certainly no reason for me to continue working on it.' Slapping his hands on his thighs, Brunetti pushed himself to his feet, eager to go off in pursuit of some new project, now that the Moro case had so neatly been settled by his colleague, Lieutenant Scarpa.

'Well,' Patta said, drawing the word out, 'perhaps it's hasty to think that things are as conclusive as Lieutenant Scarpa would like to believe.'

'I'm not sure I understand you, sir,' Brunetti lied, unwilling to let Patta off so easily and wondering to what lengths he would go to distance himself from Scarpa's eagerness to settle matters. Patta said nothing, and so an emboldened Brunetti asked, 'Is there some question about these people?

These witnesses?' By a remarkable exercise of restraint, Brunetti kept all hint of sarcasm from the last word. Still Patta said nothing, and so Brunetti asked, 'What, exactly, did he tell you, sir?'

Patta waved Brunetti to his seat again and contented himself with leaning back in his chair, and holding his chin with one hand – no doubt a non-threatening posture learned at a management seminar as a means to create solidarity with an inferior. He smiled, rubbed briefly at his left temple, then smiled again. 'I think the lieutenant might be too eager to bring closure to the boy's parents.' Surely, this was a word that had its origin in the same seminar. 'That is, it was rumoured at the school that Moro was not his normal self during the days before his death. Upon sober reflection, it occurs to me that the lieutenant might have been hasty to interpret this as proof of suicide,' Patta ventured, then added quickly, 'though I'm sure he's right.'

'Did these boys say how he was behaving?' Before Patta could answer the question, Brunetti asked a second, 'And who were these boys?'

'I'm not sure he said,' Patta answered.

'Surely it's in his report,' Brunetti said, leaning forward minimally as though expecting Patta to satisfy him by producing the lieutenant's written report.

'He gave his report orally.'

'So he didn't mention any names?' Brunetti asked.

'Not that I recall, no,' Patta said.

'Do you know if he subsequently submitted a written report?'

'No, but I doubt he'd consider that necessary, not after having spoken to me,' Patta said.

'Of course.'

'What's that supposed to mean?' Patta demanded, swiftly returning to his usual manner.

Brunetti's smile was bland. 'Only that he would have

thought he had done his duty by reporting to his superior.' He allowed a long pause to extend beyond this, then changed his expression to one he'd seen used by a tenor singing the Simpleton in *Boris Godunov*, 'What should we do now, sir?'

For a moment, he feared he'd gone too far, but Patta's response suggested he had not. 'I think it might be wise to speak to the parents again,' Patta began, 'to see if they're willing to accept the judgment that it was suicide.' There were still times when Patta's honesty was breathtaking, so absolute was his lack of interest in the truth.

Brunetti offered, 'Perhaps the lieutenant should go and speak to them, sir? '

That caught Patta's attention. 'No, it might be better if you went. After all, you've already spoken to them, and I imagine they thought you were sympathetic.' Never had that quality sounded so much like a character defect as when Patta used it in reference to Brunetti. Patta considered further. 'Yes, do it that way. Go and talk to them and see how they feel. You'll know how to handle it. Once they've accepted that it was suicide, we can close the case.'

'And turn our attention back to the *Casinò*?' Brunetti could not prevent himself from asking.

The coolness of Patta's glance not only lowered the temperature of the room; it removed Brunetti to a greater distance. 'I think the city has proven itself capable of attending to that problem,' Patta pronounced, forcing Brunetti, not for the first time, to suspect that his superior might not be as dull as he'd always found it convenient to believe him.

Upstairs, he pushed papers around on his desk until he found the thin file which contained the papers generated by the death of Ernesto Moro. He dialled the father's number, and after six rings, a man's voice answered with the surname.

'Dottor Moro,' Brunetti said, 'this is Commissario Brunetti. I'd like to speak to you again, if possible.' Moro did not answer, so Brunetti said into the silence, 'Could you tell me a time that's convenient for you?'

He heard the other man sigh. 'I told you I had nothing further to say to you, Commissario.' His voice was calm, entirely without expression.

'I know that, Dottore, and I apologize for disturbing you, but I need to speak to you again.'

'Need?'

'I think so.'

'We need very little in this life, Commissario. Have you ever considered that?' Moro asked, quite as if he were prepared to spend the rest of the afternoon discussing the question.

'Often, sir. And I agree.'

'Have you read Ivan Ilych?' Moro surprised him by asking.

'The writer or the short story, Dottore?'

Brunetti's response must have surprised Moro in turn, for there followed a long silence before the doctor answered, 'The short story.'

'Yes. Often.'

Again, the doctor sighed, after which the line lay silent for almost a minute. 'Come at four, Commissario,' Moro said and hung up.

Though reluctant to face both of Ernesto's parents on the same day, Brunetti still forced himself to phone Signora Moro. He let the phone ring once, cut the connection, then pressed the 'Redial' button, filled with relief when the phone rang on unanswered. He had made no attempt to keep a check on the whereabouts of either parent. For all he knew, she could have left the city any time after the boy's funeral two days ago; left the city, left the country, left everything behind save her motherhood.

He knew that such thoughts would take him nowhere, and so he returned his attention to the papers on his desk.

The man who let Brunetti into the Moro apartment at four

that afternoon might well have been the doctor's older brother, if such a brother were afflicted with some wasting disease. The worst signs were to be found in his eyes, which seemed covered with a thin film of opaque liquid. The whites had taken on the tinge of ivory often seen in people of advanced age, and inverted dark triangles had settled under both eyes. The fine nose had become a beak, and the thick column of his neck was now a trunk held upright by tendons that pulled the skin away from the muscle. To disguise his shock at the change in the man, Brunetti lowered his gaze to the floor. But when he noticed that the cuffs of the doctor's trousers hung limply over the backs of his shoes and dragged on the floor, he raised his eyes and looked directly at the doctor, who turned away and led him into the sitting room.

'Yes, Commissario? What is it you've come to say?' Moro asked in a voice of unwavering politeness when they were seated opposite one another.

Either his cousin had come frequently or someone else was seeing that the apartment was kept clean. The parquet glistened, the rugs lay in geometrical regularity, three Murano vases held enormous sprays of flowers. Death had made no inroads into the evident prosperity of the family, though Moro might as well have been living in the atrium of a bank for all the attention he paid to his surroundings.

'I think this has put you beyond lies, Dottore,' Brunetti said abruptly.

Moro displayed no sign that he found Brunetti's words at all unusual. 'You might say that,' he answered.

'I've thought a great deal about our last meeting,' Brunetti said, hoping to establish some connection with the man.

'I don't remember it,' Moro said, neither smiling nor frowning at the admission.

'I tried to talk to you about your son.'

'That's understandable, Commissario, as he had just died, and you seemed to be in charge of investigating his death.'

Brunetti hunted, but hunted in vain, for sarcasm or anger in the doctor's tone. 'I've thought about him a great deal,' Brunetti repeated.

'And I think of nothing but my son,' Moro said coolly.

'Is there anything among your thoughts that you can tell me?' Brunetti asked, and then amended his question by adding, 'or will tell me?'

'Of what interest could my thoughts be to you, Commissario?' the doctor asked. As Moro talked, Brunetti observed that his right hand never stopped moving, as his thumb and middle finger kept rubbing against one another, busy rolling some invisible object between them.

'As I said, Dottore, I think you must be beyond lies now, so I won't hide from you the fact that I don't think your son killed himself.'

Moro's gaze drifted away from Brunetti for a moment and then returned to him. 'Lies aren't the only thing I'm beyond, Commissario.'

'What does that mean?' Brunetti asked with conscious politeness.

'That I have little interest in the future.'

'Your own?'

'My own or, for that fact, anyone else's.'

'Your wife's?' Brunetti asked, ashamed of himself for doing so.

Moro blinked twice, appeared to consider Brunetti's question, and then answered, 'My wife and I are separated.'

'Your daughter, then?' Brunetti said, recalling a reference to the child in one of the articles he had read about Moro.

'She's in her mother's care,' Moro said with every evidence of indifference.

Brunetti wanted to say that he was still the girl's father, but he couldn't bring himself to do so. Instead, he contented himself with saying, 'That's a legal situation, a separation.'

It took Moro a long time to answer. Finally he said, 'I'm not sure I understand you.'

Until now Brunetti had paid little attention to their words, allowing his consciousness to move ahead as if on automatic pilot. His mind detached from meaning, he paid closer attention to Moro's tone and gestures, the way he sat and the pitch of his voice. Brunetti sensed that the man had moved to some place distant from pain, almost as if his heart had been put in protective custody and his mind had been left behind to answer questions. But there remained, as well, an enormous sense of fear; not fear of Brunetti but of saying something that might reveal what lay behind the façade of calm restraint.

Brunetti decided to answer what the doctor clearly intended as a question. 'I've spoken to your wife, sir, and she voices no rancour towards you.'

'Did you expect her to?'

'In the situation, yes, I think it would be understandable if she did. That way, she could somehow hold you responsible for what happened to your son. Presumably it was your decision that he attend the Academy.'

Moro shot him a stunned glance, opened his mouth as if to speak in his own defence, but stopped himself and said nothing. Brunetti averted his eyes from the other man's anger, and when he looked back, Moro's face was empty of feeling.

For a long time, Brunetti could think of nothing to say until at last he spoke entirely without thinking. 'I'd like you to trust me, Dottore.'

After a long time, Moro said, voice tired, 'And I'd like to trust you, Commissario. But I do not and will not.' He saw Brunetti preparing to object and quickly went on, 'It's not because you don't seem like a perfectly honest man but because I have learned to trust no one.' Brunetti tried to speak again, and this time Moro held up a hand to stop him.

'Further, you represent a state I perceive as both criminal and negligent, and that is enough to exclude you, absolutely, from my trust.'

The words, at first, offended Brunetti and roused in him a desire to defend himself and his honour, but in the stillness that fell after Moro stopped talking, he realized that the doctor's words had nothing at all to do with him personally: Moro saw him as contaminated simply because he worked for the state. Brunetti realized he had too much sympathy for that position to attempt to argue against it.

Brunetti got to his feet, but he did so tiredly, with none of the faked energy he had devoted to the same gesture when talking to Patta. 'If you decide you can talk to me, Dottore, please call me.'

'Of course,' the doctor said with the pretence of politeness. Moro pushed himself from his own chair, led Brunetti to the door, and let him out of the apartment.

15

Outside, he reached for his *telefonino*, only to realize he'd left it in the office or at home in another jacket. He resisted the siren song whispering to him that it was futile to call Signora Moro this late in the afternoon, that she wouldn't talk to him. He resisted it, at any rate, long enough to make two unsuccessful attempts to call her from public phones. The first, one of the new, aerodynamic silver phones that had replaced the reliable ugly oranges ones, refused to accept his plastic phone card, and the second rejected his attempts with a repeated mechanical bleat in place of a dialling tone. He yanked the card from the phone, slipped it back in his wallet and, feeling justified that he had at least made the effort, decided to go back to the Questura for what little remained of the working day.

As he stood in the gondola *traghetto* that ran between the Salute and San Marco, his Venetian knees adjusted automatically to the thrust and counter-thrust between the strokes of the *gondolieri*'s oars and the waves of the incoming tide. He looked ahead as they made their slow passage across the Canal Grande, struck by just how jaded a person could become: ahead of him lay Palazzo Ducale, and behind it popped up the gleaming domes of the Basilica di San Marco: Brunetti stared as though they were nothing more than the painted backdrop in a dull, provincial production of *Otello*. How had he got to the point where he could look on such beauty and not be shaken? Accompanied by the dull squeal of the oars, he followed this train of thought and asked himself how, equally, he could sit across from Paola at a meal and not want to run his hands across her breasts or how he could see his children sitting side by side on the sofa, doing something stupid like watching television, and not feel his bowels churn with terror at the many dangers that would beset their lives.

The gondola glided in to the landing, and he stepped up on to the dock, telling himself to leave his stupid preoccupations in the boat. Long experience had taught him that his sense of wonder was still intact and would return, bringing back with it an almost painful awareness of the beauty that surrounded him at every turn.

A beautiful woman of his acquaintance had, years ago, attempted to convince him that her beauty was in some ways a curse because it was all that anyone cared about, to the almost total exclusion of any other quality she might possess. At the time, he had dismissed it as an attempt to win compliments, which he was more than willing to give, but now perhaps he understood what she meant, at least in relation to the city. No one really cared what happened to her – how else explain her successive recent governments? – just so long as they could profit from and be seen in the reflection of her beauty, at least for as long as that beauty lasted.

At the Questura, he went up to Signorina Elettra's office, where he found her reading that day's *Gazzettino*. She smiled at his arrival and pointed at the lead story. 'The Americans' Appointed President seems to want to eliminate all restrictions on the burning of carbon-based fuels,' she said, then read him the headline: '"A SLAP IN THE FACE FOR THE ECOLOGISTS".'

'Sounds like something he'd do,' Brunetti said, not interested in continuing the discussion and wondering if Signorina Elettra had been converted to Vianello's passionate ecological views.

She looked up at him, then back to the paper. 'And this: "VENICE CONDEMNED".'

'What?' Brunetti demanded, taken aback by headline and with no idea of what it referred to.

'Well, if the temperature rises, then the ice-caps will melt, and then the seas will rise, and there goes Venice.' She sounded remarkably calm about it.

'And Bangladesh, as well, one might observe,' Brunetti added.

'Of course. I wonder if the Appointed President has considered the consequences.'

'I don't think that's in his powers, considering consequences,' Brunetti observed. It was his custom to avoid political discussions with the people with whom he worked; he was uncertain whether foreign politics were included under that ban.

'Probably not. Besides, all the refugees will end up here, not there.'

'What refugees?' Brunetti asked, not clear where the conversation was going.

'From Bangladesh. If the country is flooded and finds itself permanently under water, the people certainly aren't going to remain there and agree to drown so that they don't inconvenience anyone. They'll have to migrate somewhere, and as there's little chance they'll be allowed to go east, they'll end up here.'

'Isn't your geography a bit imaginative here, Signorina?'

'I don't mean they, the Bangladeshis, will come here, but

the people they displace will move west, and the ones they displace will end up here, or the ones that they in their turn displace will.' She looked up, confused at his slowness in understanding. 'You've read history, haven't you, sir?' At his nod, she concluded, 'Then you know that this is what happens.'

'Perhaps,' Brunetti said, his scepticism audible.

'We'll see,' she said mildly and folded the paper closed. 'What can I do for you, sir?'

'I spoke to the Vice-Questore this morning, and he seemed reluctant to put his entire faith in Lieutenant Scarpa's opinion that the Moro boy killed himself.'

'Is he afraid of a Moro Report on the police?' she asked, grasping at once what Patta himself probably refused to admit.

'More than likely. At any rate, he wants us to exclude all other possibilities before he closes the case.'

'There's only one other possibility, isn't there?'

'Yes.'

'What do you think?' She shoved the paper aside on her desk and leaned slightly forward, her body giving evidence of the curiosity she managed to keep out of her voice.

'I can't believe he committed suicide.'

She agreed. 'It doesn't make sense that a boy that young would leave his family behind.'

'Kids don't always have their parents' feelings in mind when they decide to do something,' Brunetti temporized, unsure why he did so; perhaps to muster the arguments he knew would be presented against his own opinion.

'I know that. But there's the little sister,' she said. 'You'd think he'd give her some thought. But maybe you're right.'

'How old is she?' Brunetti asked, intrigued by this mystery child in whom both parents had displayed so little interest.

'There was something about her in one of the articles about

the family, or perhaps someone I know said something about her,' Signorina Elettra answered. 'Everyone's talking about them now.' She closed her eyes, trying to remember. She tilted her head to one side, and he imagined her scrolling through the banks of information in her mind. Finally she said, 'It must be something I read because I don't have any emotional memory of having heard it, and I'd have that if someone had told me about her.'

'Have you saved everything?'

'Yes, all of the newspaper clippings and the articles from the magazines are in the file, the same one that has the articles about Dottor Moro's report.' Before he could ask to see it, she said, 'No, I'll look through them I might remember the article when I see it or start reading it.' She glanced at her watch. 'Give me fifteen minutes and I'll bring it up to you.'

'Thank you, Signorina,' he said and went to his office to wait for her. He called Signora Moro's number, but still there was no answer. Why had she not mentioned the daughter, and why, in both houses, had there been no sign of the child? He started to make a list of the things he wanted Signorina Elettra to check and was still adding to it when she came into the office, the file in her hand. 'Here it is, sir,' she said as she came in. 'Valentina. She's nine.'

'Does it say which parent she lives with?'

'No, nothing at all,' she said. 'She was mentioned in an article about Moro, six years ago. It said he had one son, Ernesto, twelve, and the daughter, Valentina, three. And the article in *La Nuova* mentions her.'

'I didn't see any sign of her when I spoke to the parents.'

'Did you say anything?'

'About the girl?'

'No, I don't mean that, sir. Did you say anything that might have given her mother the opportunity to mention her?'

Brunetti tried to recall his conversation with Signora Moro. 'No, nothing that I can remember.'

'Then it's possible she wouldn't have mentioned her, isn't it?'

For almost two decades, Brunetti had shared his home with one, then both, of his children, and he could not recall a single instant when physical proof of their existence had been absent from their home: toys, clothing, shoes, scarves, books, papers, Discmen lay spread about widely and chaotically. Words, pleas, threats proved equally futile in the no-doubt biological need of the young of the human species to litter their nest. A man of meaner spirit might have considered this an infestation: Brunetti thought of it as one of nature's ways to prepare a parent's patience for the future, when the mess would become emotional and moral, not merely physical.

'But I would have seen some sign of her, I think,' he insisted.

'Maybe they've sent her to stay with relatives,' Signorina Elettra suggested.

'Yes, perhaps,' Brunetti agreed, though he wasn't convinced. No matter how often his kids had gone to stay with their grandparents or other relatives, signs of their recent habitation had always lingered behind them. Suddenly he had a vision of what it must have been for the Moros to attempt to remove evidence of Ernesto's presence from their homes, and he thought of the danger that would remain behind: a single, lonely sock found at the back of a closet could break a mother's heart anew; a Spice Girls disc carelessly shoved into the plastic case meant to hold Vivaldi's flute sonatas could shatter any calm. Months, perhaps years, would pass before the house would stop being a minefield, every cabinet or drawer to be opened with silent dread.

His reverie was interrupted by Signorina Elettra, who leaned forward to place the file on his desk.

'Thank you,' he said. 'I have a number of things I'd like you to try to check for me.' He slid the paper towards her, listing them as he did so.

'Find out, if you can, where the girl goes to school. If she's living here or lived here with either of them, then she's got to be enrolled in one of the schools. There are the grandparents: see if you can locate them. Moro's cousin, Luisa Moro – I don't have an address for her – might know.' He thought of the people in Siena and asked her to call the police there and have them find out if the child was living with them. She ran her finger down the list as he spoke. 'And I'd like you to do the same for his wife: friends, relatives, colleagues,' he concluded.

She looked at him and said, 'You aren't going to let this go, are you?'

He pushed himself back in his chair but didn't get to his feet. 'I don't like any of it, and I don't like anything I've heard. Nobody's told me the truth and nobody's told me why they won't.'

'What does that mean?'

Brunetti smiled and said it gently. 'For the moment, all it means is that I'd like you to get me all the information I've asked for.'

'And when I do?' she asked, not for an instant doubting that she would find it.

'Then perhaps we'll start proving a negative.'

'Which negative, sir.'

'That Ernesto Moro didn't kill himself.'

16

Before he left the Questura, he made one more call to Signora Moro's number, feeling not unlike an importunate suitor growing ever more persistent in the face of a woman's continued lack of response. He wondered if he'd overlooked some mutual friend who might put in a good word for him and realized how he was returning to the tactics of former times, when his attempts to meet women had been animated by entirely different hopes.

Just as he was approaching the underpass leading into Campo San Bartolomeo, his mind on this unsettling parallel, he registered a sudden darkness in front of him. He looked up, still not fully attentive to his surroundings, and saw four San Martino cadets wheeling, arms linked, as straight across as if on parade, into the *calle* from the *campo*. The long dark capes of their winter uniforms swirled out on either flank and effectively filled the entire width of the *calle*. Two women, one old and one young, instinctively backed up against the plate glass windows of the bank, and a pair of map-embracing tourists did the same against the windows of the bar on the other side. Leaving the four shipwrecked pedestrians in their wake, the unbroken wave of boys swept towards him.

Brunetti raised his eyes to theirs – boys no older than his own son – and the glances that came back to him were as blank and pitiless as the sun. His right foot might have faltered for an instant, but by an act of will he shoved it forward and continued towards them, stride unbroken, his face implacable, as though he were alone in Calle della Bissa, the entire city his.

The boys drew closer, and he recognized the cadet to the left of centre as the one who had tried to interrogate him at the school. The atavistic urge of the more powerful male to assert his supremacy shifted Brunetti's direction two compass points until he was heading straight for the boy. He tightened his stomach muscles and stiffened his elbows, preparing for the shock of contact, but at the instant before impact, the boy next to the one who had become Brunetti's target loosened his grip and moved to the right, creating a narrow space through which Brunetti could pass. As his foot entered the space, he saw, from the corner of his eye, the left foot of the boy he recognized move minimally to the side, surely bent on tripping him. Carefully, thrusting forward with his full weight behind him, he took aim at the boy's ankle and felt a satisfying jolt as the toe of his shoe found its target, glanced off, and came down on the pavement. Not pausing for an instant, Brunetti strode on and out into the *campo*, cut left, and started for the bridge.

Because Raffi as well as Chiara was at dinner, and because he thought it unseemly to manifest pride in such mean-spirited behaviour in their presence, he said nothing about his meeting with the cadets and contented himself with the meal. Paola had brought home *ravioli di zucca* and had prepared them with salvia leaves quickly sautéed in butter, then smothered them with Parmigiano. After that, she had switched to fennel, serving it interspersed with pan-fried veal pieces that had spent the previous night in the refrigerator, marinating in a paste of rosemary, garlic, fennel seed and minced pancetta.

As he ate, delighted by the mingled tastes and the pleasant sharpness of his third glass of Sangiovese, he remembered his earlier uneasiness about the safety of his children, and the thought made him feel foolish. He could not, however, dismiss it or allow himself to scoff at the desire that nothing would ever invade their peace. He never knew if his perpetual readiness for things to change for the worse was the result of his native pessimism or of the experiences his profession had exposed him to. In either case, his vision of happiness had always to pass through a filter of uneasiness.

'Why don't we ever have beef any more?' Raffi asked.

Paola, peeling a pear, said, 'Because Gianni can't find a farmer he trusts.'

'Trusts to do what?' Chiara asked between grapes.

'To have animals he's sure are healthy, I suppose,' Paola answered.

'I don't like eating it any more, anyway,' Chiara said.

'Why not? Because it'll make you crazy?' her brother asked, then amended it to 'Crazier?'

'I think we've had more than enough mad cow jokes at this table,' Paola said with an unusual lack of patience.

'No, not because of that,' Chiara said.

'Then why?' Brunetti asked.

'Oh, just because,' Chiara answered evasively.

'Because of what?' her brother asked.

'Because we don't need to eat them.'

'That never bothered you before,' Raffi countered.

'I know it never bothered me before. Lots of things didn't. But now they do.' She turned to him and delivered what she clearly thought would be a death blow. 'It's called growing up, in case you've never heard of it.'

Raffi snorted, driving her to new defences.

'We don't need to eat them just because we can. Besides, it's ecologically wasteful,' she insisted, like someone repeating a lesson, which Brunetti thought was most likely the case.

'What would you eat instead?' Raffi asked, 'zucchini?' He turned to his mother and asked, 'Are we allowed to make mad zucchini jokes?'

Paola, displaying the Olympian disregard for the feelings of her children which Brunetti so admired, said only, 'I'll take that as an offer to do the dishes, Raffi, shall I?'

Raffi groaned, but he did not protest. A Brunetti less familiar with the cunning of the young would have seen this as a sign that his son was willing to assume some responsibility for the care of their home, perhaps as evidence of burgeoning maturity. The real Brunetti, however a man hardened by decades of exposure to the furtiveness of criminals, could see it for what it was: cold-blooded bargaining in which immediate acquiescence was traded for some future reward.

As Raffi reached across the table to pick up his mother's plate, Paola smiled upon him with favour and, displaying a familiarity with slyness equal to that of her husband, got to her feet, saying, 'Thank you so much, dear, for offering, and no, you cannot take scuba lessons.'

Brunetti watched her leave the room, then turned to watch his son's face. Raffi's surprise was patent, and when he saw that his father was looking at him, he removed that expression but had the grace to smile. 'How does she do that?' Raffi asked. 'All the time.'

Brunetti was about to offer some bromide about its being one of the powers of mothers to be able to read the minds of their children, when Chiara, who had been busy finishing the fruit on the platter, looked up at them and said, 'It's because she reads Henry James.'

In her study, Brunetti told Paola about his run-in with the cadets, deciding not to mention the rush of animal triumph he had felt when his foot made contact with the boy's ankle.

'It's a good thing it happened here,' she said when he finished, then added, 'in Italy.'

'Why? What do you mean?'

'There are a lot of places where something like that could get you killed.'

'Name two,' he said, offended that she could so cavalierly dismiss what he saw as evidence of his bravery.

'Sierra Leone and the United States, to begin with,' she said. 'But that doesn't mean I'm not happy you did it.'

Brunetti said nothing for a long time, then asked, 'Does it show, how much I dislike them?'

'Them who?'

'Boys like that, with their wealthy, well-connected families and their sense of command.'

'Families like mine, you mean?' In their early years together, before Brunetti came to realize that the shocking brutality of Paola's honesty was often entirely unaggressive, he would have been astonished by her question. Now all he did was answer it. 'Yes.'

She laced her fingers together and propped her chin on her knuckles. 'I think only someone who knows you very well would see it. Or someone who pays close attention to what you say.'

'Like you?' he asked, smiling.

'Yes.'

'Why do you think it is, that they get to me so easily?'

She considered this; it was not that she had not thought about it before, but he had never asked the question so directly. 'I think part of it is your sense of justice.'

'Not jealousy?' he asked, trying to make sure she would be complimentary.

'No, at least not jealousy in any simple sense.'

He leaned back on the sofa and latched his fingers behind his head. He shifted around, seeking a comfortable position, and when she saw that he'd found it, she went on. 'I think part of it comes from your resentment – not that some people have more than others, but that they don't realize or don't want to admit that their money doesn't make them superior or give them the right to anything they choose to do.' When he didn't query this she continued: 'And from their refusal to consider the possibility that their greater fortune is not anything they've earned or merited.' She smiled at him, then said, 'At least I think that's why you dislike them as much as you do.'

'And you?' he asked. 'Do you dislike them?'

With a ringing laugh, she said, 'There are too many of them in my family to allow me to.' He laughed along with her, and she added, 'I did, when I was young and more idealistic than I am now. But then I realized they weren't going to change, and I had come by then to love some of them so much and I knew nothing was ever going to change that, so I saw that I had no choice but to accept them as they are.'

'Love before truth?' he asked, striving for irony.

'Love before everything, I'm afraid, Guido,' she said in deadly earnest.

As he walked to the Questura the next morning, it occurred to Brunetti that he had been overlooking at least one anomaly in all of this: why had the boy been boarding at the school? So caught up had he been in the order and rules of life at the Academy that, as he searched Ernesto's room, the obvious question had not arisen: in a culture that encouraged young people to live at home until their marriage, why was this young man living away from home, when both parents lived in the city?

At the Questura, he almost bumped into Signorina Elettra

emerging from the front door. 'Are you going somewhere?' he asked.

She glanced at her watch. 'Do you need something, sir?' she asked, not really an answer, though he didn't notice.

'Yes, I'd like you to make a phone call for me.'

She stepped back inside the door and asked, 'To whom?'

'The San Martino Academy.'

With no attempt to disguise the curiosity in her voice, she asked, 'And what would you like me to tell them?' She started to walk back towards the stairs that led to her office.

'I want to know if it's obligatory for the boys to sleep in the dormitory or if they're allowed to spend the night at home if their parents live in the city. I'd like to get an idea of just how inflexible the rules are there. Perhaps you could say you're a parent and want to know something about the Academy. You can say your son is just finishing school and has always wanted to be a soldier, and as you're Venetian, you'd like him to have the opportunity to attend the San Martino because of its high reputation.'

'And is my voice to be filled with pride and patriotism as I ask these questions?'

'Choking with them,' he said.

She could not have done it better. Though Signorina Elettra spoke an Italian as elegant and pure as any he had heard, as well as a very old-fashioned Venetian dialect, she managed to mingle the two perfectly on the phone and succeeded in sounding exactly like what she said she was: the Venetian wife of a Roman banker who had just been sent north to head the Venice branch of a bank she carelessly avoided naming. After making the secretary at the Academy wait while she found a pen and pencil and then apologizing for not having them next to the phone the way her husband insisted she do, Signorina Elettra asked for particulars of the date of the beginning of the next school term, their policy on late admission, and where to have letters of recommendation and academic records sent. When the school secretary offered to provide details about school fees and the cost of uniforms, the banker's wife dismissed the very idea, insisting that their accountant dealt with things like that.

Listening to the conversation on the speaker phone, Brunetti was amazed at the way Signorina Elettra threw herself into the role, could all but see her returning home that evening after a hard day's shopping to check if the cook had found real *basilico genovese* for the pesto. Just as the secretary said she hoped that young Filiberto and his parents would find the school satisfactory, Signorina Elettra gasped, 'Ah, yes, one last question. It will be all right if he sleeps at home at night, won't it?'

'I beg your pardon, Signora,' the secretary said. 'The boys are expected to live here at the school. It's included in the fees. Where else would your son live?'

'Here with us in the *palazzo*, of course. You can't expect him to live with those other boys, can you? He's only sixteen.' Had the secretary asked her to give her life-blood, the banker's wife could have sounded no less horrified. 'Of course we'll pay the full fees, but it's unthinkable that a child that young should be taken from his mother.'

'Ah,' the secretary answered upon hearing the first part of Signorina Elettra's last sentence, managing not to register the second, 'in a few cases, with the approval of the Comandante some exceptions can perhaps be made, though the boys have to be at their first class at eight.'

'That's why we have the launch,' was Signorina Elettra's opening shot in her last volley, which drew to a close with her promise to send the signed papers and the necessary deposit off by the end of the week, followed by a polite goodbye.

Brunetti found himself filled with unwonted sympathy for Vice-Questore Patta: the man simply didn't have a chance. 'Filiberto?' he asked.

'It was his father's choice,' Signorina Elettra replied.

'And yours? Eustasio?'

'No, Eriprando.'

17

The information that exceptions to the school rules could be made at the discretion of the Comandante did not tell Brunetti anything he had not already suspected: where the children of the wealthy and powerful congregated, rules were often bent to follow the whim of their parents. What he did not know was the extent of the Comandante's subservience. Nor, he had to admit, did he have a clear idea of how this might be related to Ernesto's death.

Deciding not to speculate further, Brunetti dialled Signora Moro's phone again, and again the phone rang on unanswered. Spurred by some impulse he registered but did not question, he decided to pass by her apartment and see if any of her neighbours could give him an idea of where she was.

He chose to take the vaporetto to San Marco, then cut back towards the apartment. He rang the bell, waited, and rang again. Then he rang the bell to the left of hers, waited, then rang the others in succession, working his way across and down, like a climber rappelling down the face of a cliff. The first response came from an apartment on the first floor, the bell of which bore the name Della Vedova. A woman's voice answered, and when he explained that he was from the police and needed to speak to Signora Moro, the door clicked open. As he entered, the light in the dim hall flashed on, and a few moments later a woman's voice called from above, 'Up here, Signore.'

He ascended the steps, and noted that attached to one side of them was a system which would allow a wheelchair to move up and down. The explanation waited just inside the door at the top of the steps: a young woman in a wheelchair, an enormous grey cat resting on her lap. As he reached the landing, she smiled at him and, shifting the cat to one side, reached up with her right hand. 'Beatrice Della Vedova,' she said, 'My pleasure to meet you.'

He gave his name and rank, then she put both hands on the wheels of her chair, whipped it around in a neat half-circle and propelled herself back into the apartment. Brunetti followed her inside, closing the door behind him.

She led him into a living room in the centre of which stood an architect's drawing board that had been lowered almost a metre to a height that would allow her wheelchair to slip comfortably under it. Its surface was covered with water-colour sketches of bridges and canals, painted in the Day-Glo colours tourists seemed to favour. By contrast, the three views of the façades of churches – San Zaccaria, San Martino and San Giovanni in Bragora – that hung on the rear wall all showed a close attention to architectural detail that was absent from the paintings on the drawing board. Their muted colours captured the glowing warmth of stone and the play of light on the canal in front of San Martino and on the façades of the other churches.

She spun around and saw him studying the drawings on the wall. 'That's what I really do,' she said. Then, with a vague swipe at the paintings on the board, she added, 'And that's what I get paid to do.' She bent down to the cat and whispered in its ear, 'We've got to keep you in Whiskas, don't we, fatty?'

The cat rose slowly from her lap and jumped, with a thump that surely could be heard in the entrance hall below, to the floor. Tail raised, it walked from the room. The woman smiled up at Brunetti. 'I never know if he's offended at my comments about his weight or if he just doesn't like being made to feel responsible for those paintings.' She let this lie in the air between them, then with a smile added, 'Either position seems justified, wouldn't you say?'

Brunetti smiled in return, and she asked him to take a seat. As he did, she wheeled her chair around until it was facing him. She might have been in her late twenties, though the flecking of grey in her hair made her seem older, as did the vertical lines between her eyebrows. Her eyes were a light amber, her nose a bit too large for the rest of her face, her mouth so soft and relaxed that it seemed out of place on a face so marked with what Brunetti thought was a history of pain.

'You said you were interested in Signora Moro?' she prompted.

'Yes, I'd like to speak to her. I've been phoning but she's never home. The last time I spoke to her, she . . .'

The woman cut him off. 'When was that?'

'Some days ago. She didn't say anything about leaving the city.'

'No, she wouldn't. Say anything, I mean.'

Brunetti registered the remark and said, 'I didn't get the feeling that . . .' He paused, not certain how to express it. 'I didn't have the feeling that she had anywhere to go.'

Signora or Signorina Della Vedova looked at him with fresh interest. 'Why do you say that?'

'I don't know. I just had a very strong feeling that the city was where she belonged and that she had no interest in going anywhere. Or desire.'

When it seemed that Brunetti had no more to say, she replied, 'She didn't. Have anywhere to go, that is.'

'Do you know her well?'

'No, not really. She's been here for less than two years.'

'Since the accident?' Brunetti asked.

She looked at Brunetti, and all pleasantness disappeared from her face. 'This,' she said, flipping the fingers of her right hand across her lap to indicate the legs that rested uselessly below it, 'was an accident. What happened to Federica was not.'

Brunetti stifled any response he might have made to this and asked, calmly, 'Are you so sure of that?'

'Of course not,' she said, her voice calm again. 'I wasn't there and I didn't see what happened. But Federica, the two times she spoke to me about it, said, "When they shot me . . ." People who are in accidents don't talk about it that way.'

Brunetti had no doubt that this woman knew full well how people who were in accidents speak. 'She said this twice?'

'Yes, so far as I can remember. But simply by way of description, not complaint. I never asked her what happened, didn't want to pry. I've had enough of that myself. And I figured she'd tell me what she wanted to when she was ready.'

'And has she?'

She shook her head. 'No, only those two references.'

'Have you seen her often?'

'Perhaps every week or so. She stops in and has a coffee or simply comes down and talks for a while.'

'Did you know her before she moved into this apartment?'

'No. I knew about her husband, of course. But I suppose everyone does. Because of his report, I mean.' Brunetti nodded. 'I met her because of Gastone,' she said.

'Gastone?'

'The cat. She found him outside the front door one day and when she opened the door, he came in. When he came up and stood outside my door, she knocked and asked me if he were mine. He gets out of here sometimes and then lurks out in the *calle* until someone opens the door, or rings my bell and asks me to open the street door so they can let him in. People who know he's mine, that is.' Her face warmed in a smile. 'Good thing they do. It's not as if it's easy for me to go down and let him in.' She said this simply, and Brunetti did not hear in it an unspoken prompting to strangers to ask questions, nor did he hear an unconscious appeal for pity.

'When did you see her last?'

She had to think about this. 'The day before yesterday, and I didn't really see her, just heard her on the stairs. I'm sure of that. I'd read about the boy's death, and then, when she came in, I recognized her steps outside. I went over to the door, and I was going to open it, but then I didn't know what I could say to her, so I didn't. I just sat here and listened to her go up the stairs. Then, about an hour later, I heard her come down again.'

'And since then?'

'Nothing.' Before he could speak, she added, 'But I sleep in the back of the apartment, and I sleep very deeply because of the pills I take, so she could have come in or gone out and I wouldn't have heard her.'

'Has she called you?'

'No.'

'Is it like her to be away for two days?'

Her answer was immediate, 'No, not at all. In fact, she's almost always here, but I haven't heard her on the steps and I haven't heard her moving around in her apartment.' She said this last with a gesture towards the ceiling.

'Do you have any idea where she might have gone?'

'No. None. We didn't talk to one another like that.' When he looked puzzled, she tried to clarify things. 'I mean, we weren't friends, just lonely women who talked to one another once in a while.'

There was no hidden message in that, either, so far as Brunetti could tell: merely the truth, and the truth told clear. 'And she lived alone?'

'Yes, so far as I know.'

'No one ever visited her?'

'Not that I know of, no.'

'You never heard a child?'

'Do you mean her son?'

'No, her daughter.'

'Daughter?' she asked, her surprise answering the question for him. She shook her head.

'Never?'

Again she shook her head, as though the idea of a mother never mentioning one of her children was something too shocking to bear comment.

'Did she ever mention her husband?'

'Seldom.'

'And how? That is, how did she speak about him? With rancour? Anger?'

She thought for a moment and then answered, 'No, she mentioned him in a normal way.'

'Affectionately?'

She gave him a quick glance, rich in unspoken curiosity, then answered, 'No, I couldn't say that. She simply mentioned him, quite neutrally.'

'Could you give me an example?' Brunetti asked, wanting to get a feel of it.

'Once, we were talking about the hospital.' She stopped here, then sighed, and continued. 'We were talking about the mistakes they make, and she said that her husband's report had put an end to that, but only for a short time.'

He waited for her to clarify, but it seemed that she had said enough. Brunetti could think of nothing else to ask her. He got to his feet. 'Thank you, Signora,' he said, leaning down to shake her hand.

She smiled in response and turned her wheelchair towards the door. Brunetti got there first and was reaching for the handle when she called out, 'Wait.' Thinking she had remembered something that might be important, Brunetti turned, then looked down when he felt a sudden pressure against his left calf. It was Gastone, serpentining his way back and forth, suddenly friendly with this person who had the power to open the door. Brunetti picked him up, amazed at the sheer mass of him. Smiling, he placed him in the woman's lap, said goodbye, and let himself out of the apartment, though he did not pull the door closed until he made sure that there was no sign of Gastone between the door and the jamb.

As he had known he would do ever since Signora Della Vedova told him that there had been no sign of Signora Moro for two days, Brunetti went up the stairs to her apartment. The door was a simple one: whoever owned the apartment had no concern that his tenants should be safe from burglars. Brunetti took out his wallet and slid out a thin plastic card. Some years ago, Vianello had taken it from a burglar so successful he had become careless. Vianello had used it on more than one occasion, always in flagrant violation of the law, and upon his promotion from Sergeant to Inspector, he had given it to Brunetti in token of his realization that the promotion was due primarily to Brunetti's insistence and support. At the time, Brunetti had entertained the possibility that Vianello was merely freeing himself of an occasion of sin, but the card had since then proven so useful that Brunetti had come to appreciate it as the gift it was.

He slipped it between the door and the jamb, just at the height of the lock, and the door swung open at a turn of the handle. Long habit made him stop just inside the door and sniff the air, hunting for the scent of death. He smelled dust and old cigarette smoke and the memory of some sharp cleaning agent, but there was no scent of rotting flesh. Relieved, he closed the door behind him and walked into the sitting room. He found it exactly as he had left it: the furniture in the same position, the single book that had been lying face down on the arm of a sofa still there, still at the same page, for all he knew.

The kitchen was in order: no dishes in the sink, and when he pried the door open with the toe of his shoe, he found no perishable food in the refrigerator. He took a pen from the inner pocket of his jacket and opened all of the cabinets: the only thing he found was an open tin of coffee.

In the bathroom, he opened the medicine cabinet with the back of a knuckle and found nothing more than a bottle of aspirin, a used shower cap, an unopened bottle of shampoo, and a package of emery boards. The towels on the rack were dry.

The only room left was the bedroom, and Brunetti entered it uneasily: he disliked this part of his job as much as anything about it. On the nightstand beside the bed a thin rectangle of clear space stood outlined in the dust: she had removed a photo from there. Two more had been taken from the dresser. Drawers and closet, however, seemed full as far as he could tell, and two suitcases lay under the bed. Shameless now, he pulled back the covers on the side of the bed closest to the door and lifted the pillow. Under it, neatly folded, lay a man's white dress shirt. Brunetti pulled it out and let it fall open. It would have fitted Brunetti, but the shoulders would have fallen from Signora Moro's, and the sleeves would have come far down over her hands. Just over the heart of the man who would wear the shirt he saw the initials 'FM' embroidered in thread so fine it could only have been silk.

He folded the shirt and replaced it under the pillow, then pulled the covers up and tucked them neatly in place. He went back through the living room and let himself out of the apartment. As he passed the door to the Della Vedova apartment, he wondered if she was sitting inside, holding her cat, listening for the footsteps that carried life back and forth outside her door.

18

It was not until after the kids had gone to bed that night, when he and Paola sat alone in the living room, she reading *Persuasion* for the hundred and twenty-seventh time, and he contemplating Anna Comnena's admonition that, 'Whenever one assumes the role of historian, friendship and enmities have to be forgotten', that Brunetti returned to his visit to Signora Moro's apartment, though he did so indirectly. 'Paola,' he began. She peered at him over the top of her book, eyes vague and inattentive. 'What would you do if I asked you for a separation?'

Her eyes had drifted back to the page before he spoke, but they shot back to his face now, and Anne Elliot was left to her own romantic problems. 'If you *what*?'

'Asked for a separation.'

Voice level, she inquired, 'Before I go into the kitchen to get the bread knife, could you tell me if this is a theoretical question?'

'Absolutely,' he said, embarrassed by how happy her threat of violence had made him. 'What would you do?'

She placed the book by her side, face down. 'Why do you want to know?'

'I'll tell you that as soon as you answer my question. What would you do?'

Her look was discomfiting. 'Well?' he prodded.

'If it were a real separation, I'd throw you out of the house and after you I'd throw everything you own.'

His smile was positively beatific. 'Everything?'

'Yes. Everything. Even the things I like.'

'Would you use one of my shirts to sleep in?'

'Are you out of your mind?'

'And if it were a fake separation?'

'Fake?'

'Done so that it would look as if we were separated when in reality we weren't but just needed to look as if we were.'

'I'd still throw you out, but I'd keep all the things I like.'

'And the shirt? Would you sleep in it?'

She gave him a long look. 'Do you want a serious answer or more foolishness?'

'I think I want a real answer,' he confessed.

'Then yes, I'd sleep in your shirt or I'd put it on my pillow so that I could have at least the smell of you with me.'

Brunetti believed in the solidity of his marriage with the same faith he invested in the periodic table of the elements, indeed, rather more; nevertheless, occasional reinforcement did no harm. He found himself equally assured of the solidity of the Moros' marriage, though he had no idea what that meant.

'Signora Moro,' he began, 'is living apart from her husband.' Paola nodded, acknowledging that he had already told her this. 'But one of his dress shirts is under the pillow of the bed in which she is sleeping alone.'

Paola looked off to the left, to where an occasional light could still be seen burning in the top floor window of the apartment opposite. After a long time, she said, 'Ah.'

'Yes,' he agreed, ' "Ah," indeed.'

'Why do they have to look as if they're separated?'

'So whoever shot her won't come back and do a better job of it, I'd guess.'

'Yes, that makes sense.' She thought about this, then asked, 'And who could they be?'

'If I knew that, I'd probably understand everything.'

Automatically, not really thinking about what she said but asserting truth by habit, she said, 'We never know everything.'

'Then at least I'd know more than I know now. And I'd probably know who killed the boy.'

'You won't let that go, will you?' she asked entirely without reproof.

'No.'

'Probably wise not to,' she agreed.

'So you think he was murdered, too?'

'I always did.'

'Why?'

'Because I trust your feelings and because your feeling about it was so strong.'

'And if I'm wrong?'

'Then we're wrong together,' she said. She picked up her book, slipped a bookmark between the pages, and closed it. Setting it down, she said, 'I can't read any more.'

'Me neither,' he said, setting Anna Comnena on the table in front of him.

She looked across at him and asked, 'Is it all right if I don't wear one of your shirts?'

He laughed out loud and they went to bed.

The first thing he did the next morning was to go see Signorina Elettra, whom he found in her office. Her desk was covered with at least six bouquets of flowers, each wrapped separately in a cone of pastel paper. As he knew she had a standing order for flowers to be delivered on Monday from Biancat, he wondered if he'd got things wrong in thinking today was Tuesday or if he'd somehow invented the events of the previous day.

'Are those from Biancat?' he asked.

She ripped two of the packages open and began to place dwarf sunflowers in a green vase. 'No, they're from Rialto.' She stepped back from the desk, studied the arrangement, then added three more sunflowers.

'Then it's really Tuesday?'

She gave him a strange look and answered, 'Of course.'

'Don't the flowers usually arrive on Monday?'

She smiled, lifted the vase, and placed it on the other side of her computer. 'Yes, they usually do. But the Vice-Questore has begun to cause quite a fuss about office expenses, so, because they're so much cheaper there, I thought I'd get them from Rialto for a while, until something diverts him.'

'Did you bring them all yourself?' he asked, trying to calculate whether they'd fit in her arms.

'No, I called for a launch when I realized how many of them I'd bought.'

'A police launch?'

'Of course. It would be difficult to justify taking a taxi,' she said, snapping off the stem of a carnation.

'What with the economy drive and all,' Brunetti suggested.

'Exactly.'

Three of the other bouquets ended up together in an enormous ceramic vase, and the last, asters, went into a narrow crystal vase Brunetti could not remember ever having seen. When all three vases were placed to her satisfaction and the papers neatly folded and placed in the basket she kept for paper to be recycled, she said, 'Yes, Commissario?'

'Have you managed to find out anything about the daughter?'

Signorina Elettra pulled a notebook from the side of her

desk and flipped it open. Reading from it, she began, 'She was taken out of school two years ago, and there's been no trace of her, at least no bureaucratic trace, since.'

'Taken out by whom?'

'Her father, apparently.'

'How did that happen?'

'The school records show that her last day of school was the sixteenth of November.'

She looked at him, neither of them having to remind the other that Signora Moro had been shot one week before.

'And?' he asked.

'And that's all. The forms on file say that the parents had decided to place her in a private school.'

'Where?' Brunetti asked.

'It's not necessary to mention that, I was told.'

'And didn't they ask?' he demanded, his irritation clear. 'Don't they need to know where a child's going?'

'The woman I spoke to said that all that's required is that the parents complete and sign the proper forms, in duplicate,' Signorina Elettra recited in what Brunetti assumed was the mechanical voice of whoever she had spoken to.

'And a child's allowed to disappear and no questions asked?'

'I was told that the school's responsibility ends once the parents have filled in the forms and the child's been taken from the school by one of them.'

'Just like that?' he asked.

Signorina Elettra opened her hands in a gesture meant to show her own lack of responsibility. 'This woman said she wasn't working there when the girl was withdrawn, so the best she could do was try to explain the regulations to me.'

'So where is she? A little girl can't just disappear,' Brunetti insisted.

'She could be anywhere, I suppose,' Signorina Elettra said, then added, 'But she's not in Siena.'

Brunetti shot her an inquiring glance.

'I called the police there, and then I had a look through the records of the school system. There's no record for her, nor for any child of the Ferros.'

'The mother's missing now, too,' Brunetti said and then went on to tell her of his visit to her apartment and the inferences he had drawn from the presence of the shirt.

Signorina Elettra's face paled and just as suddenly flushed. 'His shirt?' she asked then, before he could answer, repeated the question, 'His shirt?'

'Yes,' Brunetti answered. He started to ask her what she thought of this, but when he took a closer look at her face, he realized there was only one man this could cause her to think of, and he spoke to fill the painful silence that the memory of his loss brought into the room. 'Can you think of a way to trace the child?' he finally said. When she seemed not to hear him, he said, 'There's got to be a way to find her. Some central register of children enrolled in schools, perhaps?'

As if returning from a long distance, Signorina Elettra said in a very soft voice, 'Perhaps her medical records, or if she's in the Girl Scouts.'

Before she could suggest anything else, Brunetti cut her off by saying, 'There are her grandparents. They've got to have some idea of where she is.'

'Do you know where they are?' Signorina Elettra asked with returning interest.

'No, but both of the Moros are Venetian, so they should be here in the city.'

'I'll see what I can find out,' was the only remark she permitted herself. Then: 'By the way, sir, I found out about the girl who was supposedly raped at the Academy.'

'Yes? How?'

'Friends from the past,' was the only explanation she provided. When she saw that she had Brunetti's attention, Signorina Elettra went on. 'The girl was the *fidanzata* of one of the students, and he brought her back to his room one night. Somehow, the captain of his class found out about it and went to the room. She started screaming when he came in, and then someone called the police. But there were never any charges and, from what I make of reading the original report, probably no need for any.'

'I see,' he said, not bothering to ask her how she had found that report so quickly. '*Tanto fumo, poco arrosto.*' As soon as he spoke he was aware how his dismissal of the story would seem to her, and so hastened to add, 'But thank God for the girl.'

Sounding not at all convinced by his piety, Signorina Elettra said merely, 'Indeed,' and turned back to her computer.

19

Brunetti called down to the officers' room and asked where Pucetti was, only to be told that he was out on patrol and wouldn't be back until the following morning. After he hung up, he sat and wondered how long it would take before his appreciation of Pucetti's intelligence would begin to work to the young man's disadvantage. Most of the others, even those arch-fools, Alvise and Riverre, were unlikely to turn against him: the uniformed officers were pretty much devoid of jealousy, as least so far as Brunetti could discern. Perhaps Vianello, closer to them in rank and age, would have a better sense of this.

Someone like Scarpa, however, was bound to regard Pucetti with the same suspicion with which he viewed Vianello. Even though Vianello had for years kept his own counsel, it had been obvious to Brunetti that the antipathy between the two men had been instant and fierce, on both sides. Possible motives abounded: dislike between a southerner and a northerner, between a single man and one so happily married, between one who delighted in the imposition of his will upon those around him and another who cared only to live peacefully. Brunetti had never been able to make more sense of it than that the men felt a visceral antipathy for one another.

He felt a flash of resentment that his professional life should be so hampered by the complications of personal animosity: why couldn't those who enforced the law be above such things? He shook his head at his own crazy utopianism: next he would be longing for a philosopher-king. He had only to think of the current leader of government, however, for all hopes of the philosopher-king's arrival to wither and die.

Further reflection was made impossible by the arrival of Alvise with the latest tabulations of crime statistics, which he placed on Brunetti's desk, saying that the Vice-Questore needed the finished report by the end of the day and that he wanted figures he could present to the press without embarrassment.

'What do you think that means, Alvise?' Brunetti allowed himself to ask.

'That he solved them all, I'd guess, sir,' Alvise answered straight-faced. He saluted and left, leaving Brunetti with the lingering suspicion that Lear was not the only man who had a wise fool in his following.

He worked through lunch and well into the late afternoon juggling figures and inventing new categories until he had something that would both supply the truth and satisfy Patta. When he finally glanced at his watch, he saw that it was after seven, surely time for him to abandon these concerns and go home. On an impulse, he called Paola and asked her if she felt like going out to dinner. She hesitated not an instant, said only that she'd have to prepare something for the kids and would meet him wherever he chose.

'Sommariva?' he asked.

'Oh my,' she answered. 'What brings this on?'

'I need a treat,' he said.

'Maria's cooking?' she asked.

'Your company,' he answered. 'I'll meet you there at eight.'

Almost three hours later, a lobster-filled Brunetti and his champagne-filled consort climbed the stairs to their apartment, his steps slowed by satisfying fullness, hers by the grappa she'd drunk after dinner. Their arms linked, they were looking forward to bed, and then to sleep.

The phone was ringing as he opened the door, and Brunetti for an instant thought of not answering it, of leaving whatever it was until the next morning. Had there been time to see that the children were in their rooms and thus the call unrelated to their safety, he would have let it ring on unanswered, but paternity asserted itself, and he answered it on the fourth ring.

'It's me, sir,' Vianello said.

'What's wrong?' came Brunetti's instinctive response to Vianello's voice.

'Moro's mother's been hurt.'

'What?'

Sudden static filled the line, drowning out Vianello. When it came to an end, Brunetti heard only, '. . . no idea who.'

'Who what?' Brunetti demanded.

'Did it.'

'Did what? I didn't hear you.'

'She was hit by a car, sir. I'm in Mestre, at the hospital.'

'What happened?'

'She was going to the train station in Mogliano, where she lives. At least she was walking in that direction. A car hit her, knocked her down and didn't stop.'

'Did anyone see it?'

'Two people. The police there talked to them, but neither was sure about anything other than that it was light-coloured and the driver might have been a woman.'

Glancing at his watch, Brunetti asked, 'When did this happen?'

'At about seven, sir. When the police saw that she was Fernando Moro's mother, one of them remembered the boy's death and called the Questura. They tried to get you, and then they called me.'

Brunetti's glance fell on the answering machine. A tiny pulsating light illuminated the one message that awaited him. 'Has he been told?'

'They called him first, sir. She's a widow, and his name and address were in her purse.'

'And?'

'He came out.' Both men thought of what that must have been for Moro, but neither said anything.

'Where is he now?' Brunetti asked.

'In the hospital here.'

'What do the doctors say?' Brunetti asked.

'Some cuts and bruises, but nothing broken. The car must just have brushed her. But she's seventy-two, so the doctors decided to keep her overnight.' After a pause, Vianello added, 'He just left.'

There was a lengthy silence. Finally, Vianello said, in response to Brunetti's unspoken question, 'Yes, it might be a good idea. He was very shaken.'

Part of Brunetti's mind was aware that his instinctive desire to profit from Moro's weakness was no less reptilian than Vianello's encouragement that he do so. Neither idea stopped him. 'How long ago?' Brunetti asked.

'About five minutes. In a taxi.'

Familiar sounds came from the back of the apartment: Paola moving about in the bathroom, then going down the corridor to their bedroom. Brunetti's imagination soared above the city and the mainland and watched a taxi make its way through the empty streets of Mestre and across the long causeway that led to Piazzale Roma. A single man emerged, reached back inside, shoving money at the driver, then turned away and began to walk towards the *imbarcadero* of the Number One. 'I'll go,' Brunetti said and hung up.

Paola was already asleep when he looked into the bedroom, a stream of light falling across her legs. He wrote a note then couldn't decide where to leave it. Finally he propped the sheet of paper on the answering machine, where the flickering light still called for attention.

As Brunetti walked through the quiet city, his imagination took flight again, but this time it observed a man in a dark suit and a grey overcoat walking from San Polo toward the Accademia Bridge. As he watched, the man crossed in front of the museum and made his way into the narrow *calli* of Dorsoduro. At the end of the underpass that ran beside the church of San Gregorio, he crossed the bridge to the broad *Riva* in front of the Salute. Moro's house, off to his right, was dark, though all the shutters were open. Brunetti moved along the canal and stopped at the foot of the bridge leading back over the small canal and to the door of Moro's house. From there, he would see Moro returning, whether he walked, came by taxi or took the Number One. He turned and looked across the still waters at the disorderly domes of San Marco and the piebald walls of Palazzo Ducale, and thought of the peace their beauty brought him. How strange it was: nothing more than the arrangement of lines and colours, and he felt better than he had before he looked at them.

He heard the throb of the motor of the vaporetto arriving; then saw the prow emerge from behind the wall of a building. The noise moved into a different key, and the boat glided up to the *imbarcadero*. The crewman tossed out the rope with effortless accuracy and whipped it around the metal stanchion in the centuries-old knot. A few people got off the boat, none of them Moro. The metal scraped as the gate was pulled shut; a careless flip and the rope came free, and the boat continued.

Another boat arrived twenty minutes later, but Moro wasn't on this one, either. Brunetti was beginning to think the doctor might have decided to go back to his mother's home in Mogliano when, off to the left, he heard footsteps approaching. Moro emerged from the narrow *calle* between the houses at the end of the tiny *campo*. Brunetti crossed the bridge and stood at the bottom, just short of the door to Moro's house.

The doctor came toward him, hands stuffed into the pockets of his jacket, head lowered as if he had to take particular care of where he placed his feet. When he was a few metres from Brunetti, he stopped and reached first his left hand, then his right, into the pockets of his trousers. On the second attempt, he pulled out a set of keys but looked at them as if he didn't quite understand what they were or what he was meant to do with them.

He raised his head then and saw Brunetti. There was no change in his expression, but Brunetti was sure Moro recognized him.

Brunetti walked towards the other man, speaking before he thought, surprised by the force of his own anger. 'Are you going to let them kill your wife and daughter, too?'

Moro took a step backwards, and the keys fell from his hand. He raised one arm and shielded his face with it, as though Brunetti's words were acid and he had to protect his eyes. But then, with a speed that astonished Brunetti, Moro moved up to him and grabbed at his collar with both hands. He misjudged the distance, and the nails of his forefingers dug into the skin at the back of Brunetti's neck.

He pulled Brunetti towards him, yanking so savagely that he pulled him a half-step forwards. Brunetti flung his hands out to the side in an attempt to balance himself, but it was the strength of Moro's hands that kept him from falling.

The doctor pulled him closer, shaking him the way a dog shakes a rat. 'Stay out of this,' Moro hissed into his face, sprinkling him with spittle. 'They didn't do it. What do you know?'

Brunetti, allowing Moro to support him, recovered his balance, and when the doctor shoved him to arm's length, still holding tight, Brunetti stepped back and flung his hands up, breaking the doctor's grip and freeing himself. Instinctively he put his hands to his neck: his fingers felt torn skin and the beginnings of pain.

He leaned forward until his face was dangerously close to the doctor's. 'They'll find them. They found your mother. Do you want them to kill them all?'

Again the doctor raised his hand, warding off Brunetti's words. Robot-like, he raised the other hand, now a blind man, a trapped man, seeking a place of safety. He turned away and staggered, stiff-kneed, to the door of his house. Leaning brokenly against the wall, Moro began to pat his pockets for his keys, which lay on the ground. He dug his hands into his pockets, turning them out and scattering coins and small pieces of paper around him. When no pockets remained unturned, Moro lowered his head to his chest and began to sob.

Brunetti bent and picked up the keys. He walked over to the doctor and took his right hand, which was hanging limply at his side. He turned the doctor's palm up and placed the keys in it, then closed his fingers over them.

Slowly, like a person long victim to arthritis, Moro pushed himself away from the wall and put one key, then another, then another into the lock until he found the right one. The lock turned noisily four times. Moro pushed the door open and disappeared inside. Not bothering to wait to see if lights went on inside, Brunetti turned away and started to walk home.

20

Brunetti woke groggily the next morning to the dull sound of rain against the bedroom windows and to Paola's absence from his side. She was nowhere in the apartment, nor was there any sign of the children. A glance at the clock showed him why: everyone had long since gone off to the business of their day. When he went into the kitchen, he was grateful to see that Paola had filled the Moka and left it on the stove. He stared out the window while he waited for the coffee, and when it was ready took it back into the living room. He stood looking through the rain at the bell tower of San Polo, and sipped at his coffee. When it was finished, he went back into the kitchen and made more. This time, he came back and sat on the sofa, propped his slippered feet on the table, and stared out the glass doors that led to the terrace, not really aware of the rooftops beyond.

He tried to think of who 'they' could be. Moro had been too stunned by Brunetti's attack to prepare a defence and so had made no attempt to deny or pretend not to understand Brunetti's reference to this nameless 'they'. The first possibility that occurred to Brunetti, as it would to anyone who knew even the least bit about Moro's career, was someone at the health services, the target of the Moro Report's accusation of institutionalized corruption and greed. Closing his eyes, Brunetti rested his head against the back of the sofa and tried to remember what had become of the men who had been in charge of the provincial health services at the time of the Moro Report.

One had disappeared into private law practice, another had retired, and a third currently held a minor portfolio in the new government: in charge of transportation safety or relief efforts for natural disasters; Brunetti couldn't recall which. He did remember that, even in the face of the scandal and indignation at the gross pilfering from the public purse revealed by the report, the government's response had proceeded with the stateliness of the Dead March from *Saul*. Years had passed: the hospitals remained unbuilt, the official statistics remained unchanged, and the men responsible for the deceit had moved on quite undisturbed.

Brunetti realized that, in Italy, scandal had the same shelf life as fresh fish: by the third day, both were worthless; one because it had begun to stink, the other because it no longer did. Any punishment or revenge that 'they' might have inflicted upon the author of the report would have been exacted years ago: punishment that was delayed six years would not dissuade other honest officials from calling attention to the irregularities of government.

That possibility dismissed, Brunetti turned his thoughts to Moro's medical career and tried to see the attacks on his family as the work of a vengeful patient, only to dismiss that immediately. Brunetti didn't believe that the purpose of what had happened to Moro was punishment, otherwise he would have been attacked personally: it was threat. The origin of the attacks against his family must lie in what Moro was doing or had learned at the time his wife was shot. The attacks, then, could make sense as a repeated and violent attempt to prevent the publication of a second Moro Report. What struck Brunetti as strange, when he reconsidered Moro's reaction the night before, was not that the doctor had made no attempt to deny that 'they' existed so much as his insistence that 'they' were not responsible for the attacks.

Brunetti took a sip of his coffee but found it was cold; and it was only then that he heard the phone ringing. He set the cup down and went into the hall to answer it.

'Brunetti,' he said.

'It's me,' Paola said. 'Are you still in bed?'

'No, I've been up a long time.'

'I've called you three times in the last half-hour. Where were you, in the shower?'

'Yes,' Brunetti lied.

'Are you lying?'

'Yes.'

'What have you been doing?' Paola asked with real concern.

'Sitting and looking out the window.'

'Well, it's good to know your day has started out as a productive one. Sitting and looking or sitting and looking and thinking?'

'And thinking.'

'What about.'

'Moro.'

'And?'

'And I think I see something I didn't see before.'

'Do you want to tell me?' she asked, but he could hear the haste in her voice.

'No. I need to think about it a little more.'

'Tonight, then?'

'Yes.'

She paused a moment and then said, using a voice straight

out of Brazilian soap opera, 'We've got unfinished business from last night, big boy.'

With a jolt, his body remembered that unfinished business, but before he could speak, she laughed and hung up.

He left the apartment half an hour later, wearing a pair of rubber-soled brogues and sheltered under a dark umbrella. His pace was slowed by the umbrella, which caused him to duck and bob his way between the other people on the street. The rain appeared to have lessened, not eliminated, the streams of tourists. How he wished there were some other way he could get to work, some means to avoid being trapped in the narrow zigs and zags of Ruga Rialto. He cut right just after Sant' Aponal and walked down to the Canal Grande. As he emerged from the underpass, a *traghetto* pulled up to the *Riva*. After the passengers had got off, he stepped aboard, handing the *gondoliere* one of the Euro coins he still found unfamiliar, hoping it would be sufficient. The young man handed him back a few coins, and Brunetti moved to the rear of the gondola, allowing his knees to turn to rubber and thus help maintain his balance as the boat bobbed around on the water.

When there were thirteen people, one of them with a sodden German Shepherd, standing in the gondola, all trying to huddle under the umbrellas spread above their heads in an almost unbroken shield, the *gondolieri* shoved off and took them quickly to the other side. Even in this rain, Brunetti could see people standing without umbrellas at the top of the bridge, their backs to him, while other people took their photos.

The gondola slid up to the wooden steps, and everyone filed off. Brunetti waited while the *gondoliere* at the front handed a woman's shopping cart up to her. One of its wheels caught on the side of the steps and it tilted back toward the *gondoliere*, who caught it by the handle and handed it up. Suddenly the dog jumped back into the boat and picked up something that once had been a tennis ball. With it firmly between his jaws, he leaped back on to the dock and ran after his master.

It occurred to Brunetti that he had just witnessed a series of crimes. The number of people in the boat had exceeded the legal limit. There was probably a law stating that umbrellas had to be furled while they crossed the canal, but he wasn't sure and so let that one go. The dog had worn no muzzle and wasn't on a leash. Two people speaking German had been given change only when they asked for it.

On the way up to his office, Brunetti stopped in the officers' room and asked Pucetti to come upstairs. When they were both seated, Brunetti asked, 'What else have you learned?'

Obviously surprised by the question, Pucetti said, 'You mean about the school, sir?'

'Of course.'

'You're still interested?'

'Yes. Why wouldn't I be?'

'But I thought the investigation was finished.'

'Who told you that?' Brunetti asked, though he had a good idea.

'Lieutenant Scarpa, sir.'

'When?'

Pucetti glanced aside, trying to remember. 'Yesterday, sir. He came into the office and told me that the Moro case was no longer active and that I had been assigned to Tronchetto.'

'Tronchetto?' Brunetti asked, failing to hide his astonishment that a police officer should be sent to patrol a parking lot. 'What for?'

'We've had reports about those guys who stand at the entrance and offer tourists boat rides into the city.'

'Reports from whom?' Brunetti asked.

'There was a complaint from someone at the American Embassy in Rome. He said he paid two hundred Euros for a ride to San Marco.'

'What was he doing at Tronchetto?'

'Trying to park, sir. And that's when one of those guys with the white hats and fake uniforms told him where to park and offered to show him a taxi that would take him into the city, right to his hotel.'

'And he paid?'

Pucetti shrugged and said, 'You know what Americans are like, sir. He didn't understand what was going on. So yes, he paid, but when he told the people at the hotel, they said he'd been cheated. Turns out he's something important at the Embassy, so he called Rome, and then they called us and complained. And that's why we've been going out there, to keep it from happening again.'

'How long have you been doing this?'

'I went out yesterday, sir, and I'm due there in an hour,' Pucetti said; then, in response to Brunetti's expression, he added, 'It was an order.'

Brunetti decided to make no observation on the young officer's docility. Instead he said, 'The investigation of the Moro boy's death is still open, so you can forget about Tronchetto. I want you to go back and talk to one of the boys, named Ruffo. I think you spoke to him already.' Brunetti had seen the boy's name in Pucetti's written report and recalled the young officer's comment that the boy had seemed unduly nervous during the interview. Pucetti nodded at the name and Brunetti added, 'Not at the school, if that's possible. And not while you're in uniform.'

'Yes, sir. That is, no, sir,' Pucetti said, then quickly asked, 'And the lieutenant?'

'I'll deal with him,' Brunetti answered.

Pucetti instantly got to his feet and said, 'I'll go over there as soon as I change, sir.'

That left Brunetti with Lieutenant Scarpa. He toyed with the idea of summoning the lieutenant to his office but, thinking it better to appear before him unannounced, went down two flights of stairs to the office Scarpa had insisted he be given. The room had for years functioned as a storeroom, a place where officers could leave umbrellas and boots and coats to be used in the event of a change in the weather or the sudden arrival of *acqua alta*. Some years ago, a sofa had appeared as if by magic, and since then officers on the night shift had been known to steal an hour's sleep. Legend had it that a female commissario had been introduced to the pleasures of adultery on that very sofa. Three years ago, however, Vice-Questore Patta had ordered the boots, umbrellas and coats removed; the next day the sofa disappeared, replaced by a desk made of a plate of mirrored glass supported by thick metal legs. No one lower than commissario had a private office at the Questura, but Vice-Questore Patta had installed his assistant behind that glass desk. There had been no official discussion of his rank, though there had certainly been more than ample comment.

Brunetti knocked at the door and entered in response to Scarpa's shouted '*Avanti!*' There ensued a precarious moment during which Brunetti observed Scarpa deal with the arrival of one of his superiors. Instinct asserted itself, and Scarpa braced his hands on the edge of his desk as if to push himself back and get to his feet. But then Brunetti saw him react, not only to the realization of just which superior it was, but also to the territorial imperative, and the lieutenant transformed the motion into one that did no more than propel himself higher in his chair. 'Good morning, Commissario,' he said. 'May I help you?'

Ignoring what Scarpa tried to make a gracious wave towards the chair in front of his desk, Brunetti remained standing near the door and said, 'I'm putting Pucetti on a special assignment.'

Scarpa's face moved in something that was perhaps meant to be a smile. 'Pucetti is already on special assignment, Commissario.'

'Tronchetto, you mean?'

'Yes. What's going on there is very harmful to the image of the city.'

Telling his better self to ignore the dissonance between the sentiments and the Palermitano accent in which they were voiced, Brunetti answered, 'I'm not sure I share your concern for the image of the city, Lieutenant, so I'm reassigning him.'

Again, that motion of the lips. 'And you have the approval of the Vice-Questore, of course?'

'I hardly think a detail as insignificant as where a police officer is assigned is of much interest to the Vice-Questore,' Brunetti answered.

'On the contrary, Commissario, I think the Vice-Questore is deeply interested in anything that concerns the police in this city.'

Tired of this, Brunetti asked, 'What does that mean?'

'Just what I said, sir. That the Vice-Questore will be interested to learn about this.' Like a tenor with register problems, Scarpa could not control his voice as it wobbled between civility and menace.

'Meaning you intend to tell him about it?' Brunetti asked.

'Should the occasion arise,' Scarpa answered blandly.

'Of course,' Brunetti answered with equal blandness.

'Is that all I can do for you, Commissario?'

'Yes,' Brunetti said and left the office before giving in to the temptation to say something else. Brunetti knew almost nothing about Lieutenant Scarpa or what motivated him: money was probably a safe guess. This thought called to mind a remark Anna Comnena had made about Robert Guiscard: 'Once a man has seized power, his love of money displays exactly the same characteristics as gangrene, for gangrene, once established in a body, never rests until it has invaded and corrupted the whole of it.'

An old woman lay injured in the hospital in Mestre, and

he had to concern himself with turf battles with Patta's creature and with the attempt to understand the lieutenant's motives. He walked up the stairs, inwardly fuming about Scarpa, but by the time he got back to his office he had accepted the fact that his real anger was directed at his own failure to foresee the attack on Moro's mother. It mattered little to Brunetti that this was entirely unrealistic; somehow, he should have realized the danger and done something to protect her.

He called the hospital and, adopting the harsh, authoritarian voice he had learned to use when dealing with mindless bureaucracies, announced his rank and demanded to be connected to the ward where Signora Moro was being treated. There was some delay in transferring the call, and when the nurse on duty spoke to him, she was helpful and cooperative and told him that the doctor had advised that Signora Moro be kept until the next day, when she could go home. No, there was no serious injury: she was being kept an extra day in consideration of her age rather than her condition.

Braced by this comforting sign of humanity, Brunetti thanked her, ended the call, and immediately called the police in Mogliano. The officer in charge of the investigation told him that a woman had come into the Questura that morning and admitted she had been driving the car that struck Signora Moro. Panicking, she had driven away, but after a sleepless night in which she had been the victim of both fear and remorse, she had come to the police to confess.

When Brunetti asked the other officer if he believed the woman, he received an astonished, 'Of course', before the man said he had to get back to work and hung up.

So Moro was right when he insisted that 'they' had had nothing to do with the attack on his mother. Even that word, 'attack', Brunetti realized, was entirely his own invention.

Why, then, Moro's rage at Brunetti for having suggested it? More importantly, why his state of anguished despair last night, far out of proportion for a man who had been told that his mother was not seriously injured?

21

Awareness that he had done something else to merit Lieutenant Scarpa's enmity should have troubled Brunetti, but he could not bring himself to care: there were no degrees to implacable antipathy. He regretted only that Pucetti might have to bear the brunt of Scarpa's anger, for the lieutenant was not a man likely to aim a blow, at least not an open one, at people above him. He wondered whether other people behaved like this, deaf and blind to the real demands of their professions in their heedless pursuit of success and personal power, though Paola had long assured him that the various struggles that absorbed the Department of English Literature at the university were far more savage than anything described in *Beowulf* or the bloodier Shakespearean tragedies.

He knew that ambition was accepted as a natural human trait, had for decades observed others striving to achieve what they determined to be success. Much as he knew these desires were judged to be perfectly normal, he remained puzzled by the passion and energy of their endeavours. Paola had once observed that he had been born with some essential piece missing, for he seemed incapable of desiring anything other than happiness. Her remark had troubled him until she explained that it was one of the reasons she had married him.

Musing on this, he entered Signorina Elettra's office. When she looked up, he said without introduction, 'I'd like to learn about the people at the Academy.'

'What, precisely, would you like to know?'

He considered this, then finally said, 'I think what I'd really like to know is whether any of them is capable of killing that boy and, if so, for what reason.'

'There could be many reasons,' she answered, then added, 'If, that is, you want to believe that he was murdered.'

'No, I don't want to believe that. But if he was, then I want to know why.'

'Are you curious about the boys or the teachers?'

'Either. Both.'

'I doubt it could have been both.'

'Why?' he asked.

'Because they'd probably have different motives.'

'Such as?'

'I haven't explained myself well,' she began, shaking her head. 'I think the teachers would do it for serious reasons, adult reasons.'

'For instance?'

'Danger to their careers. Or to the school.'

'And the boys?'

'Because he was a pain in the ass.'

'Seems a pretty trivial reason to kill someone.'

'Viewed from a different perspective, most reasons for killing people are pretty trivial.'

He was forced to agree. After a while he asked, 'In what way could he have been a pain in the ass?'

'God knows. I don't have any idea what bothers boys that age. Someone who is too aggressive, or not aggressive enough. Someone who is too smart and makes the others embarrassed. Or shows off, or . . .'

Brunetti cut her off. 'Those still seem like trivial reasons. Even for teenagers.'

Not the least offended, she said, 'That's the best I can come up with.' Nodding at the keyboard, she said, 'Let me take a look and see what I can find.'

'Where will you look?'

'Class lists and then members of their families. Faculty lists and then the same. Then cross-check them with, well, with other things.'

'Where did you get those lists?'

Her intake of breath was stylishly long. 'It's not that I have them, sir, but that I can get them.' She looked at him and waited for his comment; outflanked, Brunetti thanked her and asked her to bring him whatever information she could find as soon as she had it.

In his office, he set himself to attempting to recall anything he'd heard or read, over the years, about the Academy. When nothing came, he turned his reflections to the military at large, recalling that most of the faculty were former officers of one branch or other.

A memory slipped in from somewhere, tantalizing him and refusing to come into focus. Like a sharpshooter straining to see at night, he addressed his attention, not to the target that wouldn't appear, but to whatever stood beside or beyond it. Something about the military, about young men in the military.

The memory materialized: an incident from some years before, when two soldiers – paratroopers, he thought – had been directed to jump from a helicopter somewhere in, he thought, former Yugoslavia. Not knowing that the helicopter was hovering a hundred metres above the ground, they had jumped to their death. Not knowing, and not having been told by the other men in the helicopter, who had known but were members of a military corps different from their own. And with that memory came another one, of a young man found dead at the bottom of a parachute jump, perhaps the victim of a nighttime hazing prank gone wrong. To the best of his knowledge, neither case had ever been resolved, no satisfactory explanation provided for the completely unnecessary deaths of these three young men.

He recalled, as well, a morning at breakfast some years ago when Paola looked up from the newspaper which contained an account of the country's then-leader offering to send Italian troops to aid an ally in some bellicose endeavour. 'He's going to send troops,' she said. 'Is that an offer or a threat, do you think?'

Only one of Brunetti's close friends had opted for a career in the military, and they had lost touch over the last few years, so he did not want to call him. What he would ask him, anyway, Brunetti had no idea. If the Army were really as corrupt and incompetent as everyone seemed to believe it was? No, hardly the question he could ask at least not of a serving general.

That left his friends in the press. He called one in Milano but when the machine answered, he chose not to leave either his name or a message. The same happened when he called another friend in Rome. The third time, when he called Beppe Avisani, in Palermo, the phone was answered on the second ring.

'Avisani.'

'*Ciao*, Beppe. It's me, Guido.'

'Ah, good to hear your voice,' Avisani said, and for a few minutes they exchanged the sort of information friends give and get when they haven't spoken for some time, their voices perhaps made formal by a shared awareness that they usually now spoke to one another only when one of them needed information.

After everything that had to be said about families had been said, Avisani asked, 'What can I tell you?'

'I'm looking into the death of the Moro boy,' Brunetti answered and waited for the reporter to answer.

'Not suicide, then?' he asked, not bothering with polite pieties.

'That's what I want to know,' Brunetti answered.

Without hesitation, Avisani volunteered. 'If it wasn't suicide, then the obvious reason is the father, something to do with him.'

'I'd got *that* far, Beppe,' Brunetti said with an entire absence of sarcasm.

'Of course, you would. Sorry.'

'The report came out too long ago,' Brunetti said, certain that a man who had spent twenty years as a political reporter would follow his thinking and also dismiss the report as a possible cause. 'Do you know what he worked on while he was in Parliament?'

There was a long pause as Avisani followed the trail of Brunetti's question. 'You're probably right,' he said at last, then, 'Can you hold on a minute?'

'Of course. Why?'

'I've got that stuff in a file somewhere.'

'In the computer?' Brunetti asked.

'Where else?' the reporter asked with a laugh. 'In a drawer?'

Brunetti laughed in return, as though he'd meant the question as a joke.

'Just a minute,' Avisani said. Brunetti heard a click as the phone was set down on a hard surface.

He looked out of the window as he waited, making no attempt to impose order upon the information that tumbled around in his mind. He lost track of time, though it was far more than a minute before Avisani was back.

'Guido?' he asked, 'you still there?'

'Yes.'

'I haven't got much on him. He was there for three years, well, a bit less than that, before he resigned, but he was kept pretty well out of sight.'

'Kept?'

'The party he ran for chose him because he was famous at the time and they knew they could win with him, but after he was elected and they got an idea of what his real ideas were, they kept him as far out of sight as they could.'

Brunetti had seen it happen before as honest people were elected into a system they hoped to reform, only to find themselves gradually absorbed by it, like insects in a Venus' fly-trap. Because Avisani had seen far more of it than he, Brunetti drew a pad towards him and said only, 'I'd like to know what committees he worked on.'

'Are you looking for what I think you are – someone he might have crossed?'

'Yes.'

Avisani made a long noise that Brunetti thought was meant to be speculative. 'Let me give you what I have. There was a pension committee for farmers,' Avisani began, then dismissed it with a casual, 'Nothing there. They're all nonentities.' And then, 'The one that oversaw sending all that stuff to Albania.'

'Was the Army involved in that?' Brunetti asked.

'No. I think it was done by private charities. Caritas, organizations like that.'

'What else?'

'The Post Office.'

Brunetti snorted.

'And military procurement,' Avisani said with undisguised interest.

'What does that mean?'

There was a pause before he answered, 'Probably examining the contracts with the companies that supply the military.'

'Examining or deciding?' Brunetti asked.

'Examining, I'd say. It was really only a subcommittee, which means they'd have no more power than to make recommendations to the real committee. You think that's it?' he asked.

'I'm not sure there is an "it",' Brunetti answered evasively, only now forcing himself to recall that his friend was a member of the press.

With laboured patience, Avisani asked, 'I'm asking as a curious friend, Guido, not as a reporter.'

Brunetti laughed in relief. 'It's a better guess than the postmen. They're not particularly violent.'

'No, that's only in America,' Avisani said.

A moment's awkwardness fell between them, both of them aware of the conflict between their professions and their friendship. Finally Avisani said, 'You want me to follow up on this?'

At a loss as to how to phrase it, Brunetti said, 'If you can do it delicately.'

'I'm still alive because I do things delicately, Guido,' he said without any attempt at humour, gave a farewell not distinguished by its friendliness, and hung up.

Brunetti called down to Signorina Elettra, and when she answered, said, 'I'd like you to add one more thing to your . . .' he began, but was at a loss for a name for what Signorina Elettra did. 'To your research,' he said.

'Yes, sir?' she asked.

'Military procurement.'

'Could you be a bit more precise?'

'Getting and spending,' he began, and a line Paola was forever quoting rushed towards him. He ignored it and continued, 'For the military. It was one of the committees Moro was on.'

'Oh, my,' she exclaimed. 'However did that happen?'

Hearing her unfeigned astonishment, Brunetti wondered

how long it would take him to explain her reaction to a foreigner. Her response presumed Moro's honesty, and her astonishment that an honest man had been placed on any committee that would make decisions that might somehow affect the allocation of significant amounts of government funds.

'I've no idea,' he answered. 'Perhaps you could see who else served on the committee with him.'

'Certainly, sir. Government records are very easy to access,' she said, leaving him to speculate about the precise level of criminality lurking in that verb.

He looked at his watch and asked, 'Should I go and have lunch or should I wait?'

'Lunch, sir, I think,' she advised and was gone.

He walked down to Testiere, where the owner would always find him a place, and had a fish antipasto and then a piece of grilled tuna Bruno swore was fresh. For all the attention Brunetti paid to it, the fish could have been frozen or freeze-dried. At any other time, ignoring a meal this fine would have shamed Brunetti: today he could not drag himself away from his attempt to discover the connection between Moro's professional life and the suffering inflicted upon his family, and so the meal remained eaten but untasted.

He stopped at the door to Signorina Elettra's office and found her standing at her window, looking off down the canal that led toward the *Bacino*. Her attention was so absorbed in whatever she was watching that she didn't hear him come in, and he stopped, reluctant to startle her. Her arms were crossed on her breast, and she stood with her shoulder leaning against the window frame, one leg crossed in front of the other. He saw her in profile and as he watched, she lowered her head and closed her eyes for a heartbeat longer than necessary. She opened them, took a breath so deep he saw her breasts rise, and turned away from the window. And saw him watching her.

Three seconds passed. Paola had once told him that the Irish often said, in moments when consolation was necessary, 'I'm sorry for your trouble', and it was on his lips to say this when she took a step towards her desk, tried to smile, and said, 'I've got everything,' but said it in the voice of someone who had nothing.

Three more seconds passed and then he joined her at her desk, in unspoken agreement that they would ignore what had just happened.

He saw two piles of papers. Standing, she pointed to the first, saying as she did, 'That's a list of students who have fathers in the military or the government – that's the only thing I checked about the students. And under it is a list of the faculty, which branch of the military they served in, and the final rank they held. And beneath that a list of the men who served on the committee for military procurement with Dottor Moro.'

Curiosity overcame good sense and he asked, 'All right. Please tell me where you got all of this.' When she didn't answer, he held up his right hand and said, 'I promise, on the head of anyone in my family you choose to name, that I will never repeat what you tell me, will forget it the instant you tell me, will not allow Lieutenant Scarpa, no matter what means he employs, ever, to wrest it from me.'

She considered this. 'What if he makes horrible threats?'

'Like what, invites me for a drink?'

'Worse. Dinner.'

'I shall be strong.'

She capitulated. 'There's a way to access military personnel files. All you need is the code and then the service number of any member.' Because she was volunteering this, Brunetti did not ask how she got the code or the numbers. 'Parliament is too easy,' she said with contempt. 'A child could get in.' He assumed she was talking about the computer files, not the building.

'And the lists from the schools?' he asked.

She gave him a long, speculative look, and he nodded, renewing his vow of silence. She said, 'Pucetti stole them when he was there and gave them to me in case they might be useful.'

'Have you had time to study them?'

'A little. Some names occur on more than one list.'

'For example?'

She pulled a sheet of paper from the first pile and pointed to two names that she had already highlighted in yellow. 'Maggiore Marcello Filippi and Colonello Giovanni Toscano.'

'Tell me,' he said. 'It's faster.'

'The Maggiore was in the Army for twenty-seven years and retired three years ago. For the six years immediately before his retirement, he was in charge of the procurement office for the Paratroopers. His son is a third-year student at the Academy.' She pointed to the second name. 'The Colonello served as military adviser to the parliamentary committee on which Moro served. He now teaches at the Academy. He was in Paris, attending a seminar, during the week the boy died.'

'Isn't that something of a fall from grace, to go from a job in Parliament to teaching at a military academy in the provinces?'

'The Colonello retired after twenty-two years of military service under something of a cloud,' Signorina Elettra said. 'Or at least,' she immediately corrected herself, 'that's the sense I get from reading the internal files.'

Internal files, Brunetti repeated to himself. Where would she stop? 'What do they say?'

'That certain members of the committee registered less than total satisfaction with the Colonello's performance. One of them even went so far as to suggest that the Colonello was not at all impartial in the advice he provided the committee.'

'Moro?'

'Yes.'

'Ah.'

'Indeed.'

'Less than impartial in what way?' Brunetti asked.

'It didn't say, though there's not far to look, is there?'

'No, I suppose not.' If the Colonello were partial in a way which the committee did not like, it would have to be in favour of the firms which supplied the military, and the men who owned them. Brunetti's atavistic cynicism suggested here that it might just as easily mean that Toscano was in the pay of companies different from those making payments to the parliamentarians on the committee. The marvel here was not that he was partial – why else seek a position like this – but that he should have been . . . Brunetti stopped himself from saying the word 'caught', even in his mind. It was remarkable that he should have been forced to retire, for Brunetti could not imagine that a man in this position would go quietly. How obvious or excessive must his partiality have been if it had led to his retirement?

'Is he Venetian, the Colonello?' he asked.

'No, but his wife is.'

'When did they come here?'

'Two years ago. Upon his retirement.'

'Do you have any idea of how much he earns as a teacher at the Academy?'

Signorina Elettra pointed to the paper again. 'All of their salaries are listed to the right of their names.'

'Presumably, he's also receiving his military pension,' Brunetti said.

'That's listed, as well,' she answered.

Brunetti looked at the paper and saw that the sum of the Colonello's pension plus his salary at the Academy was well in excess of his own salary as a commissario. 'Not bad, I'd say.'

'They struggle though, I suppose,' she observed.

'The wife?'

'Rich.'

'What does he teach?'

'History and Military Theory.'

'And does he have a particular political stance that he brings to the teaching of history?'

She smiled at the delicacy of his phrasing and answered, 'I can't answer that yet, sir. I've got a friend whose uncle teaches Mathematics there, and he's promised to ask him.'

'It's probably a safe guess what his ideas would be,' she went on, 'but it's always best to check.'

He nodded. Neither of them had any illusions about the view of politics and, for that fact, history likely to be held by a man who had spent twenty-two years in the military. But, like Signorina Elettra, Brunetti thought it would be best to be certain.

'And the two men?' he asked. 'Did they ever serve together?'

She smiled again, as if this time pleased with his perspicacity, and pulled towards her the second pile of papers. 'It would seem that at the same time as the Colonello was giving his advice to the parliamentary committee, the newly retired Maggiore was on the board of directors of Edilan-Forma.'

'Which is?' he asked.

'A Ravenna-based company which supplies uniforms, boots and backpacks to the military, along with other things.'

'What other things?'

'I've not been able to break into their computer yet,' she said, clearly still in no doubt that this entire conversation was protected by the same dispensation. 'But it looks like they supply anything soldiers can wear or carry. It would seem, as well, that they serve as subcontractors for companies that sell food and drink to the military.'

'And all of this means?' Brunetti asked.

'Millions, sir, millions and millions. It's a money fountain, or it could be. After all, the military spends about seventeen billion Euros a year.'

'But that's insane,' he blurted out.

'Not for anyone who has a chance to take any of it home, it's not,' she said.

'Edilan-Forma?'

'Even so,' she replied, and then returned to the information she had gathered. 'At one point, the committee examined the contracts with Edilan-Forma because one of the committee members had raised questions about them.'

Though he barely thought it necessary, Brunetti asked, 'Moro?'

She nodded.

'What sort of questions?'

'The parliamentary minutes mention pricing for a number of items, also the quantities ordered,' she said.

'And what happened?'

'When the committee member resigned, the questions were not repeated.'

'And the contracts?'

'They were all renewed.'

Was he mad, he wondered, to find this so normal and so simple to understand? Or were they all mad, everyone in the country, in a way that demanded the papers lying on Signorina Elettra's desk could be read in only one way? The public purse was a grab bag, and public spoil the supreme gift of office. Moro, stupid and transparently honest Moro, had dared to question this. Brunetti was no longer in any doubt that the answer to Moro's questions had been given, not to him, but to his family.

'If you haven't already begun it, could you take a closer look at Toscano and Filippi?'

'I was just beginning that when you came in, sir,' she said. 'But my friend in Rome, the one who works in military records, has been sent to Livorno for a few days, so I won't have access to their records until the end of the week.'

Failing to remind her that she had been standing at the window, looking out sadly at her past or her future, when he came in, not beginning to work on anything, Brunetti thanked her and went back to his office.

22

By force of will, Brunetti kept himself at the Questura until the normal time for leaving. He occupied himself with reading and initialling reports, then decided that he would read only every second one, then every third, though he scrupulously wrote a careful 'GB' on the bottom of all of them, even the unread ones. As his eyes ran over the words, the columns of numbers, the endless spew of facts and figures that were as closely related to reality as Anna Anderson to Tsar Nicholas II, Brunetti's thoughts remained anchored to Moro.

Just before leaving, he called Avisani in Palermo.

Again, the journalist answered with his name.

'It's me, Beppe,' Brunetti said.

'It's not even a day, Guido. Give me some time, will you?' the journalist said waspishly.

'I'm not calling to nag, Beppe. Believe me. It's that I want to add two names to the list,' Brunetti began. Before Avisani could refuse, he continued, 'Colonello Giovanni Toscano and Maggiore Marcello Filippi.'

After a long time, Avisani said, 'Well, well, well. If there's salt, there's pepper; oil, there's vinegar; smoke, fire.'

'And Toscano, Filippi, I assume?' Brunetti asked.

'Very much so. How is it you've stumbled on those two?'

'Moro,' Brunetti said simply. 'They're both tied to the committee Moro was working on when he left Parliament.'

'Ah yes. Procurement,' Avisani said, stretching the word out as if better to enjoy the sound of it.

'Do you know anything?' Brunetti asked, though he was sure his friend did.

'I know that Colonello Toscano was encouraged to leave his position as consultant to the parliamentary committee and soon after that decided to retire from the Army.'

'And Filippi?'

'My sense is that the Maggiore decided his position had become too obvious.'

'What position was that?'

'Husband to the cousin of the president of the company from whom the Paratroopers obtained most of their supplies.'

'Edilan-Forma?' Brunetti inquired.

'Haven't you been a busy boy?' Avisani asked by way of compliment.

Honesty demanded that Brunetti make it clear that it was Signorina Elettra who had been a busy girl, but he thought it best not to reveal this to a member of the press. 'Have you written about this?' Brunetti asked.

'Time and time again, Guido,' Avisani answered with heavy resignation.

'And?'

'And what are people supposed to do? Pretend to be surprised, pretend this isn't the way they do business, too? Remember what that television comic said when they started the Mani Pulite investigation?'

'That we were all guilty of corruption and should all spend

a few days in jail?' Brunetti asked, remembering Beppe Grillo's frenetic admonition to his fellow citizens. He was a comic, Grillo, and so people were free to laugh, though what he said that night had been in no way funny.

'Yes,' Avisani said, pulling back Brunetti's attention. 'I've been writing articles about this for years, about this and about other agencies of the government that exist primarily to siphon money to friends and relatives. And no one cares.' He waited for Brunetti to react, and then repeated, 'No one cares because they all think that, sooner or later, they might get a chance at some of the easy money, so it's in their best interests that the system stay the way it is. And it does.'

Since Brunetti knew this to be the case, there was no reason to object to his friend's remarks. Returning to Avisani's original reaction, he asked, 'Is that the only way they're linked?'

'No. They graduated in the same class from the Academy in Modena.'

'And after that?' Brunetti asked.

'I don't know. I doubt it's important. What is, is that they knew one another well and that both were eventually involved in procurement.'

'And both retired?'

'Yes, pretty much at the same time.'

'Where's Filippi, do you know?' Brunetti asked.

'I think he lives in Verona. You want me to find out about him?'

'Yes.'

'How much?'

'Whatever you can.'

'And I suppose you'll pay me the same as you always do?' Avisani asked with a laugh.

'You don't want to eat my wife's cooking?' Brunetti asked with fake indignation, then, before Avisani could answer,

Brunetti said, 'I don't want you to go to any trouble with this, Beppe.'

This time it was the journalist who laughed. 'Guido, if I worried about going to trouble, or, for that matter, getting into trouble, I doubt I could do this job.'

'Thanks, Beppe,' Brunetti said, and the warmth of the other man's parting laugh told him that their friendship remained as strong as ever.

He went downstairs, and though he tried to resist the siren lure of Signorina Elettra and her computer, he failed. There was no light on in her office, and the darkened screen of the computer suggested she had not yet found what he had asked her to get. There was nothing else for him to do, short of rifling through her desk, so he went home to his family and his dinner.

The next morning he was at the Questura before eight, and when his detour past Signorina Elettra's office showed that she was not yet in, he continued to the officers' room, where he found Pucetti at a desk, reading a magazine. The young man got to his feet when he saw Brunetti. 'Good morning, Commissario. I was hoping you'd come in early.'

'What have you got?' Brunetti asked. He was vaguely conscious of motion behind him, and he saw its reflection on Pucetti's face, from which the smile disappeared. 'Only these forms, sir,' he said, reaching across his desk to the one beside it and gathering up two stacks of papers. 'I think they need your signature,' he said, his voice neutral.

Imitating his tone, Brunetti said, 'I've got to go down to see Bocchese for a minute. Could you take them up and put them on my desk for me?'

'Certainly, sir,' Pucetti said, setting one stack, and then the second, on top of his magazine and tapping them together to straighten the edges. When he picked them up, the magazine had disappeared.

Brunetti turned towards the door and found it blocked by

Lieutenant Scarpa. 'Good morning, Lieutenant,' Brunetti said neutrally. 'Is there something I can do for you?'

'No, sir,' the lieutenant answered. 'I wanted to speak to Pucetti.'

Brunetti's face lit up with grateful surprise. 'Ah, thank you for reminding me, Lieutenant: there's something I need to ask Pucetti about.' He turned to the young man. 'You can wait for me in my office, Officer. I won't be a minute with Bocchese.' With a friendly smile at the lieutenant, Brunetti said, 'You know how Bocchese loves to get an early start,' suggesting this was common knowledge at the Questura, despite the well-known truth that Bocchese spent the first hour of his day reading *La Gazzetta dello Sport* and using his email address at the Questura to place bets in three countries.

Silently, the lieutenant moved aside to let his superior pass. Brunetti waited just outside the door until Pucetti joined him and then closed the door of the office behind them.

'Oh, I suppose Bocchese can wait a few minutes,' Brunetti said resignedly. When they got to his office, Brunetti closed the door behind them and while he took off his overcoat and hung it in the closet, said, 'What did you learn?'

Pucetti kept the papers tucked under his arm and said, 'I think there's something wrong with the Ruffo boy, sir. I went over there yesterday and hung around in the bar down the street from the school, and when he came in I said hello. I offered him a coffee, but it seemed to me he was nervous about talking to me.'

'Or being seen talking to you,' Brunetti suggested. When Pucetti agreed, Brunetti asked, 'What makes you think there's something wrong with him?'

'I think he's been in a fight.' Not waiting for Brunetti to question him, Pucetti went on. 'Both of his hands were scraped, and the knuckles of his right hand were swollen. When he saw me looking at them, he tried to hide them behind his back.'

'What else?'

'He moved differently, as though he were stiff.'

'What did he tell you?' asked Brunetti as he sat down behind his desk.

'He said he's had time to think about it and he realizes now that maybe it was suicide, after all,' Pucetti said.

Brunetti propped his elbows on his desk and rested his chin on his folded hands. Silently, he waited to hear not only what Pucetti had been told but what he thought of it.

In the face of his superior's silence, Pucetti ventured, 'He doesn't believe that, sir, at least I don't think he does.'

'Why?'

'He sounded frightened, and he sounded as if he were repeating something he'd had to memorize. I asked him why he thought it might have been suicide, and he said it was because Moro had been acting strangely in the last few weeks.' Pucetti paused, then added, 'Just the opposite of what he told me the first time. It was as if he needed some sign from me that I believed him.'

'And did you give it to him?' Brunetti asked.

'Of course, sir. If that's what he needs to feel safe, and I think it is, then it's better he have it.'

'Why's that, Pucetti?'

'Because it will cause him to relax, and when he relaxes he'll be even more frightened when we talk to him again.'

'Here, do you mean?'

'Downstairs, yes. And with someone big in the room with us.'

Brunetti looked up at the young man and smiled.

The obvious choice to serve the role of enforcer was Vianello, a man who had perfected the art of disguising his essential good nature behind expressions that could vary from displeased to savage. He was not, however, to be given the chance to employ his repertory on Cadet Ruffo, for when the

Inspector and Pucetti arrived at the San Martino Academy an hour later, the cadet was not in his room, nor did the boys on his floor know where to find him. It was the Comandante who brought illumination by telling them, when their inquiries finally led them to his office, that Cadet Ruffo had been granted leave to visit his family and was not expected to return to the Academy for at least two weeks.

When asked, the Comandante remained vague as to the precise reason for Cadet Ruffo's leave, saying something about 'family matters', as if that should satisfy any curiosity on their part.

Vianello knew that the student list was in Signorina Elettra's possession, a list that would surely provide the address of Ruffo's parents, and so it was nothing more than interest in the Comandante's response that prompted Vianello to ask him to provide it. He refused, insisting that the addresses of the students constituted privileged information. Then he announced that he had a meeting to attend and asked them to leave.

After the two men returned to the Questura and reported this encounter to Brunetti, he asked Pucetti, 'What was your general impression of the cadets?'

'I'd like to say they were frightened, the way Ruffo was when I talked to him the last time, but they weren't. In fact, they seemed angry that I'd ask them anything, almost as if I didn't have a right to talk to them.' The young officer shrugged in confusion about how to make all of this clear. 'I mean, they're all seven or eight years younger than I am, but they acted like they were speaking to a kid or someone who was supposed to obey them.' He looked perplexed.

'An enlisted man, for example?' Brunetti asked.

Not following, Pucetti asked, 'Excuse me, sir?'

'As if they were speaking to an enlisted person? Is that how they spoke to you?'

Pucetti nodded. 'Yes, I think so, as if I was supposed to obey them and not ask questions.'

'But that doesn't tell us why they didn't want to talk,' Vianello interrupted.

'There's usually only one reason for that,' Brunetti said.

Before Vianello could ask what he meant, Pucetti blurted out, 'Because they all know whatever Ruffo does, and they don't want us to talk to him.'

Once again, Brunetti graced the young man with an approving smile.

By three that afternoon, they were seated in an unmarked police car parked a hundred metres from the entrance to the home listed for Cadet Ruffo, a dairy farm on the outskirts of Dolo, a small town halfway between Venice and Padova. The stone house, long and low and attached at one end to a large barn, sat back from a poplar-lined road. A gravel driveway led up to it from the road, but the recent rains had reduced it to a narrow band of mud running between patches of dead grass interspersed with mud-rimmed puddles. There were no trees within sight, though stumps stood here and there in the fields, indicating where they had been cut. It was difficult for Brunetti, stiff and cold in the car, to think of a season different from this one, but he wondered what the cattle would do without shade from the summer sun. Then he remembered how seldom cows went to pasture on the farms of the new Veneto: they generally stood in their stalls, reduced to motionless cogs in the wheel of milk production.

It was cold; a raw wind was coming from the north. Every so often, Vianello turned on the motor and put the heat on high, until it grew so hot in the car that one or another of them was forced to open a window.

After half an hour, Vianello said, 'I don't think it makes much sense to sit here, waiting for him to show up. Why don't we just go and ask if he's there or not?'

Pucetti, as befitted his inferior position, both in terms of rank and, because he was in the back seat, geography, said nothing, leaving it to Brunetti to respond.

Brunetti had been musing on the same question for some time, and Vianello's outburst was enough to convince him. 'You're right,' he said. 'Let's go and see if he's there.'

Vianello turned on the engine and put the car into gear. Slowly, the wheels occasionally spinning in search of purchase, they drove through the mud and gravel and towards the house. As they drew nearer, signs of rustic life became more and more evident. An abandoned tyre, so large it could have come only from a tractor, lay against the front of a barn. To the left of the door of the house a row of rubber boots stood in odd pairings of black and brown, tall and short. Two large dogs emerged from around the side of the house and ran towards them, low and silent and, because of that, frightening. They stopped two metres short of the car, both on the passenger side, and stared, their lips pulled back in suspicion, but still silent.

Brunetti could recognize only a few well-known breeds, and he thought he saw some German Shepherd in these dogs, but there was little else he could identify. 'Well?' he asked Vianello.

Neither of the others said anything, so Brunetti pushed open his door and put one foot on the ground, careful to choose a patch of dried grass. The dogs did nothing. He put his other foot on the ground and pushed himself out of the car. Still the dogs remained motionless. His nostrils were assailed by the acidic smell of cow urine, and he noticed that the puddles in front of what he thought to be the doors of the barn were a dark, foaming brown.

He heard one car door open, then the other, and then Pucetti was standing beside him. At the sight of two men standing side by side, the dogs backed away a bit. Vianello came around the front of the car, and the dogs backed away even farther, until they stood just at the corner of the building. Vianello suddenly stamped his right foot and took a long step towards them, and they disappeared around the corner of the building, still without having made a sound.

The men walked to the door, where an enormous iron ring served as a knocker. Brunetti picked it up and let it drop against the metal plaque nailed into the door, enjoying the weight of it in his hand as well as the solid clang it created. When there was no response, he did it again. After a moment, they heard a voice from inside call something they could not distinguish.

The door was opened by a short, dark-haired woman in a shapeless grey woollen dress over which she wore a thick green cardigan that had obviously been knitted by hand, a clumsy hand. Shorter than they, she stepped back from the door and put her head back to squint at them. Brunetti noticed that there was a lopsided quality about her face: the left eye angled up towards her temple, while the same side of her mouth drooped. Her skin seemed baby soft and was without wrinkles, though she must have been well into her forties.

'Sì?' she finally inquired.

'Is this the home of Giuliano Ruffo?' Brunetti asked.

She might have been a speaker of some other language, so long did it take her to translate his words into meaning. As Brunetti watched, he thought he saw her mouth the word, 'Giuliano', as if that would help her answer the question.

'Momento,' the woman said, and the consonants caused her great difficulty. She turned away, leaving it to them to close the door. Or just as easily, Brunetti said to himself, walk off with everything in the house or, if they preferred, kill everyone inside and drive away undisturbed, even by the dogs.

The three men crowded into the hall and stood there, waiting for the woman to return or for someone to arrive better able to answer their questions. After a few minutes they heard footsteps come towards them from the back of the house. The woman in the green cardigan returned, and behind her was another woman, younger, and wearing a sweater made from the same wool but by more skilful hands. This woman's features and bearing, too, spoke of greater refinement: dark eyes that instantly sought his, a sculpted mouth poised to speak, and an air of concentrated attention left Brunetti with a general impression of brightness and light.

'*Sì?*' she said. Both her tone and her expression made the question one that required not only an answer, but an explanation.

'I'm Commissario Guido Brunetti, Signora. I'd like to speak to Giuliano Ruffo. Our records show that this is his home.'

'What do you want to talk to him about?' the second woman asked.

'About the death of one of his fellow cadets.'

During this exchange, the first woman stood to one side of Brunetti, open mouthed, her face moving back and forth from one to the other as he spoke to the younger woman, seeming to register only sound. Brunetti saw her in profile, and noticed that the undamaged side of her face was similar to that of the other woman's. Sisters, then, or perhaps cousins.

'He's not here,' the younger woman said.

Brunetti had no patience for this. 'Then he's in violation of his leave from the Academy,' he said, thinking this might perhaps be true.

'To hell with the Academy,' she answered fiercely.

'All the more reason for him to talk to us, then,' he countered.

'I told you, he's not here.'

Suddenly angry, Brunetti said, 'I don't believe you.' The idea of what life in the countryside was like came to him, the boredom of work relieved only by the hope that some new misery would befall a neighbour. 'If you like, we can leave and then come back again with three cars, with sirens wailing and red lights flashing, and fill your courtyard and then go and ask all of your neighbours if they know where he is.'

'You wouldn't do that,' she said, far more truthfully than she realized.

'Then let me talk to him,' Brunetti said.

'Giuliano,' said the first woman, surprising them all.

'It's all right, Luigina,' the younger woman said, placing a hand on her forearm. 'These men have come to see Giuliano.'

'Giuliano,' the older woman repeated in the same dull, uninflected tone.

'That's right, *cara*. They're friends of his, and they've come to visit.'

'Friends,' the woman repeated with a crooked smile. She moved towards the bulk of Vianello, who was looming behind his colleagues. She raised her right hand and placed the open palm on the centre of his chest. She raised her face up to his and said, 'Friend.'

Vianello placed his hand over hers and said, 'That's right, Signora. Friends.'

23

There ensued a moment of intense awkwardness, at least for Brunetti, Pucetti and the younger woman. Vianello and Luigina remained linked by her hand on his chest, while Brunetti turned to the other woman and said, 'Signora, I do need to speak to Giuliano. You have my inspector's word: we're friends.'

'Why should I trust you?' she demanded.

Brunetti turned partly towards Vianello, who was now softly patting the back of the other woman's hand. 'Because she does,' he said.

The younger woman began to protest but let it drop even before she could pronounce the first word. As Brunetti watched, her face displayed her recognition of the truth of his remark. Her body relaxed and she asked, 'What do you need to ask him?'

'I told you, Signora. About the death of the cadet.'

'Only about that?' Her glance was as clear and direct as her question.

'Yes.' He could have left it at that, but he felt himself bound by Vianello's promise. 'It should be. But I won't know until I speak to him.'

Luigina suddenly took her hand from Vianello's chest. She turned to the other woman and said, 'Giuliano.' After she pronounced the name, she gave a nervous grin that tugged at Brunetti's pity as it pulled at her mouth.

The younger woman stepped close to her and took her right hand in both of hers. 'It's all right, Luigina. Nothing will happen to Giuliano.'

The woman must have understood what she heard, for the grin expanded into a smile and she clapped her hands together in undisguised happiness. She turned towards the back of the house, but before she could move the younger woman placed a hand on her arm, stopping her. 'But the gentleman needs to speak to Giuliano alone,' she began, making a business of looking at her watch. 'And while he's doing that, you can feed the chickens. It's time for that.' Brunetti knew little about country life, but he did know that chickens didn't get fed in the middle of the day.

'Chickens?' Luigina asked, confused by the abrupt change of subject.

'You have chickens, Signora?' Vianello asked with great enthusiasm, stepping forward until he was directly in front of her. 'Would you show them to me?' he asked.

Again, the lopsided smile, at the chance to show her friend the chickens.

Turning to Pucetti, Vianello said, 'The Signora's going to show us the chickens, Pucetti.' Without waiting for Pucetti to respond, Vianello placed a hand on the woman's arm and started to walk with her to the front door of the house. 'How many . . . ?' Brunetti heard the Inspector begin, and then, as if he'd realized that the act of counting was probably well beyond this woman's powers, he continued seamlessly, '. . . times have I wanted to see chickens.' He turned to Pucetti. 'Come on, let's go see the chickens.'

When they were alone, Brunetti asked the woman, 'May I ask who you are, Signora?'

'I'm Giuliano's aunt.'

'And the other signora?' he asked.

'His mother.' When Brunetti followed this with no inquiry, she added, 'She was injured some years ago, while Giuliano was still a boy.'

'And before that?' Brunetti asked.

'What do you mean? Was she normal?' she demanded, attempting an angry tone but not fully succeeding.

Brunetti nodded.

'Yes, she was. As normal as I. I'm her sister, Tiziana.'

'I thought so,' he said. 'You look very much alike, the two of you.'

'She was the beautiful one,' she said sadly. 'Before.' If this woman's neglected beauty were any indication, then Luigina must indeed have been a wonder.

'May I ask what happened?'

'You're a policeman, aren't you?'

'Yes.'

'Does that mean you can't repeat things?'

'If they're not related to the case I'm investigating, no.' Brunetti failed to tell her that it was more a case of what he chose not to reveal than what he was forbidden to, but his answer satisfied her.

'Her husband shot her. And then he shot himself,' she said. When Brunetti made no comment, she continued, 'He meant to kill her and then himself. But he failed, at least with Luigina.'

'Why did he do it?'

'He thought she was having an affair.'

'Was she?'

'No.' Her answer left no doubt in Brunetti's mind. 'But he was a jealous man, always. And violent. We all warned her not to marry him, but she did.' After a long pause, she added,

'Love,' as though asked to name the disease that had destroyed her sister.

'How long ago did this happen?'

'Eight years. Giuliano was ten.' The woman suddenly folded her arms across her stomach, her hands grabbing at the opposite arms as though seeking security there.

When it occurred to him, the idea so shocked him that he spoke before he considered how painful the question would be for her. 'Where was Giuliano?'

'No, he wasn't there,' she answered. 'At least he didn't do that to him.'

Brunetti wanted to know the full extent of the damage to the other woman, but he recognized this as the prurient curiosity it was, and so he forbore to ask. The evidence in Luigina's behaviour and asymmetrical face sufficed to indicate what was left: this woman's vitality was enough to suggest what had been taken.

As they were walking across to the back of the house, Brunetti asked, 'Why did he leave the school?'

'He said . . .' she began but then stopped, and Brunetti sensed that she was sorry not to be able to explain it to him. 'I think it would be better if you asked Giuliano that.'

'Was he happy there?'

'No. Never.' Her answer was instant and fierce.

'Then why did he go, or why did he stay?'

She stopped and turned to face him, and he noticed that her eyes, which had at first appeared dark, were in reality flecked with amber and seemed to glow, even in the dim light of the hall.

'Do you know anything about the family?'

'No. Nothing,' he said, at once regretting that he had failed to ask Signorina Elettra further to invade their privacy and ferret through their secrets. All of this would then have been far less surprising, and he would have known what information to try to get out of her.

Again, she crossed her arms in front of her and turned to face him. 'You didn't read about it, then?'

'No, not that I recall.' He wondered how he could have missed a case like this: it must have been a three-day wonder for the press.

'It happened when they were in Sardegna, on the naval base there,' she said, as though that would explain it. 'And my sister's father-in-law managed to keep it quiet.'

'Who is he, her father-in-law?' Brunetti asked.

'Ammiraglio Giambattista Ruffo,' she said.

Brunetti recognized the name instantly: the man known as the 'King's Admiral' for his avowedly monarchist sentiments and opinions. Brunetti thought Ruffo was Genovese by birth, had a vague memory of having heard people talk about him for decades. Ruffo had risen through the ranks of the Navy on merit, keeping his ideas to himself, but once his senior rank was confirmed – and Brunetti thought this had been about fifteen years ago – he had ceased to disguise or equivocate about his belief that the monarchy should be restored. The attempt on the part of the War Ministry to silence Ruffo had given him a sort of overnight celebrity, for he refused to retract any of his statements. The serious newspapers, if, in fact, any can be said to exist in Italy, quickly tired of the story, and it was relegated to those weekly magazines whose covers devote attention week by week to various parts of the female anatomy.

Given his celebrity, it was nothing short of miraculous that his son's suicide could have been kept from turning into a media feeding frenzy, but Brunetti had no memory of the case. 'How did he manage to silence it?' Brunetti asked.

'In Sardegna, at the naval base, he was in command,' she began.

'You mean the Admiral?' Brunetti interrupted to ask.

'Yes. Because it all happened there, the press could be kept out.'

'How was it reported?' Brunetti asked, knowing that, given these conditions, almost anything was possible.

'That he had died in an accident, and Luigina had been seriously injured at the same time.'

'That's all they said?' he asked, surprised at his own ingenuousness at thinking this unusual.

'Of course. The Naval police investigated, and a Naval doctor did the autopsy. Luigina wasn't even badly hurt by the bullet. It hit her in the arm. But she fell and hit her head. That's what did the damage.'

'Why are you telling me this?' Brunetti asked.

'Because Giuliano doesn't know what really happened.'

'Where was he?' Brunetti asked. 'When it happened, I mean.'

'There. But in a different part of the house, with his grandparents.'

'And no one's ever told him?'

She shook her head. 'I don't think so. At least, not until now.'

'Why do you say that?' he asked, sensitive to a sudden lessening of confidence in her tone.

She raised her right hand and rubbed at her temple, just at the hairline. 'I don't know. He asked me about it when he came home this time. I'm afraid I didn't handle it well. Instead of just telling him what we've always told him, about the accident, I asked him why he was asking.' She stopped speaking, glancing at the floor, her fingers still busy at the edge of her hair.

'And?' Brunetti prodded.

'And when he didn't answer me, I told him that he already knew what happened, that there was a terrible accident and his father was killed.' She stopped again.

'Did he believe you?'

She shrugged the question away like a wilful child refusing to deal with an unpleasant subject.

Brunetti waited, not repeating the question. Finally she said, raising her eyes to meet his, 'I don't know if he did or not.' She stopped, considering how to explain this, then went on, 'When he was younger, he used to ask about it. It was almost like a fever: it would grow and grow on him until he couldn't do anything except ask me about it again, no matter how many times I'd told him what happened. And then he'd be all right for a time, but then it would start again, and he'd refer to his father or ask questions about him, or about his grandfather, until he couldn't stand it any more, and then he'd ask about his father's death.' She closed her eyes, letting her hands fall to her sides. 'And I'd tell him the same old lie again. Until I was sick of hearing it.'

She turned away from him and started towards the back of the house again. Following her, Brunetti risked one last question: 'Did he seem different this time?'

She kept walking, but he saw the sudden rise and fall of her shoulders as she shrugged the question away. After a few more steps, she stopped just in front of a door but did not turn to face him. 'Every time he asked, he was calmer for a while after I told him what had happened, but this time he wasn't. He didn't believe me. He doesn't believe me any more.' She didn't explain why she thought this, and Brunetti didn't think it necessary to ask: the boy would be a far more reliable source.

She opened a door that gave on to another long corridor, then stopped at the second door on the right and knocked. Almost immediately it opened, and Giuliano Ruffo came out into the corridor. He saw his aunt and smiled, then turned to Brunetti and recognized him. The smile disappeared, flared up for a hopeful moment, then died away again.

'*Zia,*' he named her. 'What is it?' When she didn't answer, the boy said to Brunetti, 'You're the man who came to my room.' At Brunetti's nod, he asked, 'What do you want now?'

'The same thing I did last time, to talk about Ernesto Moro.'

'What about him?' Giuliano asked neutrally. Brunetti thought the boy should have been more disturbed to have the police pursuing him to his home to ask about Ernesto Moro. Suddenly he was conscious of the awkwardness of their situation, the three of them standing in the unheated corridor, the woman silent while Brunetti and the boy circled one another with questions. As if sensing his thoughts, the woman said, indicating the room behind her nephew, 'Shall we go somewhere warmer to talk?'

If it had been a command, the boy could not have responded more quickly. He went back inside, leaving the door open for them to follow. Entering, Brunetti was reminded of the unnatural orderliness of Giuliano's room at the Academy, but reminded only because here he saw its antithesis: clothing lay discarded across the bed and on top of the radiator; compact discs, vulnerable and naked outside of their boxes, covered the desk; boots and shoes cluttered the floor. The only thing that surprised him was the absence of the smell of cigarettes, though he saw an open pack on the desk and another on the table beside the bed.

Giuliano went to the armchair in front of the window and picked up the clothing draped over it, then told his aunt that she could sit there. He tossed the clothing on to the foot of the bed, adding it to a pair of jeans already there. He nodded his head towards the chair in front of his desk, indicating to Brunetti that he could sit there, then sat down in the space he had just made on the bed.

Brunetti began, 'Giuliano, I don't know what you've been told or have read, and I don't care what you might have told anyone. I don't believe that Ernesto killed himself; I don't believe he was the kind of boy to do it, and I don't think he had any reason to do it.' He paused, waiting for the boy or his aunt to say something.

Neither did, so he continued, 'That means either he died in an accident of some sort or that someone killed him.'

'What do you mean, accident?' Giuliano asked.

'A practical joke that went wrong, one he was playing or that someone was playing on him. If that was the case, then I think the people involved would have panicked and done the first thing that they thought of: faking a suicide.' He stopped there, hoping to provide the boy with the opportunity to agree, but Giuliano remained silent.

'Or else,' Brunetti continued, 'for reasons I don't understand, he was killed, either deliberately or, again, when something went wrong or got out of hand. And then the same thing happened: whoever did it tried to make it look like a suicide.'

'But the newspapers say it was suicide,' the aunt interrupted.

'That doesn't mean anything, *Zia*,' the boy surprised Brunetti by saying.

Into the silence that radiated from this exchange, Brunetti said, 'I'm afraid he's right, Signora.'

The boy put both hands on the surface of the bed and hung his head, as if examining the jumble of shoes and boots that lay on the floor. Brunetti watched his hands turn into fists then unfold themselves again. He looked up, suddenly leaned aside, and picked up the pack of cigarettes on the table beside him. He held it tight in his right hand, like a talisman or the hand of a friend, but he made no move to take a cigarette. He switched the pack to his left hand and finally took a cigarette from it. Standing, he tossed the pack down on the bed and came towards Brunetti, who remained motionless.

Giuliano took a disposable plastic cigarette lighter from the desk and went to the door. Saying nothing, he left the room, closing the door behind him.

His aunt said, 'I've asked him not to smoke in the house.'

'Don't you like the smell?' Brunetti asked.

She pulled a battered packet of cigarettes from the pocket of her sweater and said, holding it up to him, 'Quite the opposite. But Giuliano's father was a heavy smoker, so my sister associates the smell with him: we both smoke only outside the house not to upset her.'

'Will he come back?' Brunetti asked; he had made no attempt to stop Giuliano from leaving and was fully convinced that the boy could not be forced to reveal anything he did not want to.

'There's nowhere else he can go,' his aunt said, though not unkindly.

They sat in silence for a while, until Brunetti asked, 'Who runs this farm?'

'I do. With a man from the village.'

'How many cows do you have?'

'Seventeen.'

'Is that enough to make a living?' Brunetti asked, curious to learn how the family managed to survive, though he admitted to himself he knew so little about farming that the number of cattle could give him no indication of wealth or the ability to produce it.

'There's a trust from Giuliano's grandfather,' she explained.

'Is he dead?'

'No.'

'Then how can there be a trust?'

'He set it up when his son died. For Giuliano.'

Brunetti asked, 'What does it stipulate?' When she didn't answer, he added, 'If you'll permit me to ask.'

'I can't stop you asking anything,' she said tiredly.

After some time, she apparently decided to answer the question. 'Giuliano receives a sum every four months,' she told him.

A certain hesitation at the end of her statement led Brunetti to ask, 'Are there any conditions?'

'So long as he is actively pursuing a career in the military, he'll continue to receive it.'

'And if he stops?'

'It does, too.'

'His time at the Academy?'

'That's part of the pursuing.'

'And now?' he asked, waving a hand to indicate the unmilitary chaos of Giuliano's room.

She shrugged, a gesture he was beginning to associate with her, then answered, 'So long as he's still officially on leave, he's considered . . .' her voice trailed off.

'Pursuing?' Brunetti ventured and was pleased by her smile.

The door opened then and Giuliano came into the room, bringing with him the scent of cigarette smoke. He walked back to the bed, and Brunetti noticed that his shoes left muddy tracks on the tiles of the floor. He sat, propping his hands on either side, looked at Brunetti and said, 'I don't know what happened.'

'Is that the truth or what you decided to tell me while you were outside?' Brunetti asked mildly.

'It's the truth.'

'Do you have any idea at all?' Brunetti asked. The boy gave no sign that he had even heard the question, so Brunetti asked an even more hypothetical question: 'Or of what might have happened?'

After a long time, head still lowered and eyes still on his shoes, the boy said, 'I can't go back there.'

Brunetti did not for an instant doubt him: no one who heard him would. But he was curious about the boy's reasons. 'Why?'

'I can't be a soldier.'

'Why is that, Giuliano?' he asked.

'It's not in me. It just isn't. It all seems so stupid: the orders and the standing in line and everyone doing the same thing at the same time. It's stupid.'

Brunetti glanced at the boy's aunt, but she sat motionless,

staring at her nephew, ignoring Brunetti. When the boy spoke again, Brunetti turned his attention back to him. 'I didn't want to do it, but my grandfather said it's what my father would have wanted me to do.' He glanced up at Brunetti, who met his eyes but remained silent.

'That's not true, Giuliano,' his aunt interrupted. 'He always hated the military.'

'Then why did he join?' Giuliano snapped back, making no attempt to disguise his anger.

After a long time, as if she'd considered the effect her words were bound to have, she answered, 'For the same reason you did: to make your grandfather happy.'

'He's never happy,' Giuliano muttered.

A silence fell on them. Brunetti turned and looked out the window, but all he saw was the long expanse of muddy fields and, here and there, a tree trunk.

It was the woman who finally broke the silence. 'Your father always wanted to be an architect, at least that's what your mother told me. But his father your grandfather, insisted that he become a soldier.'

'Just like all the other Ruffos,' Giuliano spat out with undisguised contempt.

'Yes,' she agreed. 'I think that was part of the cause of his unhappiness.'

'He killed himself, didn't he?' Giuliano startled both of the adults by asking.

Brunetti turned his gaze back to the woman. She looked at him, then at her nephew, and finally said, 'Yes.'

'And before, he tried to kill *Mamma*?'

She nodded.

'Why didn't you ever tell me?' the boy asked, his voice tight and close to tears.

Tears appeared in her eyes too and began to spill down her face. She drew her mouth tight, incapable of speech, and shook her head. Finally she held up her right hand, her palm facing her nephew, as if asking him to be patient long enough for words to come back to her. More time passed and then she said, 'I was afraid.'

'Of what?' the boy demanded.

'To hurt you,' she said.

'And a lie wouldn't?' he asked, but in confusion, without anger.

She turned her palm upwards, splaying open her fingers, in a gesture that spoke of uncertainty and, in a strange way, of hope.

'What happened?' Giuliano asked. When she didn't answer, he added, 'Please tell me, *Zia*.'

Brunetti watched her struggle towards speech. Finally she said, 'He was jealous of your mother and accused her of having an affair.' As the boy showed no curiosity about this, she went on. 'He shot her and then himself.'

'Is that why *Mamma* is the way she is?'

She nodded.

'Why didn't you tell me? I always thought it was a disease you were afraid to tell me about.' He stopped and then, as if carried forward on the current of his own confessions, added, 'That it was something in the family. And it would happen to me, too.'

This broke her, and she started to cry openly, silently, save for an occasional deep intake of breath.

Brunetti turned his attention to the boy and asked, 'Will you tell me what you think happened, Giuliano?'

The boy looked at Brunetti, at the weeping woman, and then back at Brunetti. 'I think they killed him,' he finally said.

'Who?'

'The others.'

'Why?' Brunetti asked, leaving for later the question of who 'they' were.

'Because of his father and because he tried to help me.'

'What did they say about his father?' Brunetti asked.

'That he was a traitor.'

'A traitor to what?'

'*La Patria*,' the boy answered, and never had Brunetti heard the words spoken with such contempt.

'Because of his report?'

The boy shook his head. 'I don't know. They never said. They just kept telling him his father was a traitor.'

When it seemed that Giuliano had reached a halting place, Brunetti prodded him by asking, 'How did he try to help you?'

'One of them started talking about my father. He said he knew what had happened and that my mother was a whore. That there wasn't any accident, and that she'd gone crazy when my father killed himself because it was her fault that he did.'

'And what did Moro do?'

'He hit him, the one who said this, Paolo Filippi. He knocked him down and broke one of his teeth.'

Brunetti waited, not wanting to press him, afraid that it would break the thread of the boy's revelations.

Giuliano went on. 'That stopped it for a while, but then Filippi began to threaten Ernesto, and then a bunch of his friends did, too.' Brunetti's attention was riveted by the name Filippi, the third-year student whose father supplied material to the military.

'What happened?'

'I don't know. I didn't hear anything that night, the night he died. But the next day they all seemed strange – worried and happy at the same time, like kids who have a secret or a secret club.'

'Did you say anything? Ask anyone?'

'No.'

'Why?'

Giuliano looked straight at Brunetti as he said, 'I was

afraid', and Brunetti was struck by how much courage it took for him to say that.

'And since then?'

Giuliano shook his head again. 'I don't know. I stopped going to classes and stayed in my room most of the time. The only people I talked to were you and then that policeman who came to the bar, the nice one.'

'What made you leave?'

'One of them, not Filippi, but one of the others, saw me talking to the policeman, and he remembered him from when he was asking questions at the Academy, and then Filippi told me if I talked to the police I better watch out . . .' His voice trailed off, leaving the sentence unfinished. He took a deep breath and added, 'He said I should be careful and that talking to the police could drive a person to suicide, and then he laughed.' He waited to see what effect this would have on Brunetti, and then said, 'So I left. I just walked out and came home.'

'And you're not going back,' his aunt startled them both by interrupting. She got to her feet, took two steps towards her nephew, and stopped. Looking across at Brunetti, she said, 'No more. Please, no more of this.'

'All right,' Brunetti agreed, standing. For a moment, he debated whether to tell the boy he would have to make a formal statement, but this was not the time to try to force anything from him, especially not with his aunt present. In future, they could deny that this conversation had taken place or they could admit it. Which they chose to do was irrelevant to Brunetti: what interested him was the information he had obtained.

As they made their way back to the front hall, he heard the deep, comforting bass of Vianello's voice, interspersed with a light female warbling. When Brunetti and the others entered the room, Giuliano's mother turned to greet them, her face aglow with joy. Vianello stood in the middle of the room, a wicker basket full of brown eggs dangling from his right hand. Giuliano's mother pointed to Viarello and said, 'Friend.'

24

On the way back to Venice, Brunetti explained that, although they now had enough to warrant calling the Filippi boy in for questioning, he would prefer them to dedicate their energies to seeing what they could find out about his father.

Vianello surprised him by suggesting he take a few hours the next day to have a look on the Internet to see what he could discover. Brunetti forbore from comment on his phrase, 'have a look', which sounded to him like vintage Signorina Elettra, when he considered the relief that would come to him if someone other than Signorina Elettra, someone to whom he was less beholden by the heavy demands of past favours, were to be the one to discover sensitive information.

'How will you do it?' he asked Vianello.

Keeping his eyes on the traffic that filled the roads leading towards Venice, Vianello said, 'The same way Signorina Elettra does: see what I can find and then see what my friends can find.'

'Are they the same friends as hers?' Brunetti asked.

At this question, Vianello took his eyes from the road and permitted himself a quick glance in Brunetti's direction. 'I suppose.'

'Then perhaps it would be faster to ask Signorina Elettra,' a defeated Brunetti suggested.

He did so the following morning, stepping into her office and asking her if her military friend was back from Livorno and, if so, whether he would allow her to have a look at their files. As if she had known upon rising that the day would cause her to engage the military, Signorina Elettra wore a dark blue sweater with small buttoned tabs on the shoulders not unlike epaulettes.

'You wouldn't happen to be wearing a sword, would you?' Brunetti asked.

'No, sir,' she answered, 'I find it very inconvenient for daytime wear.' Smiling, she pressed a swift series of keys on her computer, paused a moment, then said, 'He'll start working on it now.'

Brunetti went back to his office.

He read two newspapers, calling it work, while he waited for her, then made a few phone calls, not attempting to justify them as anything other than maintaining good relations with people who might some day be asked to provide him with information.

When there had been no sign of Signorina Elettra before lunchtime, he left the Questura without calling her, though he did call Paola to say he would not be home for lunch. He went to da Remigio and ate insalata di mare and coda di rospo in tomato sauce, telling himself that, because he drank only a *quartino* of their house white wine and limited himself to a single grappa, it was a light meal and would entitle him to have something more substantial that evening.

He looked into Signorina Elettra's office on his way up to his own, but she was gone. His heart dropped, for he feared that she had left for the day and he would have to wait until the following day to learn about Filippi. But she did not disappoint. At three-thirty, just as he was considering going down to ask Vianello to have a look on the computer, she came into his office, a few papers in her hand.

'Filippi?' he asked.

'Isn't that the name of a battle?'

'Yes. It's where Bruto and Cassio were defeated.'

'By Marc' Antonio?' she asked, not at all to his surprise.

'And Ottaviano,' he added for the sake of correctness. 'Who then went on, if memory serves, to defeat Antonio.'

'It serves,' she said, placing the papers on his desk, adding, 'A tricky lot, soldiers.'

He nodded at the papers. 'Do they lead you to that conclusion, or does the battle of Filippi?'

'Both,' she answered. She explained that she would be leaving the Questura in an hour because she had an appointment and left his office.

There didn't seem to be more than a dozen sheets of paper, but they contained an adequate summary of both men's rise through the ranks of the military. After graduating from the San Martino Academy, Filippi went on to the formal military academy in Mantova, where he proved to be a mediocre cadet. Filippi finished in the middle of his class, beginning a career that had little to do with battle or its many dangers. He had spent his early years as 'resource specialist' in a tank regiment. Promoted, he had served for three years on the staff of the military attaché to Spain. Promoted again, he was posted as executive officer in charge of procurement for a regiment of paratroopers, where he remained until his retirement. Glancing back at Filippi's first posting, Brunetti's attention was caught by the word, 'tank', and his mind flew instantly to his father and the rage into which that word would catapult him. For two of the war years, while the Army staggered under the command of General Cavallero, ex-director of the Ansaldo armaments complex, Brunetti's father had driven one of their tanks. More than once he had seen the men of his battalion blown to fragments as the armour plating shattered like glass under enemy fire.

Toscano had enjoyed a similarly un-bellicose career. Like Filippi, he had risen effortlessly through the ranks, as though helped along by gentle puffs of wind from the cheeks of protecting cherubs. After years in which he had certainly never been disturbed by the sound of shots fired in anger, Colonello Toscano had been appointed to serve as military adviser to Parliament, the position from which he had been encouraged to retire two years before. He now served as professor of history and military theory at the San Martino Academy.

Beneath the two pages bearing the letterhead of the Army were two more containing lists of property owned by Filippi and Toscano and by members of their families, as well as copies of their most recent bank statements. Perhaps they both had rich wives; perhaps both came from wealthy families; perhaps both had been careful with their salaries all those years. Perhaps.

Years ago, when he first met Paola, Brunetti had limited himself to phoning her only every few days in the hope of disguising his interest and in the equally vain hope of maintaining what he then defined as his male superiority. The memory of this awkward restraint came to him as he dialled Avisani's number in Palermo.

But Avisani, when he heard Brunetti's voice, was as gracious as Paola had been, all those years ago. 'I've wanted to call you, Guido, but things are crazy here. No one seems to know who's in charge of the government.'

Brunetti marvelled that a reporter as experienced as he should think anyone would find this worthy of comment but said only, 'I thought I'd call. And nag.'

'It's not necessary,' Avisani answered with a laugh. 'I've had a trawl through the files, but the only thing I could come up with – aside from what I told you last time – is that both of them, Filippi and Toscano, own enormous amounts of stock in Edilan-Forma.'

'What does "enormous" mean?'

'If you've managed to convert to thinking in Euros, perhaps ten million each.'

Brunetti made a low humming noise of interest then asked, 'Any idea how they acquired it?'

'Toscano's really belongs to his wife. At least it's listed in her name.'

'You told me Filippi was married to the President's cousin.'

'Yes. He is. But the stock is in his name, not hers. It seems that he was paid in stock while he was on the board.'

Neither spoke for a long time until finally Brunetti broke the silence by saying, 'It would be in both of their interests to see that the price of the stock didn't drop.'

'Exactly,' agreed Avisani.

'A parliamentary investigation might have just that effect.'

This time it was the journalist who answered with a noise, though his was more a grunt than a hum.

'Did you check the stock?' Brunetti asked.

'Steady as a rock, well, as a rock that continues to move upward and that gives out steady dividends.'

The phone line was silent, but both of them heard the tumble and roll of the other's calculations and conclusions. Finally Avisani said, sounding stressed, 'I've got to go, Guido. We might wake up tomorrow morning with no government.'

'It's a pity Tommaso d'Aquino is no longer with us,' Brunetti observed mildly.

Confused, Avisani asked, 'What?' then amended it to 'Why?'

'He might have added that to his proofs of the existence of God.'

Another muffled noise and Avisani was gone.

But how, Brunetti wondered, to penetrate the world of the cadets? He had long held the view that it was no accident that the Mafia had grown in the home of the Vatican, for both demanded the same fidelity from their followers and both punished betrayal with death, either earthly or eternal. The third in this trinity of twisted loyalty was undoubtedly the military: perhaps the business of imposing death upon the enemy made it easy to impose it upon their own.

He sat for a long time, dividing his gaze between the wall of his office and the façade of San Lorenzo, but on neither surface saw he any way to penetrate the code that reigned at San Martino. Finally he picked up the phone and called Pucetti. When the officer answered, Brunetti asked, 'How old is Filippi?'

'Eighteen, sir.'

'Good.'

'Why?'

'We can talk to him alone.'

'Won't he want a lawyer?'

'Not if he thinks he's smarter than we are.'

'And how will you make him think that?'

'I'll send Alvise and Riverre to bring him in.'

Brunetti was very pleased by the fact that Pucetti refrained from laughter or comment, seeing in his discretion sign of both the young man's intelligence and his charity.

When Brunetti went downstairs an hour later, he found Paolo Filippi in the interview room, sitting at the head of the rectangular table, facing the door. The young man sat straight in the chair, his spine at least ten centimetres from the back, his hands carefully folded on the desk in front of him, like a general who has summoned his staff and waits impatiently for them to arrive. He wore his uniform and had placed his cap, neatly folded gloves carefully set on its crown, to his right. He looked at Brunetti when he and Vianello came in but said nothing to acknowledge their presence. Brunetti recognized him instantly as the boy whose ankle he had so delighted in kicking, and he saw that the recognition was mutual.

Taking his cue from Filippi's silence, Brunetti walked to one side of the table, Vianello to the other. Brunetti carried a thick blue file, which he placed in front of him as he sat down. Ignoring the boy, he reached out and turned on the microphone, then gave the date and the names of the three people present in the room. He turned to face the boy and, in a voice he made sound as formulaic as possible, asked Filippi if he wanted a lawyer to be present, hoping that to the young man's ears it would sound like the sort of offer a brave man would spurn.

'Of course not,' the boy said, striving for the tone of bored superiority used by mediocre actors in bad war movies. Brunetti gave silent thanks for the arrogance of the young.

Quickly, using the same formulaic tone, Brunetti disposed of the standard questions about name, age, place of residence, and then asked the boy what he did.

'I'm a student, of course,' Filippi answered, as though it were unthinkable that someone his age, from his background, could be anything other than this.

'At the San Martino Academy?' Brunetti asked.

'You know that,' the boy said.

'I'm sorry, but that's not an answer,' Brunetti said calmly.

In a sulky voice, the boy said, 'Yes.'

'In what year are you?' Brunetti asked, though he knew the answer and believed the information to be irrelevant. He wanted to see if Filippi had learned to answer questions without dispute.

'Third.'

'Have you spent all three years at the Academy?' Brunetti asked.

'Of course.'

'Is it part of your family tradition?'

'What, the Academy?'

'Yes.'

'Of course it is. The Academy and then the Army.'

'Is your father in the Army, then?'

'He was. He's retired.'

'When was that?'

'Three years ago.'

'Do you have any idea why your father retired?'

Irritated, the boy asked, 'Who do you want to know about, me or my father? If you want to know about him, then why don't you bring him in and ask him?'

'In due course,' Brunetti said calmly, then repeated, 'Do you have any idea why your father retired?'

'Why does anyone retire?' the boy shot back angrily. 'He had enough years and he wanted to do something else.'

'Serve on the board of Edilan-Forma?'

The boy waved away the possibility with his hand. 'I don't know what he wanted. You'll have to ask him.'

As if it followed in logical sequence, Brunetti asked, 'Did you know Ernesto Moro?'

'The boy who killed himself?' Filippi asked, Brunetti thought unnecessarily.

'Yes.'

'Yes, I knew him, though he was a year below me.'

'Did you take any classes together?'

'No.'

'Did you participate in sports together?'

'No.'

'Did you have friends in common?'

'No.'

'How many students are there at the Academy?' Brunetti asked.

The question puzzled Filippi, who turned to take a quick

look at the silent Vianello, as if the other man might know why this question was being asked.

When nothing was forthcoming from Vianello, the boy said, 'No. Why?'

'It's a small school, fewer than a hundred students.'

'If you knew that, why did you ask me?' Brunetti was glad to see that the boy was irritated at having been asked a question to which the police obviously already knew the answer.

Ignoring Filippi's question, Brunetti said, 'I understand it's a good school.'

'Yes. It's very hard to get in.'

'And very expensive,' Brunetti observed neutrally.

'Of course,' Filippi said with no attempt to disguise his pride.

'Is preference given to the sons of former students?'

'I should hope so,' Filippi said.

'Why is that?'

'Because then the right people get in.'

'And who are they?' Brunetti asked with mild curiosity, conscious as he spoke that, if his own son were to use the phrase, 'the right people', in that same tone, he would feel himself to have failed as a parent.

'Who?' Filippi demanded.

'The right people.'

'The sons of officers, of course,' the boy answered.

'Of course,' Brunetti repeated. He opened the file and glanced at the top sheet of paper, which had nothing to do with Filippi or Moro. He looked at Filippi, back at the paper, then again at the boy. 'Do you remember where you were the night that Cadet Moro was . . .' he began, deliberately hesitating after the last word before correcting it to, 'died?'

'In my room, I assume,' the boy answered.

'You assume?'

'Where else would I be?'

Brunetti permitted himself to look across at Vianello, who gave the most minimal of nods. Brunetti slowly turned the page over and glanced at the next.

'Was anyone in the room with you?'

'No.' The answer was immediate.

'Where was your roommate?'

Filippi reached out and adjusted the folded gloves until they ran directly from the centre of the peak to the back of the cap. 'He must have been there,' the boy finally said.

'I see,' Brunetti said. As if unable to resist the impulse, he glanced across at Vianello. The Inspector gave another slight nod. Brunetti looked again at the paper and, from memory, asked, 'His name's Davide Cappellini, isn't it?'

Filippi, suppressing any sign of surprise, answered, 'Yes.'

'Is he a close friend of yours?' Brunetti asked.

'I suppose so,' Filippi said with the petulance that only teenagers can express.

'Only that?'

'Only what?'

'That you suppose it. That you aren't sure.'

'Of course I'm sure. What else would he be if we've shared a room for two years?'

'Exactly,' Brunetti permitted himself to observe and bent his attention to the papers again. After what he realized was a long time, he asked, 'Do you do things together?' Then, before Filippi could ask who he meant, Brunetti clarified, 'You and your roommate, Cadet Cappellini?'

'What do you mean?'

'Do things together,' Brunetti repeated. 'Study? Sports? Other things?'

'What other things?' Filippi demanded suspiciously.

'Hunting?' Vianello surprised them both by suggesting.

Almost as if he had forgotten the presence of the other policeman, Filippi whipped his head towards Vianello and demanded, his voice slipping up an octave, 'What?'

'Fishing? Hunting?' Vianello asked with innocent curiosity, then added, 'Soccer?'

Filippi reached a hand in the direction of the gloves but stopped himself and folded both hands together on the desk in front of him. 'I want to have a lawyer here with me,' he said.

Mildly, as though Filippi had asked for a glass of water, Brunetti said, 'Of course,' leaned forward, gave the time, and said into the microphone that the interview was being broken off.

25

When he said that he didn't know a lawyer, the boy was left alone in a room and allowed to call his father. A few minutes later he came out and said that his father would be there with a lawyer in about an hour. Brunetti called an officer to take the boy back to the room where he had been questioned and told Filippi that he would be left there, undisturbed, until his father arrived. Politely, Brunetti asked if he would like anything to eat or drink, but the boy refused. In the manner of his refusal, Brunetti saw generations of B movie actors spurning the handkerchief offered by the commander of the firing squad.

As soon as the boy was led away, Brunetti told Vianello to wait for Major Filippi and the lawyer and to delay them as long as he could before letting them see the boy.

Calling to Pucetti, he told him to go down and wait at the launch, that he'd be down in a moment.

'Where are you going?' interrupted a puzzled Vianello.

'Back to the Academy. I want to talk to the Cappellini boy before they get to him,' Brunetti said. 'Let them talk to the boy alone as long as they want. If you have to, let them take him away. Just see that it all takes as long as possible. Do anything you can to delay them.' He was gone even before Vianello could make any acknowledgement.

The launch stood before the Questura, the pilot gunning the engine in response to Pucetti's excitement. Pucetti had already untied the moorings and stood on the dock, holding the boat close to the pier. Brunetti jumped on board, followed a second later by Pucetti, who lost his footing on the already-moving boat and had to steady himself with a hand on Brunetti's shoulder. Full throttle, the launch sped out into the *Bacino*, straight across, then turned into the open mouth of the Canale della Giudecca. The pilot, warned by Pucetti, used the flashing blue light but not the siren.

The first thrill of excitement was followed almost immediately by Brunetti's embarrassment that, in the midst of death and deceit, he could still revel in the simple joy of speed. He knew this was no schoolboy holiday, no cops and robbers chase, but still his heart soared with delight at the rush of wind and the rhythmic thump of the prow against the waves.

He glanced at Pucetti and was relieved to see his own feelings reflected on the younger man's face. They seemed to flash by other boats. Brunetti saw heads turn and follow their swift passage up the canal. Too soon, however, the pilot pulled into the Rio di Sant' Eufemia, slipped the motor into reverse, and glided silently to the left-hand side of the canal. As he and Pucetti jumped off, Brunetti wondered if he had been rash to bring this sweet-tempered young man with him instead of someone like Alvise who, if equally decent, at least had the professional advantage of looking like a thug.

'I want to frighten this kid,' Brunetti said as they started up the *Riva* towards the school.

'Nothing easier, sir,' Pucetti replied.

As they walked across the courtyard, Brunetti sensed some sort of motion or disturbance to his right, where Pucetti was. Without breaking his stride, he took a quick glance at him and was so surprised that he almost stopped. Somehow, Pucetti's shoulders had thickened, and he had adopted the stride of a boxer or roustabout. His head jutted forward on a neck that, to Brunetti, looked suddenly thicker. Pucetti's hands were curled, almost as if poised for the command that they be turned into fists, and his steps were, each one, a command that the earth dare not resist his passage.

Pucetti's eyes roved around the courtyard, his attention turning with predatory haste from one cadet to another. His mouth looked hungry, and his eyes had lost all trace of the warmth and humour which usually filled them.

Brunetti automatically slowed his pace, allowing Pucetti to cut ahead, like a cruise ship in the Antarctic that moves aside to allow an ice breaker to slip in front of it. The few cadets in the courtyard fell silent as they passed.

Pucetti took the steps to the dormitory two at a time, Brunetti following at a slower pace. At the door to Filippi's room, Pucetti raised his fist and banged on it twice, then quickly twice again. From the end of the corridor, Brunetti heard the yelp from inside and then saw Pucetti open the door and shove it back on its hinges so that it banged against the wall.

When Brunetti got to the door, Pucetti was standing just inside, his hands raised almost to the level of his waist; his shoulders looked, if this were possible, even thicker.

A thin blonde boy with acne-pitted cheeks was on the top bunk, half sitting, half lying, but pressed back against the wall, his feet pulled towards him, as though he were afraid to leave them hanging in the air so close to Pucetti's teeth. As Brunetti came in, Cappellini raised a hand, but he used it to wave Brunetti closer, not to tell him to stop.

'What do you want?' the boy asked, unable to disguise his terror.

At the question, Pucetti turned his head slowly to Brunetti and raised his chin, as if asking if Brunetti wanted him to climb up on the bed and hurl the boy down.

'No, Pucetti,' Brunetti said in a voice generally used to dogs.

Pucetti lowered his hands, but not by much, and turned his head back to face the boy on the bed. He kicked the door shut with his heel.

Into the reverberating silence, Brunetti asked, 'Cappellini?'

'Yes, sir.'

'Where were you on the night Cadet Moro was killed?'

Before he thought, the boy blurted out, 'I didn't do it,' voice high and himself too frightened to realize what he'd just admitted. 'I didn't touch him.'

'But you know,' Brunetti said in a firm voice, as if repeating what he'd already been told by someone else.

'Yes. But I didn't have anything to do with it,' the boy said. He pushed himself farther back on the bed, but his shoulders and back were flat against the wall, and there was no place for him to go, no way he could escape.

'Who was it?' Brunetti added, stopping himself from suggesting Filippi's name. When the boy hesitated, he demanded, 'Tell me.'

Cappellini hesitated, calculating whether this current danger were worse than the one he lived with. Obviously he decided in Brunetti's favour, for he said, 'Filippi. It was his idea, all of it.'

At the admission, Pucetti lowered his hands, and Brunetti sensed a general relaxing of his body as he allowed the menace of his presence to slip away. He had no doubt that, were he to take his eyes off Cappellini, he would see that Pucetti had managed to return to his normal size.

The boy calmed down, at least minimally. He allowed

himself to slip down lower on the bed, extended his legs and let one of his feet hang off the side. 'He hated him, Filippi. I don't know why, but he always did, and he told us all that we had to hate him, too, that he was a traitor. His family was a family of traitors.' When he saw that Brunetti made no response to this, Cappellini added, 'That's what he told us. The father, too. Moro.'

'Do you know why he said that?' Brunetti asked in a voice he allowed to grow soft.

'No, sir. It's what he told us.'

Much as Brunetti wanted to know who the others were, he was aware that it would break the rhythm, so he asked, instead, 'Did Moro complain or fight back?' Seeing Cappellini's hesitation, he added, 'When Filippi called him a traitor?'

Cappellini seemed surprised by the question. 'Of course. They had a couple of arguments, and one time Moro hit him, but somebody stopped it, pulled them apart.' Cappellini ran his right hand through his hair, then propped himself up on both hands, letting his head sink down between his shoulders. There was a long pause. Pucetti and Brunetti might just as easily have been two stones.

'What happened that night?' Brunetti finally prodded him.

'Filippi came in late. I don't know whether he had permission or he used his key,' Cappellini explained casually, as if he expected them to know about this. 'I don't know who he was with; it might have been his father. He always seemed angrier, somehow, when he came back from seeing his father. Anyway, when he came in here . . .' Cappellini paused and waved his hand at the space in front of him, the same space now filled by the motionless bodies of the two policemen. 'He started talking about Moro and what a traitor he was. I'd been asleep and I didn't want to hear it, so I told him to shut up.'

He stopped speaking for so long that Brunetti was finally prompted to ask, 'And then what happened?'

'He hit me. He came over here to the side of the bed and reached up and hit me. Not really hard, you understand. Just sort of punched me on the shoulder to show me how mad he was. And he kept saying what a shit Moro was and what a traitor.'

Brunetti hoped the boy would continue. He did. 'And then he left, just turned and walked out of the room and went down the hall, maybe to get Maselli and Zanchi. I don't know.' The boy stopped and stared at the floor.

'And then what happened?'

Cappellini looked up and across at Brunetti. 'I don't know. I fell asleep again.'

'What happened, Davide?' Pucetti asked.

With no warning, Cappellini started to cry, or at least tears started to roll down his cheeks. Making no attempt to brush them away he spoke through them. 'He came back later. I don't know how long it was, but I woke up when he came in. And I knew something was wrong. Just by the way he walked in. He wasn't trying to wake me up or anything. Just the opposite, maybe. But something woke me up, as if there was energy all over the place. I sat up and turned on the light. And there he was, looking like he'd just seen something awful. I asked him what was wrong, but he told me it was nothing and to go back to sleep. But I knew something was wrong.'

The tears slid down his face, as if independent of his eyes. He didn't sniff, and he still made no attempt to wipe them away. They ran down his cheeks and fell on to his shirt, darkening it.

'I suppose I went back to sleep, and the next thing I knew, people were running down the halls shouting and making a lot of noise. That's what woke me up. Then Zanchi came in and woke Filippi up and told him something. They didn't speak to me, but Zanchi gave me a look, and I knew I couldn't say anything.'

He stopped again, and the two policemen watched his tears fall. He nodded at Pucetti. 'Then you all came and started asking questions, and I did what everyone else did, said I didn't know anything.' Pucetti made a sympathetic patting gesture in the air with his right hand. The boy raised a hand and wiped away the tears on the right side of his face, ignoring the others. 'It's what I had to do.' He used the inside of his elbow to wipe all of the tears away; when his face emerged, he said, 'And then it was too late to say anything. To anybody.'

The boy looked at Pucetti, then back at Brunetti, then down at his hands, clasped in his lap. Brunetti glanced at Pucetti, but neither of them risked saying anything.

Beyond the door, footsteps went by, then came back after a minute or so but did not stop. Finally Brunetti asked, 'What do the other boys say?'

Cappellini shrugged away the question.

'Do they know, Davide?' Pucetti asked.

Again, that shrug, but then he said, 'I don't know. No one talks about it. It's almost as if it never happened. None of the teachers talks about it either.'

'I thought there was some sort of ceremony,' Pucetti said.

'Yes, but it was stupid. They read prayers and things. But no one said anything.'

'How has Filippi behaved since then?' Brunetti asked.

It was as if the boy hadn't considered it before. He raised his head, and both Brunetti and Pucetti could see how surprised he was by his own answer. 'Just the same. Just the same as ever. As if nothing's happened.'

'Has he said anything to you about it?' Pucetti asked.

'No, not really. But the next day, that is, the day they found him, when all of you came here to the school and started asking questions, he said he hoped I realized what happened to traitors.'

'What do you think he meant by that?' Brunetti asked.

With the first sign of spirit the boy had shown since the two men came into his room, Cappellini shot back, 'That's a stupid question.'

'Yes, I suppose it is,' Brunetti admitted. 'Where are the other two?' he asked. 'Zanchi and Maselli.'

'Their room is down to the right. The third door.'

'Are you all right, Davide?' Pucetti asked.

The boy nodded once, then again, leaving his head hanging down, looking at his hands.

Brunetti signalled to Pucetti that they should leave. The boy didn't look up when they moved, nor when they opened the door. Outside, in the corridor, Pucetti asked, 'Now what?'

'Do you remember how old they are, Zanchi and Maselli?' Brunetti said by way of answer.

Pucetti shook his head, a gesture Brunetti interpreted to mean they were both underage and thus obliged to have a lawyer or parent present when they were questioned, at least if what they said were to have any legal weight at all.

Brunetti saw then the futility of having rushed here to speak to this boy; he regretted the folly of having given in to his impulse to follow the scent laid down by Filippi. There was virtually no hope that Cappellini could be led to repeat what he had just said. Once he spoke to cooler heads, once his family got to him, once a lawyer explained to them the inescapable consequences of an involvement with the judicial system, the boy was certain to deny it all. Much as Brunetti longed to be able to use the information, he had to admit that no sane person would admit to having had knowledge of a crime and not going to the police; much less would they allow their child to do so.

It struck him that, in similar circumstances, he would be reluctant to allow his own children to become involved. Surely, in his role as police officer, he would offer them the protection of the state, but as a father he knew that their only hope of emerging unscathed from a brush with the *magistratura* would be his own position and, more importantly, their grandfather's wealth.

He turned away from the boys' room. 'Let's go back,' he told a surprised Pucetti.

26

On the way back to the Questura, Brunetti explained to Pucetti the laws regarding statements from underage witnesses. If what Cappellini told them was true – and Brunetti's bones told him it was – then he bore some legal responsibility for his failure to tell the police what he knew. This, however, was only negligence; the actions of Zanchi and Maselli – if they were involved – and of Filippi, were active and criminal and, in the case of Filippi, subject to the full weight of the law. But until Cappellini confirmed his statement in the presence of a lawyer, his story had no legal weight whatsoever.

Their only hope, he thought, was to attempt the same strategy with Filippi as had worked with his roommate: pretend to have full knowledge of the events leading to Moro's death and hope that, by asking questions about the small details that still remained unexplained, they could lead the boy to a full explanation of just what had happened.

Holding the mooring rope, Pucetti jumped on to the Questura dock and hauled the boat up to the side of the pier.

Brunetti thanked the pilot and followed Pucetti into the building. Silent, they went back to the interrogation rooms, where they found Vianello standing in the corridor.

'They still here?' asked Brunetti.

'Yes,' Vianello said, glancing at his watch, then at the closed door. 'Been in there more than an hour '

'Hear anything?' Pucetti asked.

Vianello shook his head. 'Not a word. I went in a half-hour ago to ask them if they wanted anything to drink, but the lawyer told me to get out.'

'How'd the boy look?' Brunetti asked.

'Worried.'

'The father?'

'The same.'

'Who's the lawyer?'

'Donatini,' Vianello said in a studiedly neutral voice.

'Oh, my,' Brunetti answered, finding it interesting that the most famous criminal lawyer in the city should be chosen by Maggiore Filippi to represent his son.

'He say anything?' Brunetti asked.

Vianello shook his head.

The three men stood in the corridor for a few minutes until Brunetti, tiring of it, told Vianello he could go back to his office and himself went up to his own. There he waited until, almost an hour later, Pucetti phoned and told him that Avvocato Donatini said his client was ready to talk to him.

Brunetti called Vianello and told him he'd meet him at the interrogation room but deliberately made no haste in going downstairs. Vianello was there when he arrived. Brunetti nodded, and Vianello opened the door and stood back, allowing his superior to pass into the room before him.

Donatini stood and extended his hand to Brunetti, who shook it briefly. He smiled his cool smile, and Brunetti noticed that he had had extensive dental work since last they met. The Pavarotti-style caps on his upper front teeth had been replaced with new ones that better corresponded to the proportions of his face. The rest was the same as ever: skin, suit, tie, shoes all joining in a hallelujah to wealth and success and power.

The lawyer gave Vianello a curt nod but did not offer his hand. The Filippis, father and son, looked up at the policemen but did not acknowledge their arrival with even a nod. The father wore civilian clothes, but it was a suit that, like Donatini's, spoke so eloquently of wealth and power that it might as well have been a uniform. He was perhaps Brunetti's age but looked a decade younger, the result of either natural animal grace or hours in a gym. He had dark eyes and the long, straight nose that was mirrored on the face of his son.

Donatini, staking a claim to the proceedings, waved Brunetti to a seat at the opposite end of the rectangular table and Vianello to a chair across from the father and son. Thus he himself faced Brunetti, while the other two looked at Vianello.

'I won't waste your time, Commissario,' Donatini said. 'My client has volunteered to talk to you about the unfortunate events at the Academy.' The lawyer looked to his side, where the cadet sat, and the boy gave a solemn nod.

Brunetti gave what he thought was a rather gracious one.

'It would seem that my client knows something about the death of Cadet Moro.'

'I'd be very eager to hear what that is,' Brunetti said with a curiosity he allowed to be tempered with *politesse*.

'My client was . . .' Donatini began, only to be stopped by Brunetti, who held up a hand, but gently and not very high, to suggest a moment's pause. 'If you don't mind, Avvocato, I'd like to record what your client has to say.'

This time it was the lawyer who responded with *politesse*, which he conveyed by the merest inclination of his head.

Brunetti reached forward, conscious as he did so of how

often he had done the same thing, and switched on the microphone. He gave the date, his name and rank, and identified all of the people in the room.

'My client . . .' Donatini began again, and again Brunetti saw fit to stop him with a raised hand.

'I think it would be better, Avvocato,' Brunetti said, leaning forward to switch off the microphone, 'if your client were to speak for himself.' Before the lawyer could object or question this, Brunetti went on with an easy smile, 'That might give a greater appearance of openness on his part, and it would certainly then be easier for him to clarify anything that might seem confusing.' Brunetti smiled, aware of how elegant had been his implication that he reserved the right to question the boy as he spoke.

Donatini looked at Maggiore Filippi, who until now had remained motionless and silent. 'Well, Maggiore?' he asked politely.

The Maggiore nodded, a gesture his son responded to with what appeared to be an involuntary half-salute.

Brunetti smiled across at the boy and turned the microphone on again.

'Would you tell me your name, please?' he asked.

'Paolo Filippi.' He spoke clearly and louder than he had spoken the last time, presumably for the benefit of the microphone.

'And are you a third-year student at the San Martino Military Academy in Venice?'

'Yes.'

'Could you tell me what happened at the Academy on the night of November third of this year?'

'You mean about Ernesto?' the boy asked.

'Yes, I'm asking specifically about anything concerning the death of Ernesto Moro, also a cadet at the Academy.'

The boy was silent for so long that Brunetti finally asked, 'Did you know Ernesto Moro?'

'Yes?'

'Was he a friend of yours?'

The boy shrugged that possibility away, but before Brunetti could remind him about the microphone and the need to speak, Paolo said, 'No, we weren't friends.'

'What was the reason for that?'

The boy's surprise was obvious. 'He was a year younger than me. In a different class.'

'Was there anything else about Ernesto Moro that prevented him from being a friend of yours?'

The boy thought about this and finally answered, 'No.'

'Could you tell me about what happened that night?'

When the boy did not answer for a long time, his father turned minimally towards him and gave a slight nod.

He leaned towards his father and whispered something, the last words of which, 'have to?' Brunetti couldn't help but overhear.

'Yes,' the Maggiore said in a firm voice.

The boy turned back to Brunetti. 'It's very difficult,' he said, his voice uneven.

'Just tell me what happened, Paolo,' Brunetti said, thinking of his own son and the confessions he had made over the years, though he was sure none of them could compare in magnitude to what this boy might have to say.

'I was,' the boy began, coughed nervously, and began again. 'I was with him that night.'

Brunetti thought it best to say nothing and so did nothing more than look encouragingly.

The boy glanced up to the top of the table at Donatini, who gave an avuncular nod.

'I was with him,' he repeated.

'Where?'

'In the showers,' the boy said. Usually, it took them a long time to get to the confession. Most people had to build up to it with a long set of details and circumstances, all of which would make what finally happened seem inevitable, at least to themselves. 'We were there,' the boy said and then stopped.

Brunetti looked at Donatini, who drew his lips together and shook his head.

The silence went on so long that at last Donatini was driven to say, 'Tell him, Paolo.'

The boy cleared his throat, looked at Brunetti, started to glance at his father but stifled the gesture and looked back at Brunetti. 'We did things,' he said, and stopped.

For a moment that seemed all he was going to say, but then he added, 'To one another.'

Brunetti said, 'I see. Go on, Paolo.'

'A lot of us do it,' the boy said in a voice so soft Brunetti doubted the microphone would pick it up. 'I know it's not right, not really, but nobody gets hurt, and everybody does it. Really.'

Brunetti said nothing, and the boy added, 'We have girls. But at home. And so it's . . . it's hard . . . and . . .' His voice stopped.

Brunetti avoided the eyes of the boy's father and turned to Donatini. 'Am I to understand that these boys engaged in sexual acts with one another?' He thought he might as well be as clear as he could and hoped he was right.

'Masturbation, yes,' Donatini said.

It had been decades since Brunetti had been as young as this boy, but he still failed to understand the strength of Paolo's embarrassment. They were boys in late adolescence, living among other boys. Their behaviour didn't surprise him: the boy's reaction did.

'Tell me more about it,' Brunetti said, hoping that whatever he heard would help this to make sense to him.

'Ernesto was strange,' Paolo said. 'It wasn't enough for him to, well, just to do what we do. He always wanted to do other things.'

Brunetti kept his eyes on the boy, hoping with his attention to spur him on to explain.

'That night, he told me that . . . well, he told me he'd read about something in a magazine. Or a newspaper.' Paolo stopped and Brunetti watched him worry at this detail. Finally he said, 'I don't know where he read it, but he said he wanted to do it that way.' He stopped.

'To do what?' Brunetti finally asked. 'What way?' For an instant, he took his eyes from the boy and saw his father, sitting with his head lowered, looking down at the table as if he were willing himself not to be in the room where his son had to admit this to a policeman.

'He said the thing he read said it made it better, better than anything,' the boy went on. 'But it meant he had to put something around his neck and choke himself a little bit when he . . . well, when he did it. And that's what he wanted me there for, to be sure that nothing went wrong, when it happened.'

The boy gave an enormous sigh, pulling air into his lungs, preparing himself for the final leap. 'I told him he was crazy, but he wouldn't listen.' He brought his hands together and folded them primly on the table.

'He had the stuff there in the bathroom, and he showed me the rope. It was where it was . . . I mean, where it was after, when they found him. It was long, so he could sort of crouch on the floor in there and pretend to fall over. And that would make him choke. And that's why it was so good. The choking, or something. Or that's what he said.'

Silence. From beyond the wall, everyone in the room could hear a low humming noise: computer? tape recorder? It hardly mattered.

Brunetti remained absolutely silent.

The boy began again. 'So he did it. I mean, he had this bag and put it over his head and over the rope. And then he started laughing and tried to say something, but I couldn't understand what he said. I remember he pointed at me and laughed again, then he started to . . . and after a while, he crouched down and sort of fell over to the side.'

The boy's face grew suddenly red and Brunetti watched his hands grip at one another. But he went on, unable to stop himself from telling it all until it was finished. 'He kicked a few times and his hands started to wave around. And then he started to scream or something and kick real hard. I tried to grab him, but he kicked me so hard he knocked me out of the shower. But I went back and I tried to untie the rope, but the plastic bag was tied over it, so I couldn't get to the rope, and when I did, I couldn't untie the knot because he was yanking around so much. And then, and then, he stopped kicking, but when I got to him it was too late, and I think he was dead.'

The boy wiped at his face, which was covered with sweat.

'And then what did you do, Paolo?' Brunetti asked.

'I don't know. For the first minute, I just was there, next to him. I never saw a dead person before, but I don't remember what I did.' He glanced up, then immediately down. As Brunetti watched, his father reached out and placed his left hand on top of his son's clenched hands. He squeezed them once and left his hand there.

Encouraged by that pressure, Paolo went on. 'I guess I panicked. I thought it was my fault because I hadn't been able to save him or stop him. Maybe I could have, but I didn't.'

'What did you do, Paolo?' Brunetti repeated.

'I wasn't thinking much, but I didn't want them to find him like that. People would know what happened.'

'And so?' Brunetti prodded.

'I don't know where I got the idea, but I thought if it looked like a suicide, well, it would be bad, but it wouldn't be as bad as . . . as the other.' This time, Brunetti didn't press, hoping that the boy would continue by himself

'So I tried to make it look like he hanged himself. I knew I had to pull him up and leave him there.' Brunetti's eyes fell to their clasped hands; the father's knuckles were white. 'So that's what I did. And I left him there.' The boy opened his mouth and pulled air into his lungs as though he'd been running for kilometres.

'And the plastic bag?' Brunetti asked when his breathing had grown calmer.

'I took it with me and threw it away. I don't remember where. In the garbage somewhere.'

'And then what did you do?'

'I don't remember much. I think I went back to my room.'

'Did anyone see you?'

'I don't know.'

'Your roommate?'

'I don't remember,' he said. 'Maybe. I don't remember how I got back to my room.'

'What's the next thing you do remember, Paolo?'

'The next morning, Zanchi woke me up and told me what had happened. And then it was too late to do anything.'

'Why are you telling me this now?' Brunetti asked.

The boy shook his head. He separated his hands and grabbed at his father's with his right. Finally in a soft voice, he said, 'I'm afraid.'

'Of what?'

'Of what will happen. Of what it could look like.'

'What's that?'

'That I didn't want to help him, that I let it happen to him because I didn't like him.'

'Did people think you didn't like him?'

'That's what he told me to do,' Paolo said, turning minimally away from his father, as if fearful of what he would see on his face, but not letting go of his hand. 'That's what Ernesto told me to do. So people wouldn't know about the other thing.'

'That you were, well . . . ?'

'Yes. All of us do it, but we usually do it with different

guys. Ernesto just wanted to do it with me. And I was ashamed of that.'

The boy turned to his father. '*Papà*, do I have to say any more?'

The Maggiore, instead of answering his son, looked across the table at Brunetti. Instead of replying, Brunetti leaned forward, gave the time, and said that the interview was over.

Silently, all five of them got to their feet. Donatini, who was closest to the door, went and opened it. The Maggiore wrapped his right arm around his son's shoulders. Brunetti pushed his chair under the table, nodded to Vianello that they would leave now, and moved towards the door. He was just a step from the door when he heard a noise behind him, but it was only Vianello, who had stumbled against his chair.

Seeing that Vianello was all right, Brunetti took a final glance at the father and son, who were facing one another. And as he watched he saw Paolo, who had his father's complete attention, close his right eye in a single wink of triumphant, sly satisfaction. In the same instant, the father's right hand came up and gave the boy an approving punch on the right biceps.

27

Vianello hadn't seen it; he had been facing away from that millisecond of complicit understanding between father and son. Brunetti turned towards the door and passed in front of a silent Donatini. In the hall, he waited until Vianello emerged, followed by the two Filippis and their lawyer.

Brunetti closed the door of the interrogation room, moving slowly to give himself time to think.

Donatini spoke first. 'It's your decision, Commissario, about what to do with this information.' Brunetti was entirely unresponsive, didn't even bother to acknowledge that the lawyer had spoken.

In the face of Brunetti's silence, the Maggiore spoke. 'It might be better if that dead boy's family were left with the memory of him that they have,' he said solemnly, and Brunetti was shamed to realize that, had he not seen the momentary flash of triumph between him and his son, he would have been moved by the man's concern for Ernesto's family. He was swept by a desire to strike the man across the mouth but instead turned away from all of them and started down the corridor. From behind him, the boy called out, 'Do you want me to sign anything?' and then a moment later, intentionally delayed, 'Commissario?'

Brunetti kept walking, ignoring them all, bent on getting back to his office, like an animal that has to return to its cave in order to feel safe from its enemies. He closed the door behind him, knowing that Vianello, however confused by his superior's behaviour, would leave him alone until called.

'Check and mate and game at an end,' he said aloud, so much the victim of the energy surging in him that he could not move. Clenching his hands and closing his eyes didn't help at all: he was left with the image of that wink, that sustaining punch. Even if Vianello had seen it, he realized, it would make no difference for them, nor for Moro. Filippi's story was credible, the entire performance perfectly pitched. He cringed at the memory of how he had been moved by the boy's embarrassment, how he had superimposed upon his halting account what he imagined would be his own son's response in the same circumstances and seen fear and remorse where there had been only low cunning.

Part of him longed to hear Vianello's voice at the door so that he could tell him how they had been duped. But there would be no purpose, he realized, and so he was glad that the Inspector stayed away. His own rashness in going off to talk to Cappellini had given the Filippis time to concoct their story; not just to concoct it but to work on it and to put into it all of the ingredients that were sure to appeal to the sentimentalism of anyone who heard it. What cliché did they leave untouched? Boys will be boys. My shame is greater than my guilt. Oh, spare from further pain the suffering mother of the lad.

Brunetti turned and kicked the door, but the noise and the jolt of pain in his back changed nothing. He confronted the fact that anything he did would have the same effect: nothing would change, regardless of how much pain was endured.

He looked at his watch and saw that he'd lost all track of time while questioning the boy, though the darkness outside should have told him how late it was. He'd given no orders, but there was certainly no reason to hold Filippi, and Vianello must surely have let him go. He wanted desperately not to see any of them when he left, so he forced himself to stand there, eyes closed and head leaning back against the door, for another five minutes, and then he went downstairs.

Cowardice made him avoid the officers' room, though he could see light coming from the door as he went silently down the steps. Outside he turned to the right and walked to the *Riva* to take a vaporetto, suddenly desiring the distraction presented by the many people on board at this hour.

One was just pulling away as he arrived at the *imbarcadero*, so as he waited for the next he had ten minutes to study the people who arrived, most of them Venetian by the look of them. When it came, he boarded the boat, crossed to the far side and stood at the rail, back turned to the glory of the city.

When at last he arrived at the door to his apartment, he paused, hoping that some remnant of humanity would be waiting for him inside. What if he came home to a son like Paolo? How to praise a son like that without having first created him? He opened the door and let himself into the apartment.

'I will not buy you a *telefonino* because they create a race of spineless weaklings; it would make you even more dependent than you already are,' he heard Paola say and rejoiced in the heartless rigour with which she denied her children their desires.

Her voice came from the direction of the kitchen, but Brunetti went, instead, down the hall toward Paola's study. He knew that years of lying awake for the sound of the footsteps of returning children would alert her to his arrival, so he had no doubt that she would soon come and find him.

She did, and they talked. Rather, he talked and she

listened. After a long time, when he had explained everything and named the choices open to him, he asked, 'Well?'

'The dead can't suffer,' was all she said, an answer that confused him at first.

Familiar with her habits of thought, he considered the remark for some time and finally asked, 'And the living can?'

She nodded.

'Filippi and his father,' he said, then added, 'who should. And Moro and his wife.'

'And daughter, and mother,' Paola added, 'who shouldn't.'

'Is this a contest of numbers?' he asked soberly.

She flicked this away with a quick motion of her hand. 'No, no, not at all. But I think it matters, not only because of the number of people who will be affected but for the amount of good it would do.'

'Neither choice will do anyone any good,' he insisted.

'Then which will do less harm?'

'He's dead,' Brunetti said, 'no matter what the official verdict is.'

'This isn't about the official verdict, Guido.'

'Then what is it about?'

'It's about what you tell them.' The way she spoke, she made it sound self-evident. He had shied away from accepting that, had almost succeeded in preventing himself from thinking about it, yet the instant the words fell from her lips, he realized that it was the only thing any of this was about.

'You mean what Filippi did?'

'A man has the right to know who killed his child.'

'You make that sound so simple. Like something from the Bible.'

'It's not in the Bible, to the best of my knowledge. But it is simple. And true.' Her tone was a stranger to uncertainty.

'And what if he does something about it?'

'Like what? Kill Filippi? Or his father?'

Brunetti nodded.

'From what I know of him and what you've said, I doubt that he's the kind of man who would do something like that.' Before he could say that one never knew, she said, 'But you never know, do you?'

Once again, Brunetti had the strange sensation of being adrift in time. He looked at his watch and was stunned to see that it was almost ten. 'Have the kids eaten?'

'I sent them out to get a pizza when I heard you come in.'

He had gradually, as he told her the story of his meeting with the Filippis and their lawyer, sunk lower and lower on the sofa until he was now lying with his head on a pillow. 'I think I'm hungry,' he said.

'Yes,' Paola agreed. 'Me, too. Stay here for a while and I'll make some pasta.' She got to her feet and went to the door. 'What will you do?' she asked.

'I'll have to speak to him,' Brunetti said.

He did so the next day, at four in the afternoon, a time chosen by Dottor Moro, who had insisted on coming to the Questura rather than have Brunetti come to his home. The doctor was on time to the minute, and Brunetti stood up when a uniformed officer ushered him into his office. Brunetti came around his desk and extended his hand. They exchanged strained courtesies and then, as soon as he was seated, Moro asked, 'What is it you want, Commissario?' His voice was level and calm, devoid of curiosity or, for that fact, interest. Events had washed him clean of such things.

Brunetti, who had retreated behind his desk more out of habit than choice, began by saying, 'There are some things I think you should know, Dottore.' He paused, waiting for the doctor to respond, perhaps with sarcasm, perhaps with anger. But Moro said nothing.

'There are certain facts regarding the death of your son that

I think . . .' Brunetti began, then flailed to a stop. He looked at the wall behind Moro's head, then began again. 'That is, I've learned some things and want you to know them.'

'Why?'

'Because they might help you decide.'

'Decide what?' Moro asked tiredly.

'How to proceed.'

Moro shifted to one side in the chair and crossed his legs. 'I have no idea what you're talking about, Commissario. I don't think there are any decisions I can make, not now.'

'About your son, I think.'

Brunetti saw something flash into Moro's eyes.

'No decision can affect my son,' he said, making no attempt to disguise his anger. And then, to hammer the message home, he added, 'He's dead.'

Brunetti felt the moral heat of what Moro had just said sweep over him. Again, he looked away, then back at the doctor, and again he spoke. 'I've come into the possession of new information, and I think you should be aware of what it is.' Without giving Moro a chance to comment, he went on. 'Paolo Filippi, who is a student at the Academy, maintains that your son died by accident and that, to avoid embarrassment for him, and for you, he arranged it to look like suicide.'

Brunetti waited for Moro to ask if that would not also be an embarrassment, but instead the doctor said, 'Nothing my boy did would embarrass me.'

'He maintains your son died as the result of homosexual activity.' Brunetti waited for the other man to respond.

'Even though I'm a doctor,' Moro said, 'I have no idea of what that can mean.'

'That your son died in an attempt to increase his sexual excitement by near-strangulation.'

'Autoerotic asphyxiation,' Moro said with clinical detachment.

Brunetti nodded.

'Why should that embarrass me?' the doctor said calmly.

After a long silence, Brunetti realized that Moro was not going to prompt him, so he said, 'I don't think what he told me is true. I think he killed your son because his father had persuaded him that Ernesto was a spy or a traitor of some sort. It was his influence, perhaps even his encouragement, that led the boy to do what he did.'

Still Moro said nothing, though his eyes had widened in surprise.

In the face of the other man's silence, the best Brunetti could do was say, 'I wanted you to know what story Filippi will give if we pursue the case.'

'And what is this decision you've called me in here to make, Commissario?'

'Whether you want us to bring a charge of involuntary manslaughter against Filippi.'

Moro studied Brunetti's face for some time before he said, 'If you think he killed Ernesto, Commissario, then involuntary manslaughter is not much of a charge, is it?' Before Brunetti could reply, Moro added, 'Besides, this should be your decision, Commissario. Not mine.' His voice was as cool as his expression.

'I wanted to give you the choice,' Brunetti said in what he thought was a calm voice.

'So you wouldn't have to decide?'

Brunetti bowed his head but turned the motion into a nod. 'In part, yes, but it's also for you and your family.'

'To spare us embarrassment?' Moro asked with heavy emphasis on the last word.

'No,' Brunetti asked, worn down by Moro's contempt. 'To spare you danger.'

'What danger?' Moro asked, as though he were really curious.

'The danger that would come to all of you if this went to trial.'

'I don't understand.'

'Because the report you suppressed would have to be produced as evidence, or at least you would have to testify as to its existence and contents. To justify Filippi's behaviour and his father's anger. Or fear, or whatever it was.'

Moro put a hand to his forehead in what seemed to Brunetti an artificial gesture. 'My report?' he finally asked.

'Yes. About military procurement.'

Moro took his hand away. 'There is no report, Commissario. At least not about the Army or procurement or whatever it is they're afraid I've done. I abandoned that when they shot my wife.'

Brunetti was amazed to hear Moro speak so calmly, as though it were a truth universally acknowledged that his wife had been shot deliberately.

The doctor went on. 'I started doing research on their spending and where the money went as soon as I was appointed to the committee. It was obvious where all the money was going; their arrogance makes them very sloppy bookkeepers, so their trail was very easy to follow, even for a doctor. But then they shot my wife.'

'You say that as though there's no question,' Brunetti said.

Moro looked across at him and said in a cold voice. 'There's no question. I was called even before she reached the hospital. And so I agreed to abandon my research. The suggestion was made at the time that I retire from politics. And I did. I obeyed them, Commissario.'

'You knew they shot her?' Brunetti asked though he had no idea who 'they' were, at least no idea so clear that a specific name could be attached.

'Of course,' Moro said, his voice slipping back towards sarcasm. 'I'd done at least that much research.'

'But then why arrange the separation from your wife?' Brunetti asked.

'To be sure they left her alone.'

'And your daughter?' Brunetti asked with sudden curiosity.

'In a safe place,' was the only answer Moro was willing to provide.

'Then why put your son there, at the Academy?' Brunetti asked, but as he did it came to him that perhaps Moro had thought it would be best to hide the boy in plain sight. The people who shot his wife might think twice about creating bad publicity for the Academy; or perhaps he had hoped to fool them.

Moro's face moved in something that might once have been a smile. 'Because I couldn't stop him, Commissario. It was the greatest failure of my life that Ernesto wanted to be a soldier. But that's all he ever wanted to be, ever since he was a little boy. And nothing I could ever do or say could change it.'

'But why would they kill him?' Brunetti asked.

When Moro eventually spoke, Brunetti had the sense that he was relieved, at long last, to be able to talk about this. 'Because they are stupid and didn't believe that it was so easy to stop me. That I was a coward and wouldn't oppose them.' He sat thinking for a long time and added, 'Or perhaps Ernesto was less of a coward than I am. He knew I had once planned to write a report, and perhaps he threatened them with it.'

Though his office was cool, Brunetti saw that sweat stood on Moro's brow and was slowly sliding down his chin. Moro wiped at it with the back of his hand. Then he said, 'I'll never know.'

The two men sat for a long time, the only motion Moro's occasional attempt to wipe the sweat from his face. When, finally, his face was dry again, Brunetti asked, 'What do you want me to do, Dottore?'

Moro raised his head and looked at Brunetti with eyes that had grown even sadder in the last half-hour. 'You want me to make the decision for you?'

'No. Not really. Or not only. To make it for yourself. And for your family.'

'You'll do whatever I say?' Moro asked.

'Yes.'

'Regardless of the law or justice?' Moro's emphasis, a very unkind emphasis, was on the last word.

'Yes.'

'Why? Don't you care about justice?' Moro's anger was undisguised now.

Brunetti had no taste for this, not any longer. 'There's no justice here, Dottore,' he said, frightened to realize that he meant not only for this man and his family, but for this city, and this country, and their lives.

'Then let it be,' Moro said, exhausted. 'Let him be.'

Everything that was decent in Brunetti urged him to say something that would comfort this man, but the words, though summoned, failed to come. He thought of Moro's daughter and then of his own. He thought of his own son, of Filippi's son, and of Moro's, and then the words came: 'Poor boy.'